R. J. Gadney was born in Cross Hills, Yorkshire. He lives

THE WOMAN IN SILK

R. J. GADNEY

Quercus

First published in Great Britain in 2011 by

Quercus
55 Baker Street
7th Floor, South Block
London
W1U 8EW

A CIP catalogue record for this book is available
from the British Library

ISBN 978 0 85738 259 7

10 9 8 7 6 5 4 3 2 1

Typeset by Ellipsis Digital Limited, Glasgow

Printed and bound in Great Britain by Clays Ltd, St Ives plc

For Fay and my grandchildren Nell, Jago, Toby
and Elliot (when they are older) with love.

When I breathe in
there is a sound in my body
sadder than the winter
wind.

ISHIKAWA TAKUBOKU

ONE

I have, indeed, no abhorrence of danger,
except in its absolute effect – in terror.

EDGAR ALLAN POE

Someone once said: 'One never knows what goes on in a brave man's head.'

Hal Stirling often wondered when he'd heard the remark. Not for a minute, of course, thinking it might apply to him.

When he saw the lizard on the patch of desert shale pretending to be dead, he blinked.

The lizard flinched.

Then it sprang into a tangle of bamboo roots narrowly avoiding the dusty package. Wise move, *trapelus agilis*.

Covered with hardened insulating foam, the package was roughly the size of two ammunition boxes, large enough to contain two small steel cylinders of plastic explosive. He reckoned it must have been there for six months or more.

Also present among the visible and invisible usual suspects was another silent creature, member of a different tribe, *Macrovipera lebetina*, with a triangular head and blunt snout, a Levantine viper. Levantine vipers rarely go into action in daytime. Hazard Warning. They're unpredictable.

Two more lovers of the desert were showing interest in the stranger. Motionless fellow-travelling scorpions from the *Buthidae* tribe. Long sleek butts ending in bulbous stingers. Eight legs excluding pincers. Smaller the scorps, more powerful the sting. These were small, very small and unpredictable.

Brave desert stranger kept his focus on his grip, hand-hold steady. He was staring at his fingers before he moved them, watching for any involuntary twitch, making certain no nerve was signalling fear, visualizing how he'd take the packaged bomb apart, what might need touching, where to move things, how to achieve the disconnection, exactly where he'd make the cut of the wire to disable it.

He was on the verge of Success + E = Euphoria or being taken by the big N: as in nada nil zero zippo Nothin' = N = big 0e0. Nothing. And, to state the obvious, he wouldn't know anything about N. His eyes were inches from the thing . . . *if it goes up* . . . *it's N.* Oblivion.

Flat on his stomach, mindful of the sultry viper, he looked for a battery and a wire and the best place to break the circuit to the detonators. He could withdraw the detonators, unravel the wires, and disable the electronics. Be Warned: cutting into the hardened foam causes dangerous vibration.

Or he could retreat to a safe distance, relax and simply blow the whole thing up by remote control. But every bomb-maker leaves a signature and this was a bomb to collect intact and hand in to the forensic experts.

So he disabled the electrical circuit. Then he very slowly opened a plastic bag and stared at the viper. No doubt about it – definitely a Levantine viper.

He spent time calming himself. This was his Calmness Ritual: lie still. *Think blue skies. Breathe sweet fresh air. Think ocean beach and ocean waves. Remind Myself I'm Nothing But A Nomad.* He'd begun to resemble a nomadic kuchi: a Pashtun from east and south-west Afghanistan whose double-headed drums and lutes have been silenced by the foreigners. Like the kuchi, he too was constantly on the move through sand and dust, the shale and stones: like the lizard, the scorps and the viper, always in transit.

His scalp itched. His body felt thinner than it had ever been, his muscles harder. Now a size too large, his combat 95 multi-terrain-pattern camouflage uniform was stained and malodorous. His veined and bloodshot eyes ached.

He looked at his broken fingernails, at his raw knuckles. He hoiked up phlegm, twisted his lips, and spat the glob to get rid of the flies exploring the desert scum that pitted his burned unshaven jaw. He looked at the beautiful viper. The beautiful viper looked at him. You're half-asleep, beautiful. Goodnight, viper.

Right elbow and left hand taking his weight, he edged still closer to the trophy.

He reached out for it with his pliers and nipped its wrinkly throat.

The viper hissed. Its teeth sank into the ball of his right thumb. It used its jaws to pump venom into him. He used the pliers to crush its snout—

Plunged his knife straight into its arching head.

A moment later a radio signal told him there were more IEDs up the riverbed, about ninety metres distant.

He thought of reporting to his team that the viper had got him. Imagine the sniggers. *'Now what's he gone and bloody done . . . sat on a bloody snake − ha-ha-bloody-ha!'*

He decided to collect the dead viper once he'd dealt with the other IEDs. He might. Might not.

He began to crawl further up the riverbed. The dry mud stank of fly-ridden shit. It stank because the locals shit in the open. The pain in his hand increased. Cold sweat stung his eyes, dung flies flicked against his exposed skin. He couldn't stop his hands shaking.

The sun was dazzling him. The heat was taunting

him. Every shape he saw harboured danger. A blackened thorn became another slithering viper; a knot of dried grass, a scorp, then turned into a wire; a wire connected to another IED.

It was becoming difficult to distinguish what was real from what was imaginary.

He could ignore the real or phoney snake. He could cut the telltale wire. *If it is a wire. Might be a come-on. Could be others buried beneath connected to yet another IED.* Wires that had most probably degraded rendering the bombs unstable. Moving in the lightest breeze, the wires might produce an electrical short and trigger an explosion.

He found made-up batteries, more wires; blasting caps inserted into stable explosive charges, perhaps a mixture of fertilizer mixed with aluminium-based paint or military explosive from unexploded ordnance or conventional land mines and pressure plates. They acted as switches. When a foot or a hand or vehicle pressed them down, the circuits closed, the battery current activated the blasting caps, ignited them and the bomb exploded.

Next bombs he found were encased in large plastic containers; one an ice cooler; another a cooking-oil container.

They appeared to be attached to pressure pads on either side of the riverbed. Clever that. The patrol wouldn't go up the shallow V of the riverbed. It would keep to the sides.

The threat of the unexpected forced him to lie still and breathe in slowly. Dust he inhaled made him wheeze like he'd wheezed as a child when asthma worked its black magic. A whistling sounded in his throat; then deeper in his chest.

Struggling to control his shaking fingers, he probed the shale; fissile rocks of fine-grain clay sediment and shit. The combination of probing, edging forward along the riverbed, telling himself to take control of the situation: dust, extreme nervous tension: all of this made him retch.

He paused to look at his fingers. Fingers that had felt gently round the countless IEDs he'd disabled. Now, even in the colossal heat, his fingertips felt cold. He couldn't keep them still.

Maybe it was fear that induced the adrenalin rush. He craved fear like the gambler or the mountaineer climbing some Alpine rock face without a safety harness.

His radio came to life again and he heard his No. 2 asking about progress.

'Taking stock.'

'Say again.'

He tasted acidic saliva scum on his cracked lips. The taste of fear.

'Taking stock.'

Then he the saw the flash. Heard the thunder. Felt the shockwave. The desert erupted.

He saw the carnage through binoculars and went back to help.

Vehicle parts lay across the ground with equipment in flames, severed limbs and at least one detached head. Soldiers caught in the storm of shrapnel staggered about in the grey and yellow smoke. One man was choking on his vomit. Arms and hands were drenched in blood. Men were preparing to self-inject morphine. The screaming was terrible. He'd heard it more times than he cared to remember.

Among the dead and dying was a soldier who'd lost a hand and most of his leg. Someone was trying to apply a tourniquet but the soldier was protesting. The pressure would cause his leg to die.

Blood poured from the Patrol Commander's shattered arm. The lower arm dangled from a twisted sinew like meat on a slaughterhouse hook. He could smell the heated blood.

Fingers pinched the artery trying to stem the flow.

Helping the Patrol Commander to his Land Rover, there seemed to be three of them. The Patrol Commander, his trousers soaked in blood; the dangling arm; and his own throbbing hand.

He did his best to calm the general panic and made sure the wounded and shocked survivors were safe.

He heaved the Patrol Commander into the passenger seat and settled the semi-detached arm in the man's bloodied lap. He was ashen, his forehead cold. Droplets of sweat were collecting in his furrowed brow. '*Water. Water*,' he begged. Signs of very serious shock.

He retrieved a strip of plastic normally used to tie up detainees' wrists and tightened it around the stump of the upper arm to stem the flow of blood.

Someone must have already called the Medical Emergency Response Team so the four airborne medics and their protection squad would be on the way to the emergency in a Chinook.

The Patrol Commander was thinking the same thing. 'The MERT,' he croaked. 'Take charge – make sure ...'

'Say again.'

'. . . make sure – make sure my men are safe.' He was trying to make the sign of the cross and his throat went into spasm. He looked like a frightened child.

Several of the howling blood-drenched survivors had shat themselves. The scene reeked of diarrhoea, burning human flesh and plastic. Others, choking on the fumes, poured water over their heads.

Soldiers who'd escaped the blast formed a protective

screen of snipers and heavy machine guns. A voice said the MERT was finally on its way in the Chinook.

The chaos and panic lessened. He tried to turn his mind to the collection of forensic evidence from the blood-soaked clothing, body parts and crushed equipment, to establish the trail of evidence to lead to the bomb-makers, the owners of the clandestine workshops and the explosives smugglers.

Then his No. 2 told him more about those IEDs up the riverbed. He'd spotted what looked to be a water-proofed command wire. 'There are tripwires all over the fucking shop,' he said.

A soldier, eyes wide open, pupils dilated, was shouting: '*Fuck. Fuck. FUCK.*'

Fear-fuck's contagious, so he looked away.

The IEDs had to be disabled. The longer they detained the patrol the more likely the soldiers would be sitting sniper targets. To say nothing of the bomb disposal experts who were priority targets. Another reason for not wearing his telltale protective bomb suit.

He told his team to stay with what was left of the patrol. He was going back up the riverbed alone.

No matter he'd honed his skills during eight years of intensive training. An asset to counterterrorist operations back home, he'd passed the Parachute

Regiment's Pegasus Company course at Catterick with distinction. He was far from the sort of soldier his peers would expect to fall apart. Like him, they too were on permanent ten-minute stand-by at the base under unimaginable strain. But his hand was aching and his fingers twitching.

Keeping in touch with his team by radio, he set off.

He dragged himself back up the stinking riverbed. The noise of the screaming and the *Fuck-Fuck* faded.

The rocks and stones were jagged, the thorns vicious, the stench nauseating. Looking left, looking right, peering close ahead; he crawled with a sort of wild care.

His arms stiffened. The sweat in his eyes was sometimes hot, sometimes cold.

A question nagged him. What's the name for what happens to your fingertips when you hyperventilate, when too little blood and too few nutrients jam the nerve cell signals to your brain?

What's it called?

No answer.

Horse flies and wasps bombarded him, defeating his usually effective Ultrathon insect repellent. The idea death's sting was waiting round the corner didn't occur to him.

Got it. Paresthesia.

Pins and needles.

*

For the second time he saw the apocalyptic flash. Heard the thunder. Felt the shockwave. The desert erupted in yellow clouds.

The world turned upside-down-inside-out.

Could've been the other way about.

The sun was screaming – *BURN!*

Drifting in and out of consciousness, he saw the rise of blinding suns, veils of blood, felt the constant throbbing pain, the blows hammering inside his skull.

'Two-Two Alpha, Two-Two Alpha, this is Two-Zero Charlie, Two-Zero Charlie. I have six times T One casualties. My location – I need immediate CASEVAC. Immediate. Over—'

Another voice said:

'He's going to die.' Another: 'You're going to be okay, Sir. You're going to be okay . . .'

The noise of the Chinook's howling engines, beating rotors, *thwack-thwack-thwacking* front-and-back deafened him. Its downdraughts forced up giant veils of sand and dust. At any second the vibrations in the ground might trigger metal plates and blow the aircraft to smithereens. Someone on a radio was losing his cool, yelling advice to base that the Chinook should get the hell away.

He saw the Royal Air Force Sergeant, the helicopter's loadmaster, give a thumbs-up, then wait a moment for the cable to be dropped allowing the injured to be winched up.

For some reason, the Chinook flew away. It turned, kept on turning, and lowered to make its landing. Can't believe it. Can't believe the pilot would be so dozy to attempt to land in what any fart could see was a minefield.

He saw the ramp lowering and someone signalling in semaphore with his arms to the loadmaster. The loadmaster had his eyes elsewhere.

He realized he was being ferried hurriedly on a stretcher born by a quad bike and trailer and lifted into the helicopter.

Aboard the Chinook, the Medical Emergency Response Team was ready to do its best. Eight soldiers were assisting a consultant anaesthetist, an accident and emergency specialist and two medical orderlies.

They were about an hour away from the Camp Bastion field hospital. Someone said Apache Longbow helicopter gunships were circling overhead on the *kay-vee*.

A medic struggled to take his pulse; another tried to get a cannula into him to deliver an intravenous drip of saline fluid. If he was about to die the odds were on his doing so within the next thirty to forty minutes.

'*Blink if you can hear me?*' a voice shouted.

He blinked.

'*Full name, rank and regiment ... Captain Hal Stirling ... 101 Engineer Regiment, Explosive Ordnance Disposal. Counter-IED Task Force. Since we departed Nahr-e Saraj you've bloody died twice.*'

He didn't think so. They were nowhere near Nahr-e Saraj. *We won't let you die a third time.*

And for the third time you rose from the dead
Ascended into heaven
And sitteth on the right hand of the Father
Whence he cometh to judge the living and the dead.

Did you pack this case yourself? In case of your death, will your insurance company pay for the return of your body to the United Kingdom?

He must have lost consciousness—
the next thing he knew
the ambulance crew was stretchering him out of the Chinook.

He was being ferried to the emergency department. He remembered the rising Chinook's rotors howling. Whooshing clouds of dust.

The helicopter rose skywards like some airborne beast: And I beheld, and, lo, in the midst of the throne and of the four beasts, and in the midst of the elders, stood a Lamb as it had been slain, having seven horns and seven eyes, which are the seven Spirits of God sent forth into all the earth.

And I saw when the Lamb opened one of the seals, and I heard, as it were the noise of thunder, one of the four beasts saying – Come and see.

Fuck-Fuck-Fuck.

Hold Thou Thy cross before my closing eyes;
Shine through the gloom and point me to the skies.
Heaven's morning breaks, and earth's vain shadows flee;
In life, in death, O Lord, abide with me.

4

Apart from St John the Divine and Fuck-Fuck in his head he heard other friendly and familiar voices, sometimes his mother's calling to him, echoing across the moors beyond The Towers; or his lover whispering on his pillow.

He thought he saw faces cut from blood oranges in the crimson mist before his eyes. Inches in front of him: the veined faces turned rubbery and the toothless mouths opened and screamed.

'Headley Court will set his head straight,' a voice said.
  'There's nothing wrong,' he said – *without a sound* – 'with my fucking head.'
  'That's what you think,' another voice said.
  Except that's what he *thought* he heard.

That was Helmand then
  – the Desert of Death
  – where your brain gets paresthesia
  – said to be where God comes to cry

TWO

You wonder what I am doing? Well, so do I, in truth. Days seem to dawn, suns to shine, evenings to follow, and then I sleep. What I have done, what I am doing, what I am going to do, puzzle and bewilder me. Have you ever been a leaf and fallen from your tree in autumn and been really puzzled about it? That's the feeling.

FROM HAL TO SUMIKO, FROM THE LETTER BY
T. E. LAWRENCE TO ERIC KENNINGTON
(6 MAY 1935)

Headley Court, the Defence Medical Rehabilitation Centre, is a ten-minute drive from Epsom through the Surrey countryside.

The agreed arrangement for his treatment was that he could rest and convalesce at home and make the longish journeys to see the doctors at Headley Court.

Home was The Towers, the family house near Carlisle.

When he arrived at Headley Court he had a variety of minor shrapnel wounds and a mid-shaft tibia and fibula fracture. There were other servicemen at Headley Court in far worse physical and mental states. Thanks to treatment with antivenom the effects of the Levantine viper's hit had been neutralized. The physical damage could be repaired.

Still showing symptoms of trauma, he was referred to a civilian psychological counsellor attached to the Defence Medical Services.

The counsellor must have realized it would require a small miracle to return Hal to active service as an effective Army bomb disposal expert. The counsellor didn't say as much; he said he wanted to help Hal heal his wounds himself. He entertained 'a genuine conviction, given time and care, the most serious scars, the scars of trauma' would mend.

He congratulated Hal for showing 'an acute and intelligent interest' in his problems and in what might be their origins. Hal said he knew about the origins. They didn't warrant medical attention. It was normal to be drawn to fear and its attendant pain: the pain of fear.

When he wondered vaguely why fear induced euphoria, the counsellor gabbled on about 'the power of endorphins, the body's painkiller or analgesic, the opioid like morphine produced in the brain and spinal cord and elsewhere . . .'

Hal dismissed the idea he might be a victim of Traumatic Brain Injury or TBI, one of those catch-all phrases employed to describe 'signature injuries' of the conflict in Afghanistan; particularly injuries caused by IEDs. The viper might have accentuated his latent phobia for such creatures. Other than that he maintained there was nothing wrong in his head.

The counsellor treated him with professional gentleness. Hal was 'facing a difficult time. What with the approach of Christmas, the darkness falling in the early afternoons and the threat of severe cold and snows, Christmas frequently induces a melancholy frame of mind.'

More than his own condition, Hal said it was his mother's that was giving him cause for concern. She was suffering from a combination of heart disease, rheumatic arthritis, respiratory problems and the onset of dementia.

'What will you feel when she dies?' the counsellor asked.

'What d'you think I'll feel?'

'In practical terms, what will the future hold for you?'

'I take responsibility for the family home and all that entails.'

'What do you feel about that?'

'What anyone would.'

'What, in a word, does The Towers conjure up for you?'

'Silence.'

'When you think of it, what do you see?'

'Bleak moorland near Carlisle shrouded in darkness. The façade of blackened stone.'

'What does it embody?'

'A presence. Presences.'

'What presences?'

'Brooding spirits. Spirits that my mother sees that persuaded her to recognize her gifts of mediumship.'

'Do they trouble you?'

'The spirits? I don't know. I can't say they are pleasant.'

'Unpleasant?'

'Perhaps.'

'What physical form do they take?'

'God knows. They're intangible. My mother maintains they speak to her during séances; as well as to one or two women similarly possessed of the powers of mediumship. She established contact with the other world when I was small soon after my father died. She held regular séances to listen to what my father had to say from the great beyond. She even established contact with the first owner of The Towers, Sir Glendower Stirling. Like my father before her, Mother has more friends and acquaintances on the other side in the spirit world than in the real one.'

'You feel your mother is imprisoned by the spirits?'

'No idea. Could be. You'd have to ask her. Mind you, if any of the spirits, my father's among them, have advised my mother to sell off the family land to increase the finances required for the upkeep of the house, well, she hasn't done much about it.'

'You want to preserve the house?'

'Yes, I do.'

'No matter that it harbours spirits?'

'We all have our burdens. If you were to tell me the house is insane, I'd agree.'

'Houses,' the counsellor declared, 'are neither sane nor insane.'

Hal was about to say: 'You should listen to what it has to say. Perhaps you could help it heal itself—' then thought better of it. The counsellor was doing his best to help. Yet there was a curious sense of disengagement about their conversations. The two men talked at each other rather than to each other. The counsellor didn't seem to get to the heart of Hal's problem.

During their final session before Christmas, Hal said: 'I don't want to give you the impression there's something wrong with my mind.'

The counsellor affected to ignore the comment. 'Perhaps,' he said, 'you'd like to stay here for a while – stay away from home a bit? I can recommend you be given a room.'

'No thanks.'

'The idea doesn't appeal to you?'

'Not much. Quite honestly, I can't take the sight of the officers and men walking around with legs and hands missing. The amputees staring at the walls. The barracks humour. The mucky sex jokes. The relentless kindness of the orderlies and nurses. The bloody wheelchairs humming and careering about in all directions. The padre and the visitors telling me I'm a hero. *Hero?* You get a bang on the head and you're a goddamn *hero*. The doctors asking: "How are you?" How do they *think* I am? Can't they bloody *see* how I am? They're paid to tell me how I am. I hate the dependency. I want my freedom back. Anyway, I have my mother to think of.'

The counsellor suggested he should head for home.

'You're through with me?'

'Of course not.'

'I'm sorry,' Hal said. 'I didn't mean to lose my cool. These days it seems to be the norm.'

'I understand what you're going through.' The counsellor's tone was saccharine. 'I think home will be the place for you to spend Christmas. It'll do you good. Your mother will want you there. I hope she improves. Go home before the weather gets any worse. Safe journey.'

Take your problems with you, he might as well have added.

Hal left Headley Court downcast.

Mother wasn't going to improve and the weather had already got worse.

On the spur of the moment, he decided to break his journey home and call on Sumiko to raise his spirits.

6

He found a crowded afternoon train at King's Cross bound for Cambridge. There he hired a car and drove the fifteen miles to Sumiko's cottage in the Hertfordshire village of Ashwell.

A previous customer had left a homemade tape in the cassette player. Over and over it played Elton John's duet with Aretha Franklin, 'Through The Storm'.

It was dark by the time he arrived in Ashwell.

By way of an immediate welcome, she said: 'You must go.' Judging from previous visits when she answered her door in her kimono with her hair still wet from a bath, he could tell she wanted him to stay.

She reached past him and dropped the door's lock and as she did so she kissed him. She kissed his lower lip; he her upper lip, and then he slowly kissed her ears and neck. Lowering her face, she took his hand and led him to the bedroom.

Omedetou Christmas
Omedetou Christmas
Omedetou Christmas
Oiwaishimashou

She untangled herself from his arms and threw off the duvet. She hurriedly dressed in a white T-shirt and jeans.

'Yukio's village friends,' she said. 'I must give them something . . .'

Minnashite asobi mashou
Omadetou Christmas
Oiwaishimashou

– followed by the carol singers' happy shouts. 'We wish you a Merry Christmas.'

He heard the front door open and 'Happy Christmas.' Then: '*Arigatou gozaimasu.*'

'Thank you. Merry Christmas,' Sumiko said. 'Meerii Kurisumasu.'

He heard the door close and the light tread of her footsteps coming up the stairs.

She glanced at the bedside clock, its greenish digital numbers flickering like a warning. 'Yukio's coming back soon,' she said. 'Her father's bringing her home. You have to leave before they get here.'

'They won't get far in the snow.'

'You managed.'

'Only just.'

He stroked her hair. 'Then let's at least have dinner at the hotel – you and me?'

'I have to be here for Yukio.'

'She can come to dinner too.'

'She can't. She's only eight. You must leave.'

'I'll call the hotel and get a room for the night.'

'For you. For one. A single room, Hal.'

'Let's wait and see.'

They dressed and went downstairs.

He reserved a table for dinner in half an hour. He was about to book a room in the hotel when the telephone rang. Sumiko spoke curtly in Japanese. '*Hai – ii esa-yōnara* – Yes. No. Goodbye.'

'What was that about?' he asked.

'My husband. The snow. Too dangerous to drive. Yukio's staying over with her father tonight.'

'So we can have dinner.'

In spite of the snow, he insisted on driving her to the hotel.

'You have no suitcase,' she said, delighted at the patterns of the snow falling across the windscreen.

'I have everything I need at The Towers. Everything, that is – except you. I planned to get home tonight. I'll try tomorrow.'

It was only half true. He'd planned the visit. He longed

31

to stay the night with her. The Towers would still be there waiting for him.

There were two Range Rovers parked outside the hotel. He noticed each had large Hertfordshire Farmers Federation stickers in the rear window.

They were the only people in the dining room except for four large men the worse for wear from drink, young farmers hooting about rugby football.

'How's your mother?' she asked.

'Very weak, I'm afraid. Not long for this earth. It'll be a merciful release when she goes.'

'Is she in a lot of pain?'

'She's drugged to the eyeballs.'

'And still has those nurses looking after her?'

'Teresa and Francesca. Thank God for the sainted mother and her daughter. More governesses than nurses. Otherwise she'd be in hospital. Except, as you can imagine, she refused to be admitted.'

They toyed with a shared salad and plates of roast chicken. He ordered a bottle of claret and drank most of it.

'And you, Hal-san ... how are you – how are you really?'

'Much better for seeing you.'

She reached across the table for his hand. It seemed a good sign. But the intimacy was interrupted by raucous laughter from the drunken gang of four. One of them had the tips of his forefingers to the sides of his eyelids and was drawing his eyes sideways. Hal could tell the men were taunting Sumiko.

'Would you mind lowering your voices?' he asked.

The men continued talking in theatrical whispers.

'Don't worry,' she said. 'If I were black they wouldn't make those remarks. But you British have an open season as far as we're concerned. Don't get involved, Hal. *Horei* – keep cool. Tell me about yourself. How are you – really?'

'Fine. Believe me.'

'Is that what the doctors say?'

'More or less. I'll be back in harness soon.'

'And then . . . you'll go back to Afghanistan?'

'If you allow me to.'

'I allow you to do anything you want,' she said.

'But you wouldn't allow me to have my heart broken, would you?'

'It's your heart, Hal. And . . .'

'And . . . what?'

She smiled. 'I too have a heart.' She took her mobile telephone from her shoulder bag. 'Here. I want to take a photo of you.'

'Good idea,' said Hal. 'Me too.'

They took photographs of each other.

'No flash photography,' came the shout from the far table.

The waiter asked if they'd enjoyed the food. Was there

anything else they wanted? Sumiko ordered mint tea. Hal a glass of brandy.

Across the room the four men were quarrelling with the waiter about their bill. Finally, one of them slammed a wad of notes onto the table. A glass toppled to the floor and smashed.

'You look tired, Hal,' Sumiko said softly. 'You must get some sleep. I'm going to pay for dinner.'

'No, you're not – no, Sumiko. *Please*. Let me—'

'You're my guest.' She called for the bill.

'I'll drive you home,' he offered.

'You've had too much to drink.'

Once she'd settled the bill he took her hand and led her to the doorway. He asked the hotel receptionist where the men's room was and told Sumiko to wait for him.

He was washing his hands when two of the men barged past him towards the urinals. Hal noticed one of them urinating across the floor. The other man laughed and shouted: 'Look who's here. Hey, c'mon – c'mon . . .' He made an obscene gesture with his fingers. 'C'mon. What's Madam Butterfly like in bed – eh?'

Hal dried his hands. His fury rising, he made for the door. He felt his hands began to shake, his mouth dry.

The thug blocked his exit. 'Hey – I ask a gentleman a question he answers it, right? I asked you a question – yes?'

'Excuse me,' Hal said quietly.

The other drunk was throwing up over the floor.

'If you want to leave this pisshole alive you fucking answer my fucking question.'

Hal reached out to open the exit door. The man barred his way. He leaned so close to Hal's face his malodorous spit fell against Hal's cheek. 'Tell you what, matey. You've her smell on your dick.'

The man being sick had crawled through his vomit into one of the cubicles and was coughing with such violence that he never saw what happened when Hal struck the man blocking his way. He delivered two very sharp blows, one with his knee, straight up into the big man's genitals. As the man's mouth opened to howl, Hal thwacked his jaw with his fist.

The man's head crashed back against the door. He collapsed onto the tiles, his bloodied face lowering into the pool of his companion's pee.

He hurried through the hotel to where Sumiko was waiting by the main exit. The two remaining men made an exaggerated show of gallantry, opening the door for her.

One raised his hands as if hoping to receive The Sacrament of Communion and asked for a tip.

Hal led Sumiko to the car.

'What's wrong?' she asked.

He told her about the confrontation with the drunken racist. 'You hit him – you left him lying there unconscious?'

'He'll survive.'

'You shouldn't have done it on my behalf. Suppose he's seriously injured?'

'He's lucky I didn't have a bayonet.'

'Oh, Hal.' She shook her head. 'Wherever you go there's danger. It's best to walk away. And look—' She was staring at his knuckles. 'They're bleeding. You'd better let me clean you up.'

'I should've punched him harder.'

'You shouldn't have punched him in the first place.'

'Others can judge.'

'I judge you've had too much to drink.'

'I lost my temper. These days it flares up suddenly. Never used to.'

'That's one of the things I loved about you.'

Loved. He wondered if the past tense was intentional.

'Your level head,' she said. 'I love your level head. You mustn't cause yourself unnecessary stress, Hal. In your condition . . .'

'Let's not talk about my condition.'

Outside her cottage the snow lay deep.

Leaving the car, he saw one of the Range Rovers draw up at the end of the street. Its headlights were raised and the light dazzled him.

The headlights were suddenly turned out. The Range Rover stayed put.

Sumiko's Jack Russell terrier began to bark and Sumiko was fiddling with her keys. He decided not to alarm her, to say nothing about the Range Rover. Its lights came on again and it began to drive slowly towards the cottage.

Once inside he slipped the chain lock in place. Sumiko had walked through the living area to the small kitchen at the back. She was talking rapidly to the yelping Jack Russell. '*Takahiro. Takahiro.* Good dog. *Out you go* – and you sit down, Hal. I'm going to make some tea. Then I'll see to that hand of yours.'

'It's nothing.'

'If you'd been on your own it wouldn't have happened. It's my fault.'

'It's not your fault, Sumiko.'

She smiled. 'You shouldn't have done it on my account. Anyway, you can't drive anywhere tonight. Put some logs on the fire.'

He called National Rail Enquiries. There were innumerable cancellations and the chance of services tomorrow was slim. He decided to make arrangements with the hire car firm to drive north in the morning.

He parted the window blinds. The road was quiet; the snow still, and there was no sign of the Range Rover.

Sumiko returned with tea. 'How long will you stay up there?' she asked.

'I don't know. Until I get a hundred per cent fit. Sometimes, like now, I feel fine. Then I get tired for no apparent reason. I get cold in the legs. The fracture may have healed but it aches. My head spins. I think it's the medication. The morphine has ugly side effects.'

She cleaned his grazed knuckles and dressed them with Elastoplast. 'It's a pity The Towers is so far away from anywhere. Don't you find it lonely?'

'It's the only home I know. The fact is – if the Army doesn't work out – when Mother dies ... The Towers is what's left. I'll be there alone. The reality is that, in Mother's case, that day's fast approaching.'

'You'll be happy up there alone?'

'It's fine in spring and summer. Autumn's okay too. It's only in the winter the whole place seems so isolated. The silence can be disturbing. I've been thinking, perhaps I'll get myself a housekeeper.'

'Why not a Romanian girl? I get endless e-mails from Romanian girls asking for domestic jobs.'

'Maybe. You once said you'd love to live there with me and with Yukio too.'

She sat looking at him straight in the eyes. 'Things have changed, Hal, haven't they? That's the truth. You and me. Things have changed. Anyway, Yukio couldn't bear to be parted from Takahiro.'

'Then bring Takahiro. There are plenty of rats and rabbits for him to hunt.'

'It's too far removed from civilization. And there are the voices your mother hears. Don't you remember how frightened Yukio was? We lay together, you and me, listening to the wind whispering. Don't you remember? We heard the rain talking. And in the morning you took photos of me standing by the window. "Two girls in silk kimonos," you said. "Both beautiful, one a gazelle . . ." I was jealous of the other one.' She paused. 'What happened to those photos?'

'They're in my bedroom desk drawer along with strands of your hair. Under lock and key.'

'You've never shown them to anyone else?'

'Of course I haven't.'

'My husband showed me photos of his previous lovers.'

'I haven't got any of mine. And there isn't another woman.'

'Promise me, Hal.'

'Cross my heart.'

'Swear to God?'

'Swear to God.'

'Has your mother seen them?'

'The photos?'

'I'm naked in them.'

'I know. Beautiful.'

'Are you sure she hasn't seen them?'

'*Sumiko* – of course she hasn't seen them.'

'Aren't you frightened of her any more?'

'Frightened of her?'

'She frightened me,' Sumiko said.

'She only took against you because you're not an English rose. You know her sort.'

'Old English ladies who believe in ghosts . . .'

'Lonely souls are the only people who see ghosts.'

'Isn't that what you want – to be alone?'

'Perhaps. I might, well, I might fear being alone for the rest of my life.'

'Isn't that what you want?'

'If I can't have you, Sumiko, there's nothing I can do about it.'

'I know. And you are special to me, Hal. You always have been. Ever since you bumped against my arm in that restaurant in Kensington and spilled the cranberry juice over my white dress and offered to pay for it to be cleaned.'

'I did pay, didn't I?'

'I can't believe you don't remember.'

'Of course I remember.'

'And you wrote down your address on the menu. Stirling Towers, Moster Lees, Carlisle, Cumbria.'

'And you spent a very long time looking at it.'

'My husband took the menu and tore it up.'

'Even then you never mentioned him by name.'

'Because I don't like him.'

'A month later you were in my bed.'

'*Two* months later.' She took his hand and held it

against his cheek. 'You used to say you'd dreamed things about me.'

She stared at the wood fire and as if listening to the silence, she frowned. 'I can't hear Takahiro.'

'I'll go and find him.'

He left the cottage by the back door. The snow had stopped and the night sky was clear. When he breathed in the cold air it hurt his lungs. He thought he heard footsteps, a distant squeal of rubber on ice, the crunching of frozen grit, a departing car. The light in Sumiko's bedroom went on. He looked up and saw her close the curtains.

The effect of the alcohol had lessened yet his throat was dry and he felt his heart beating. He gave a low whistle. 'Takahiro? Come. Come . . .' He gazed into the dark, shivered and called out: *Takahiro* one last time. To no avail. He went back into the warmth of the cottage locking the door after him.

'Come upstairs,' Sumiko called.

The lights in the living area had been turned out and she had lit a candle in her bedroom and wore the white silk kimono, the one he had given her as a birthday present two years before. 'When the fire burns low the house gets cold,' she said as if it were a proverb. She drew back the duvet.

'There's no sign of Takahiro,' he said.

'Don't worry. He often wanders off into the night. He'll have found somewhere safe to sleep.'

Sunlight woke him.

She was whispering. 'I've run a bath for you.' She was dressed in the white silk kimono. 'There's coffee, toast and marmalade for you. Then – you must go. Yukio and her father will be here in an hour from now.'

She stood by the window silhouetted against the sunlight. He saw she'd folded his clothes. A familiar sign, something she did when she wanted him to stay. Without another word she went downstairs.

As she went he thought *she has no feet*. Traditionally, Japanese ghosts have no feet. Western ghosts have feet and they are transparent. Japanese ghosts are shadowy things.

He had frequently asked her to explain the reasons for things she did and she'd laugh at him and shake her head and look at him with amusement. The one thing predictable about Sumiko was her unpredictability. He loved her for it. Sumiko the Unexpected. He looked at the windows edged with crystalline frost patterns.

*

After he'd bathed and dressed he joined her for breakfast in the kitchen. 'No sign of Takahiro?' he asked.

'He'll have gone to my neighbours. They spoil him.'

'What made you change your mind, Sumiko?'

'Sorry?'

'About last night?'

'*Taisetsu*.'

'What's that?'

'It means you're precious.'

'Does that mean you'll come and stay?'

'It depends on your mother, doesn't it?'

'It depends on me.'

'We'll see. We'll see.'

Which equally meant Yes or No.

Wrapped in her cashmere coat, she stood by the door to watch him leave. 'Telephone me ... tell me when you've arrived there safely. Promise?'

'I promise.'

The snow and ice creaked beneath his feet. The car was covered in snow and there was a white mound on the car's bonnet.

He brushed away the snow and his fingers touched the animal's open mouth.

Takahiro's throat had been slit from ear to ear.

As in summer, as in winter.

The arrangement of her garden consisted not so much of the snow-covered rocks, trees and plants. The space between them also counted like the silence between her words. The winter shapes matched the flower arrangement inside the house.

She didn't protest against the inevitable. 'Even when things can't be helped,' she used to say. 'Things can be helped.' So the death of Takahiro made her smile. Not that she wasn't profoundly upset; rather she exhibited no emotion. The smile was a smile. Just that. 'The absence of emotion causes no nuisance.'

He helped her bury the corpse at the end of the quiet garden. Given the frozen earth, no easy task.

His first reaction was to go back to the hotel and establish the identity of the men who'd been in the restaurant. He wondered if they intended to return. But any minute now her husband and daughter would show up and Sumiko insisted he leave.

'I'm very sorry,' he said.

'It's not your fault. I'll tell Yukio that a car hit Takahiro and I buried him. You must go. You're not going to drive the whole way to Carlisle? Go by train, Hal. Please.'

'If you promise to visit me. There's always Christmas. If the sun shines it's beautiful at Christmastime.'

'I'll have Yukio with me.'

'It's not as though I'm short of guest rooms. Bring her too. And I have a plan. I'll get her a puppy as a Christmas present. A Jack Russell puppy.'

She smiled. 'I hope you get a train.'

'So do I. I'm sorry, Sumiko . . .'

'Hurry up and call the station. Perhaps there are trains still running.'

He followed her inside the house and called National Rail Enquiries. The train timetables had been thrown into chaos. Few trains were running. There might possibly, he learned, be a midday train from Cambridge via Euston to Carlisle. Service couldn't be guaranteed.

'Now go, Hal. Please.'

'I seem to bring you bad luck,' he told her.

'I don't believe in the wheel of fortune,' she said. 'You must go home to your mother. Call me once you're safe at home – promise?'

Promise echoed in his head throughout the journey.

The wheel of fortune Sumiko disbelieved determined that the rail system had not entirely ground to a halt. By now the battery of his mobile telephone was running very low. It was only when he changed trains at Peterborough during the long wait for the Leeds train that he succeeded in making a call home from a public telephone.

The line was poor and he could barely hear the whispery voice of his mother's nurse. 'This is The Towers,' she said. She spoke very quietly with a genteel Yorkshire accent.

'Sister Vale?'

'Oh, Hal. I didn't recognize your voice. We've been trying to reach you.' He could tell from her quavering tone that something was wrong. 'Please, Hal, you must come home.'

'I'm doing my best. I'm at Peterborough. I've been delayed. Waiting for the Leeds train. How's my mother?'

'She's very weak, Hal. The doctor's with her. He thinks the end is nearing.'

'How near?'

'She's sinking. Francesca and me have stayed at her bedside round the clock. She's drifting in and out of consciousness. She's been asking for you, Hal. For your father too. She thinks he's seated by her bed. She can see him. He talks to her.' Her voice grew tearful. 'I don't think she recognizes me any more. We're so looking forward to having you back. There's a lot to be seen to before Christmas.'

'Be sure to tell my mother I'm on my way.'

'She thinks you're here already. She's seen you playing outside in the snow. Building bonfires and snowmen . . .'

'If it makes her happy then don't disabuse her.'

'She asks – "Is Hal talking to me from beyond?" She thinks you've passed over.'

'Put her right.'

'Francesca and me will make your room nice and comfy.'

'That's very kind,' said Hal impatiently. 'We can talk in the morning. Don't wait up.'

He stood on the platform watching two teenagers seated on a platform bench: the boy with a harmonica, the girl with a battered guitar.

They were singing: *When you walk through the storm – Hold your bonce up high—*

It took him back to Helmand. He tried to shut his

ears – *Walk on, through the wind* – *And you'll get shit in your eyes. Walk on, through the piss and you'll die of pneumonia* . . .

Snowflakes whisked about, settling on his face, and the cold burned his skin.

The sky lowered like a trap. He felt completely alone and loneliness inflamed the sense of impending loss: fear that he might lose Sumiko.

Walk on, walk on, with hope in your heart . . .

He felt a rare stab of homesickness, longing for a home possessed of warmth, friendliness and unconditional love. Things he'd never known.

He glanced at the rail tracks, yellow light flickering, silken, shining, the rails creaking with the train's approach.

The voice on the tannoy announced: 'The train now approaching Platform One is . . .'

The train rolled and juddered its way slowly north through Grantham, Newark and on to Retford, Doncaster and Wakefield.

For most of the journey he was the sole passenger in the carriage. His mobile phone, its battery flat, was of no use. The power point for charging it provided by the rail company was out of order.

Catching sight of his reflection in the window he saw his face now bore few signs of his time in Afghanistan. In his dark grey overcoat, black silk scarf and worn leather cap there was, he thought, the look of a stateless person about his appearance that gave no indication of his profession.

He wondered – as lately he often had – if his military career might be at an end, quite what the future held in store. As now seemed inevitable, if his mother had only a short time left, he told himself his indefinite future lay at The Towers. That's where he'd have to get a life.

It was a daunting prospect. The whole place was in need of repair. It would require an extensive structural survey and the cost of essential building works might prove prohibitive.

On the other hand, there were, if only reputedly, paintings and tapestries and furniture of considerable value and he had always supposed that their sale might yield enough capital to carry out the necessary works. He was far from clear how the place could ever produce an income.

It had been his mother's wish, also indeed his solemn promise, that he would live there throughout his lifetime. In so far as he hadn't actually set eyes on a copy of her Will, he was unclear what might happen if he were to sell up – except she'd said, with stern conviction, that 'the person or persons responsible for its sale *will*' – not '*would*' – become '*insane, be struck down, committed to eternal damnation and hell-fire*'.

Naturally, he gave slight credence to this view, except

since his return from Afghanistan she had perceived, possibly even actually seen, malignant spirits. Reasonably enough, he'd put these sightings of hers down to the wanderings of her mind.

In truth, they'd occurred with greater regularity since his father died, frequently during his mother's deranged outbursts inflamed by the structural deterioration of The Towers.

One of the more painful nightmares that visited him was the sight of her open mouth, separated from her face like a pair of false teeth set in rubber, moaning *The Towers The Towers The Towers* like Poe's bells: *How the danger sinks and swells, by the sinking or the swelling in the anger of the bells of the bells of the bells, bells, bells, bells, bells.*

Over the tracks. Homewards bound. Over the tracks. Click and clack. *Sumiko – Sumiko—*

A word in his ear: 'Sir?'
  '*What*—?'
  'You're going to Carlisle?'
  He looked up at the conductor. 'Carlisle? Yes.'
  'This service is terminating at Leeds.'
  'No trains whatsoever?'
  'You wish. You're lucky to have got this far.'

LEEDS CITY STATION

A Salvation Army band played 'Silent Night'. He tossed a pound coin in the collection box and heard a familiar voice. 'Captain Stirling.'

'MacCullum. Good to see you.'

'How are we, Sir?'

'Fine, thanks. You?'

'Bloody weather.'

Of indeterminate middle age, Ryker MacCullum was a dour figure no more than five feet six inches tall. He wore a jacket cut too long to make him took taller. Tonight, as well as the usual long black coat with a velvet collar, he wore a funereal black hat. There was the look of the weasel about him.

Like his father before him, MacCullum owned the village garage, the Moster Lees undertaking business and ran a sideline breeding pedigree saddleback pigs he butchered himself in his garden sheds. 'Sister Vale's asked me to collect you,' he said. 'No more trains tonight. Not tomorrow either, I dare say, or the day after that.'

'The roads passable?'

'We'll try 'em. Vectra's in car park. We'll get you home. Take a while, mind.'

'When did you get here?'

'Mid-morning. Funeral in Leeds.'

'Anyone local?'

'Not local you might say from Moster Lees. It were a twelve-year-old girl.' He fiddled with the band of white silk thread around his wrist from which a small ornament dangled. 'Congenital brain damage. Never get over a child going. Mother's suffering from traumatic grief. Can't think of worse. It's upset the wife. She were at school with the lass's aunt. I always say it's family what matters. Back home's where we belong. That's why we'll be getting you home safely, Sir. No sweat. Like I say, Vectra's in the short-term car park.'

The Vauxhall Vectra was a grey six-speed air-conditioned hearse.

'If snowploughs have been out we may make it in just above of three or four hours.' He drove the hearse down the car park's ramps. 'If the snow gets worse I'll be making sure The Towers doesn't get cut off. If you've no objection I'll be collecting the wife. Got to pick her up from the Queens Hotel. I've a folding seating deck in the back that the wife doesn't mind.'

MacCullum led his portly wife out of the hotel. In a black coat and hat she leaned heavily on his arm. Once she was installed with a pile of shopping bags in the back of the hearse it soon became clear to Hal she'd been drinking heavily.

'Sorry, Sir. I'm so sorry.'

He thought she was talking about his repatriation. 'It could be worse.'

'Yes. She could've lingered on in pain.'

'Not now, Betsy,' MacCullum snapped.

'Your mother . . .' Betsy said.

52

MacCullum brought the hearse to a sudden stop. 'Bloody hell. You heard what Teresa said.'

'It's not going to bring her bloody back.'

'My mother . . .?' Hal said quietly.

'She were lovely.'

MacCullum hissed: 'Shut up.' He turned to face Hal. 'I'm sorry. Sister Vale gave us orders. She wanted to be the one to tell you—'

'Tell me what?'

'Your mother passed over two days ago. Rest her soul.'

'But Sister Vale said she was alive a few hours ago.'

'She wanted to keep it secret from you,' MacCullum said. 'Until you got back to The Towers. So she could tell her yourself. They seemed to know she was sinking.'

'I'd have thought . . .' Mrs MacCullum said, 'they'd have moved heaven and earth to tell you, Captain Stirling – you of all people, what with you her only son. She being so ill and all.'

'The solicitor had us prepare her for the crematorium,' MacCullum said. 'We had the funeral yesterday.'

'Sun came out,' said Mrs MacCullum. 'Just for a minute. Your mother, Captain, you know something? She always did want the best for you. Saw to it you never wanted for any little thing. She was so proud of you.' She choked back tears. 'We're proud of all you boys in uniform.'

MacCullum pulled out into the road and headed into the snow. 'Sorry about all that,' he said.

Mrs MacCullum sucked her teeth. 'Did I say something? Seems Mrs Stirling only wanted nice Sister Vale and her daughter at the graveside. They've been wonderful to your mother. Francesca's an angel. And the Vicar did it perfect in spite of his having the Asian 'flu. Solicitor was there too seeing to your mother's wishes. She left orders. No fuss.'

Hal stared at the snow falling across the yellowish streetlights.

'Say if you want to stop off for a hot drink,' MacCullum said.

'There's a nice place in Skipton,' said Mrs MacCullum.

'We aren't going to Skipton.'

'Barnoldswick then?'

'No, Betsy. Barnoldswick neither.'

Tears overcame her. 'Things have changed. I don't like change.' She began to rummage in her handbag. 'I need a fag.'

'No smoking in the hearse,' MacCullum said.

All arms and elbows, Mrs MacCullum couldn't prevent the handbag spewing its contents across the floor.

The airless hearse was overheated and Mrs MacCullum fell asleep.

'Do you want me to share the driving, MacCullum?'

'Best keep going. The Towers – won't be the same with your mother gone, Captain. Be different, won't it?'

'It will stay about the same, MacCullum.'

'Daresay the future of the old place is now in your hands, Captain. There'll be changes up there, then?'

'I don't think so.'

'Moster doesn't welcome change. So there'll just be you and Sister Vale and her daughter up there? They'll look after you, Captain. Salt of the earth. Strange that Teresa never married again. She's classy, softhearted. More the governess type. You wonder where she sprang from. Mind, there's plenty of fellers in the locality that fancy her. Voluptuous is the word, isn't it? Keeps herself to herself, mind. Francesca's a cracker too. And you, Sir, if you don't mind me asking . . . will you be courting, then?'

'Being in the Army, you know, it isn't easy.'

'Now you're back you can settle down at home. Or will you be going back to Afghanistan?'

'We'll see.'

'A good rest at The Towers over Christmas will do you the world of good. Christmas always lifts the spirits.' He fell silent a while and then suddenly added: 'Country really appreciates what the boys are doing out there. Not that I could put me finger on the map and show you where Afghanistan is. Leeds, yes. Bradford, yes. Sheffield. Carlisle. London. Not Afghanistan. Must be a right shit-hole.'

Hal made no comment and MacCullum concentrated on his driving.

He thought of distant Helmand.

*

Heated rocks. Whirling dust storms. Apocalyptic thunder. Lightning streaking across the mountains.

True, to some people, the Afghan helter-skelter landscape is terrifying. Not to him.

The violent beauty of its colours beguiled him: scarlets, ultramarine, gold and silver; like colours from Byzantine icon paintings or crusaders' coats of arms.

Carmine, magenta and ruby. Venetian and Indian red, cherry and rose madder.

No matter it inspires internecine warfare, breeds plagues of flies and locusts and gives you disabling diarrhoea.

It's home to the Levantine vipers, the lizards and the scorps, the nomadic kuchis.

In another life I could've made a home there too.

'Shit-hole,' MacCullum said.

'It's actually rather beautiful.'

'Not as beautiful as Moster Lees. You want my opinion?'

Hal was sure he'd get it whether he wanted it or not.

'Moster Lees,' MacCullum announced, ' . . . and The Towers is the most enchanted place on earth. I'd even say – when you see The Towers in the snow you might think you'd arrived at the gates of Heaven. Pure holy magic. And at Christmastime. You could say, in the snow . . . beneath the moon . . . Watched over by womankind. White magic.'

*

He stared at the condensation on the window and saw the blurred image of his mother forming. She'd have liked MacCullum's turn of phrase. *White magic.* He heard her quavering voice: *A savage place! as holy and enchanted As e'er beneath a waning moon was haunted By woman wailing for her demon-lover! And from this chasm, with ceaseless turmoil seething, As if this earth in fast thick pants were breathing—*

MacCullum was saying: ' . . . remember you as a young lad like it were yesterday. Yesterdays were better days. You remember?'

He remembered.

Sleep denied him by the rainwater dripping from cracked ceilings clacking like metronomes into rusted buckets.

Long and pleasantly anxious afternoons alone talking to himself about the disappointments of the world elsewhere: mooching, head down, shoulders bent, eyes on the alert like a detective investigating the perpetual twilight of empty rooms; listening outside the heavy door to the family crypt beneath the Chapel for any voices from the vaults, home to the skeletons of his forebears, home to the noiseless communities of rats and maggot hordes.

Standing motionless, watching the play of watery sunlight shafts forming twisted rainbows in the fractures of the windows that hadn't been boarded up, trying to interpret their signals as though they were part of a semaphore system bringing good news.

A world more intense, more real and more human than that offered by the boarding schools whose teachers tried to educate him: tried to educate him, because he'd been born to educate himself and had spent most of his schooldays doing so.

The more perceptive of his teachers judged him to be a boy who'd always been middle-aged, very much the only son, a solitary from the past, unselfish, courteous, kindly and hard-working; a small useful pillar of a small society with the makings of, say, a diligent provincial solicitor; even, because there was something of the fossil about him, a museum palaeontologist.

They seemed to know he belonged to a family shipwrecked on an island where news from the outside world never seemed to reach.

If and when any of them raised the subject of The Towers, he said it was The Place of Fear.

They said he was young for his age when he achieved four Grade As in A levels, entered RMA Sandhurst, distinguished himself in military, practical and academic subjects; and at the end of the Sovereign's Parade marched up the steps of Old College to be commissioned Ensign in the Coldstream.

Out of the blue, one former teacher wrote to him saying that was exactly what he'd foreseen in his 'crystal ball'. He signed off: 'Nulli Secundus', the Coldstream motto. Second to None.

Hal had acquired the taste for handling bombs at Sandhurst. And though he loved the Coldstream and was intensely proud to be serving in the oldest regiment in continuous active service, he was already listening to the bombs and surrendering to the whispering of their siren songs.

In a different world, The Towers might have been Home Sweet Home: a world of unforgotten moments, his first kiss, where he first fell in love; where someone first told him that they loved him. The truth was different.

He remembered his mother had been his father's prisoner there. When he died she ruled over it. A barren place of dereliction, The Towers was the residence of broken souls. Time after time it drew the Stirlings back. It embraced and held them like a spider's shroud.

MacCullum continued talking: preoccupied with a story about the sighting of a ghost at the church in Haydon Bridge intriguing Teresa Vale.

'St Cuthbert's bones are buried there,' he said. 'Most of them are in Durham. But his skull and pelvis are buried near the altar. They were bricked up in the mists of time so as the Vikings wouldn't take them. There was this lass who wanted a lovely coat of crimson velvet to attract a boy and when she saw the local tailor making a coat for some lady or other she asked if the tailor would run a crimson velvet one up for her as well. The tailor said he would. No fee. You know what he had her do?'

'I never heard.'

'All she had to do was go to the church and steal the St Cuthbert Prayer Book from the altar for him. "Do that," he says, "and I'll make the coat up for you." So she creeps into the church the same night, takes the Prayer Book and as she's leaving, she hears these whispers in the entrance. Terrified, she hides herself behind the font and then she sees these two men coming into the church carrying a woman's corpse with an arrow in her breast and she sees them jemmy up the flagstones and lower the body on ropes down into the crypt. They replace the flagstones. You know what's next? The woman was alive. They'd bloody buried her alive. Then they ran for it. They'd had their way with her, the both of them, three-in-a-bed, and didn't want her to tell on them.

'Petrified, the girl runs home, trips on something, falls and twists her ankle. Then as she stands up she sees the thing she's tripped over, a longbow. And she knows whose. You know whose? Her lover's.

'Next day when he calls on her she's in her new coat and her lover tells her he's leaving her. Good riddance. Narrow escape. She might've got a lovely coat. But she's lost her lover. Then she went mad.

'She's the lass who appears every time there's a burial at the church. That's why Sister Vale wants to go there. She's asked me to take her there.'

'Why?'

'To get a sight of her, that's why.'

'Do you believe this, MacCullum?'

'She saw her.'

'Perhaps.'

'She bloody did. I saw her too.'

There were no lights in the windows of The Towers.

Battered by the whirling snow, Home was impenetrable, its windows hooded, its dark eyes watching the desolate moorland near Carlisle.

THREE

Horror. The state of mind expressed by this term implies terror, and is in some cases almost synonymous with it. He who dreads, as well as hates a man, will feel, as Milton uses the word, a horror of him.

CHARLES DARWIN
The Expression of Emotions in Man and Animals

Seen from a distance, it could easily be mistaken for a forbidding country house that had seen better days. As you approached it seemed to be more suited to those the world prefers to ignore: recluses, solitudinarians withdrawn from worldliness and public notice, supernatural beings and the mad. Perhaps, because it stood high on a hill in isolation, it looked larger than it was. Its size and shape only served to emphasize its aura of menace and fearfulness, mute repository of secrets and vague undercurrents of suppressed terror.

Its quartet of neo-Gothic towers comprised the square Victoria Tower at the south end, the octagonal spire of the Central Tower; the East Tower; and the Bell Tower at the north end. When seen against the dying sun in silhouette its windows resembled ranks of suspicious eyes. In winter, veiled by ice and snow, they gazed at you like the living dead.

MacCullum refused to take any payment for delivering him to the main entrance and he stayed resolutely at the wheel of the hearse with its engine turning over. It was as if he didn't want to venture too close. He kept the hearse's headlights on to make it easier for Hal to stumble through the blizzard towards the entrance.

He passed the stone statue of the house's creator standing in the portico. The likeness of the self-aggrandizing Sir Glendower Stirling was held to be the work of a follower of Sir Francis Legatt Chantrey. The family motto, *Capax Infiniti* or *Capable of the Infinite*, was carved into its marble pedestal. Sir Glendower's fortunes, amassed in South East Asia, had funded The Towers' original construction. Day and night Sir Glendower's blank eyes gazed into the distance with the expression of an anxious soul hearing troubled voices.

Hal struggled to unlock the entrance door. His hands were cold and he fumbled with the key. Finally the door opened and the snow and particles of ice seemed to follow him inside nipping at his ankles.

The hearse's headlights briefly illuminated the hallway and Hal turned, the glare dazzling him; and he gave a salute of cursory thanks to MacCullum who acknowledged the gesture with two dismissive hoots of the vehicle's horn and drove away.

He turned a light on in the hallway and began his walk across the flagstone floor to the dim passages leading to the Victoria Tower. The only sounds were of his shoes rapping against the stone, then muffled when he crossed threadbare floor rugs.

Passing the wooden staircase rising to the gallery on the floor above, he smelled the familiar scent of damp soot. The Towers, it seemed to him, had always smelled of damp soot. Soot was the smell of home, the odour of dark memories.

In a vain attempt to bring some life back to it, his mother had agreed to lease it as a country retreat, but the idea was soon abandoned, the result of visits by surveyors and officials from the Health and Safety Executive. One of them had been heard to say it was unfit for human habitation.

Priscilla Stirling retaliated: 'We Stirlings have lived here perfectly happily for a hundred and fifty years. As long as there is a Stirling, we will continue to do so until hell freezes.'

The route to his room in the Victoria Tower took him through the interior of the Central Tower.

Beneath the darkened ceilings he heard his father's voice. *'Recite the history after me ...'* His father had demanded that from an early age his son knew the history of the place. If the boy failed to offer a word-perfect recitation, the father would clip the child's knuckles with his Parker pen and call him an *ignoramus*.

He often found himself reciting one or other of his father's summaries. To do so kept the devils of terror and ill fortune at bay. Like not stepping on pavement cracks. Not walking under ladders. Not keeping the exact total of the IEDs you'd disabled. '*Sir Edward Elgar played the Music Room's piano after a visit to the waterfall Catrigg Force as the guest of his friend Dr Charles Buck in Settle, some eighty miles to the south. There's the Stone Drawing Room containing works by Rubens, Van Dyck and Claude Lorrain . . .*'

Elgar, keeper of a semi-secret mistress, had intrigued his father. Had his father similarly kept some lover secret from the world?

He tried to rid his mind of that high-pitched voice. It was a long time since he'd heard it and, with the passing of the years, the fabric of his life, like the fabric of The Towers, had changed

Passing years during which those old master paintings had been revealed to be of doubtful provenance; the floor of the Music Room had collapsed and the 'Elgar Piano' leaned like a broken coffin against curtained double doors more suited to a crematorium.

For as long as he could remember, the furniture in the Stone Drawing Room, Entrance Hall and Billiard Salon had stood covered in dust sheets resembling shrouds and the yards of leather-bound volumes in the Gothic Library's glass-fronted bookcases had remained unread.

His mother had forbidden access to the attics, said to offer sanctuary for pipistrelle bats from the *vesper-*

tilionidae family. The doors to the basement cellar where Hal's father's scientific archive was stored also remained locked.

There was a small derelict swimming pool connected to the ornate Turkish baths.

He paused by the barred entrance to the lower floor that housed them. The abandoned Turkish baths particularly intrigued him. Like his forebears, he entertained dreams of bringing both pool and baths back into use. One day, well, even the Stirling family Crypt and Chapel might be restored to their former neo-Gothic glory.

Low thudding brought him up sharply. Was it the snow beating against the windows behind the shutters?

He thought he heard an owl cry out.

Nearing the windows he saw one of the shutters had been parted from its hinges. A pane of glass had split and snow was blowing in across the windowsill.

He glanced outside.

No sign of the grazing land or the moors beyond. No sign of Moster Lees.

No tiny sparks of light from the hamlets further afield, no signs of life in Stonsey, Gretan or Warely. Wall upon wall of falling snow was building an impenetrable barrier between The Towers and the world beyond.

*

Here he was. Home.

The home that had tormented him as child because he'd never understood its darkest places.

What he hadn't understood had frightened him and he'd been too proud to ask his mother or any of the temporary cleaners or maintenance men who befriended him for explanations.

There'd been no one whom he might approach for confirmation or denial of the dark spirits sharing his home. They made him fearful.

'What is fear?' he'd once asked his father.

'Fear? Fear is Nothing. Fear of Fear is Everything.'

The door to the kitchen in the Victoria Tower opened with a creak.

A single night-light illuminated the wooden table in the centre of the room.

The nurses had left out two paper plates of sandwiches at the head of the table.

Propped against an unopened bottle of wine was an envelope addressed simply H.S. On the kitchen gas stove stood a saucepan of tomato soup.

He switched on the main lights and saw a small Christmas tree had been placed in front of the shuttered windows.

Mother and daughter must have been busying themselves in the family storerooms for they had decorated

the tree with angels, animals, wise men, shepherds and
the Baby Jesus he'd made as a child.

At the top of the tree stood the faded paper cut-out
he'd made of Sir Glendower's statue. Sir Glendower was
dressed as Father Christmas.

Remembering his promise to Sumiko to call her
he plugged in his mobile phone charger and then walked
unsteadily to the larder in search of a bottle of whisky.

Over supper for one – ham and cheese sandwiches,
tomato soup and neat whisky – he read the letter.

Dear Hal, I hope you have arrived home safely
without a hitch in this truly terrible weather. It
is with great sadness that I have to tell you your
mother passed over.

I wanted to tell you in person as your mother
so wished and before you heard the news from
anyone else but Francesca and I are very tired
and we have taken ourselves to bed.

Your mother passed over peacefully two days
ago in her sleep and as she instructed her
funeral took place with all speed.

We tried to make urgent contact with you but
what with the phone service being unreliable
and so on we couldn't.

Mr MacCullum and the Vicar and the Solicitor
and his clerk helped Francesca and me arrange
the small cremation and her ashes are scattered

in the Moster Lees churchyard again according to her instructions.

We took the liberty of laying a wreath from you upon the grave. I give you my greatest sympathy as does Francesca and if it is all right with you we would like to stay here until we can make new living arrangements in the New Year.

I hope you find your room warm enough. We lit a fire in the grate. We look forward to seeing you in the morning for breakfast.

With sympathy from us both, Teresa and Francesca

PS. Don't forget to take your medication. The nice doctor from Headley Court has spoken with me and I look forward to continue helping with your convalescence that's going so well and taking good care of you.

He sat staring at the reflected lights flickering on the surface of the tiles above the cooking range. He dumped the paper plates and soup bowl in the kitchen bin and took the bottle of whisky and a glass to his room.

A shadow, his own, stretched to the kitchen doorway. It seemed to move, to form a face.

He stood still listening. Tap. Tap. Tap. Dripping water from a leak? His shadow was the shadow of a hanging man.

He leaned heavily against the kitchen table. *All be better in the morning. Call Sumiko then. Take a Chinook to the Land of Nod. Take a bloody Lormetazepam.*

Which was what he did.

His feet began to hurry for the staircase and at first his body refused to follow suit. The staircase was wooden. Like most of the floorboards, it issued its special creaks of warning.

The door to his mother's room faced him and he felt drawn to look inside.

The walls were a patchwork of old silk and stucco stained by years of penetrative damp. He glanced at the paraphernalia of twenty-first-century geriatric care. Height-adjustable bed rails. Waterproof maintenance pads. Electric mobility wheelchair. Four-wheel walker with detachable shopping basket. Care kit as good as new.

This was where she'd died. The room where he'd heard the doctor ask a hundred times: 'How are we today?' As if he didn't know. *She's dying.*

The Vicar would drift in. Always he said, oddly with great slowness: 'In a bit of a dash – can't stay long, my lamb.' A gaunt figure, a shepherd's kindly son and former probation officer who'd seen The Shining and followed Glory's Light. 'How's our spirits this day?' he'd enquire with a look of pain. If Mother knew she didn't say. *'There's no one here at present. If you leave your name and number we'll get back to you.'* Like hell we will.

The fire in his bedroom grate burned low.

Here I am, home for the first time without Mother. He tried and failed to remember when last he'd stayed at The Towers without her.

Here I am. Standing in the centre of my room, once my nursery: along with its Japanese six-panel folding screen, the early nineteenth-century *byobu* of the Edo period, its delicate black-and-white images of figures dancing on a golden floor holding fans. Here were the familiar African hides, the Indian rugs, lace curtains, the crochet blankets on the formidable mahogany bed.

The wallpaper had been there for decades. The patterns of gathered and wreathed feathery flowers had long since faded. They'd been chosen by his mother who believed they'd calm the young Hal's over-whelming fear of darkness. When they failed to do so she'd leave the bedroom door ajar so the landing light's beam might do the trick. Leaving on a landing light remained an occasional nocturnal habit he never kicked. Yet the dull light still created shadows in the recesses of the high ceiling, creeping shadows that presaged nightmares.

Either Sister Vale or her daughter had arranged his cotton pyjamas on the goosedown pillows.

He changed out of his clothes and ran the hot tap of the large Victorian washbasin. Its stained glaze had webs of cracks and there were patches of green behind the heavy taps. The tepid brackish water spluttered across the basin, an intermittent putrid gush, producing a clanging in the water pipes somewhere within the wall.

He filled a china beaker and swallowed his pills; then remembered he'd left his supply of Lormetazepam downstairs in the kitchen, and his promise to telephone Sumiko. It would have to wait till morning. Or would it?

He wanted to hear her voice.

Rehearsing the lines to persuade her to join him for Christmas, he returned downstairs to the kitchen.

Then he froze – mesmerized by the power plug above the skirting board. The mobile phone charger wasn't there. Neither was the phone.

The landline would come into its own. But it didn't. Stone dead.

What in the name of God Almighty had he done with his mobile phone?

He opened the kitchen drawers. Not there. He poked about in the waste bin beneath the china sink. Not there either.

Once more he climbed the staircase to his bedroom paying no attention to the creaks, the rattling of the shutters, the distant voices moaning in the snows.

At nine o'clock next morning, trying not to wake him, Francesca Vale opened the shutters in his room onto the landscape magnificent in sun and snow. Welcome sunbeams filled the room raising sparkles on the gilt frame of the mirror that faced his bed.

'Good morning ... Hal,' she said, perhaps unsure whether to call him Hal or Captain Stirling. 'It's a lovely day.'

'Snow stopped?'

'Yeah. Sun'll soon melt the rest. Don't mind me making up the fire? Mam's bringing you breakfast in bed.' She broke open a packet of firelighters. 'I'm so sad,' she sighed, 'about Priscilla. I was there when she died. She didn't suffer. And the funeral was lovely. Small, mind. You know, private. Not so many flowers being as it's near Christmas and all. I shed buckets. Whatever ... Mam said it was the loveliest she'd ever been at. We had drinks and nibbles here afterwards. You couldn't get here, could you?'

'Alas. No.'

She spread out old newspapers round the grate and the dust made her sneeze.

'Francesca, you didn't by any chance see my mobile phone in the kitchen?'

'Mobile phone. No. Lost it, have we?'

'Yes. And the landline isn't working.'

'It is.'

'It wasn't last night.'

'It is now. Mam's been on the phone to the solicitor. He phoned early. And he's calling in at noon.'

'Warren is?'

'Mr Warren and his personal assistant. Sophie Peach. That's if the drive's been cleared of the snow in time. Ryker's using a snowplough.'

Edged with sunlight, her shoulder-length dark hair was lustrous like her mother's. He listened to her chattering, watching her crouched over the grate.

'Don't know what Mam and me would've done without Ryker the last few days. Deep, ever such deep snow drifts. Like a Christmas card—'

'Good morning, Hal,' a voice called from the open door.

Sister Vale was carrying a large breakfast tray.

She set it down and straightened his bedclothes. 'Porridge and cream. Bacon and eggs. Toast, marmalade and a glass of freshly squeezed juice. Coffee and hot milk. Breakfast for a prince.'

Tall, like her daughter, she had a slow smile. Her voice was low. It drew you close to her. It wasn't hard to see why MacCullum had said men fancied Teresa Vale.

They were dressed in similar nurse's cardigans: Teresa's bright red; Francesca's, pale lilac. Their short-sleeved dresses were cut below the knee; their waist belts fastened by nickel-plated clasps. Teresa's dress was bright white; Francesca's pale blue. Both wore nurse's shoes with leather linings and slip-resistant soles. Both of them wore identical bands of white silk thread around their left wrists.

'Look at your hands,' Teresa said. 'What've you been doing to them?'

'It's nothing. I caught them . . . in a door.'

'Dressings need changing: I'll do it for you later. We'll look after you, won't we, Francesca?'

'Yes, Mam.'

'That's what Priscilla would've wanted of us, isn't it?' Teresa said. 'You read my letter?'

'Yes, of course. Thank you for it.'

'She was a beautiful soul. She'll be much missed by all her friends. I used to say you've more friends, Priscilla, on earth and on the other side than anyone I've known. She'd say: "*Love is composed of a single soul inhabiting two bodies.*" And she said: "I put it down to one's infinite capacity for love of my fellow human beings. And to one's ability to accept love. Love is all."' She sighed deeply. 'What a way with words she had. Made me weep. Now she's gone. The Towers is empty. Silent, you know.

I always say you can't put out the flame of love. Francesca and I miss her – don't we, love? Mind, we have heard her loving whispers. Memory plays tricks, doesn't it? You must be feeling it very deeply, Hal.' She tapped her heart. 'Must be hurting inside.'

'To be honest, I found it hard to see her in so much pain. We have to think of her going as a mercy—'

'I told Hal,' Francesca interrupted, 'about the funeral, Mam.'

Teresa stared at him. 'Believe me, I tried to have the solicitor and the Vicar postpone it. There was reasons for getting it over with as they did. Out of respect for your mother's wishes. I was worried you'd be upset, you know. I mean, you not being there to say goodbye.'

She turned her attention to Francesca. 'Hal will be wanting his morning bath. You run it for him slowly, dearie. Nice warm bath'll do you the world of good, Hal.'

'You mean there's hot water?'

'I'm keeping it on in the mornings. Then again in the evening for an hour or so. We don't want frozen pipes causing us more misery. You have your breakfast while it's still hot.'

Francesca smiled at Hal with coy approval. 'I've taken the liberty of pressing your shirts,' she said maternally. 'Everything's freshened up in the wardrobe too.'

'C'mon, young lady,' said Teresa. 'Leave the master to his business. And don't you forget your Velamorphine.'

'I'll try not to.'

With that they left, closing the door after them with deliberate quietness.

Mother and daughter had made a world for themselves at The Towers. A world that was, as it were, neither upstairs nor downstairs. Now his mother was gone, it was difficult to define exactly where they belonged.

Teresa was a governessy creature of admonition. Behind the dark eyes there seemed to be a well of silence. She kept up appearances. Niceness was the norm. She aspired to refinement and the genteel, yet fell a little short of gentility.

She very probably harboured social expectations for her daughter. So far Francesca wasn't showing signs of the conformity her mother apparently admired. Francesca wore her heart on her sleeve. It was harder to say quite where Teresa wore hers.

Breakfast and the hot bath cheered him. The steam seemed to bring the nervy excitement of a new journey beginning. Everything, more or less, felt back to normal.

Standing by the bedroom window he relished the warmth on his face. In the distance he could see clouds of snow filling the air. The sun played happy tricks, edging the white flurries with the colours of the rainbow.

Yes. He'd ask Teresa and Francesca to stay for Christmas and the New Year. There was a more than sporting chance Sumiko would yield to his plea to join him along with Yukio and time enough to get the replacement Jack Russell puppy in Carlisle and deck the halls with holly.

He dressed in a shirt Francesca had ironed, chinos, Tricker's Keswick Commando shoes, blue cashmere jumper and Donegal tweed jacket.

Striding along the landing he gazed out across the snows to where the snowplough was breaking through the last of the white piles blocking the sweep of the drive. It moved aside to let a silver Mercedes pass.

Hal recognized the car. Warren the solicitor was early.

'Sincere condolences, Captain,' Warren said, advancing across the entrance hall. 'Sad business.'

Hal didn't know St John Warren well and what he saw of him he'd never much liked.

Known generally as Warren, he was what his mother used to call 'a character'. Frequently, depending on the season, with a buttonhole in his lapel, he sported a pinstripe suit. The practised harbinger of bad news, Warren invariably affected a sour smile, perhaps the mark of the man for whom life's turned out to be a disappointment.

'Your mother was a favourite at my firm,' he said.

'One of the family. Never heard a bad word said about her. The sort of woman who remembered staff birthdays with flower seeds she'd dried herself.'

That was the first Hal had heard about his mother drying flower seeds.

Warren grinned and the grin stayed fixed. 'Wherever she may be watching us . . . ' he continued with a priestly tone. 'She'll be deeply missed by all. We mean that very sincerely.' He might have been signing off a lawyer's letter. 'May I introduce my personal assistant, Sophie Peach?'

'You have my sympathies,' she said. She removed her tartan scarf and carefully folded it before putting it in her handbag. She was a tall woman, about Hal's age, with very fair hair, green eyes and a fine straight nose above full lips. 'My father thought the world of Mrs Stirling.'

'Your father – a friend of my mother's?' said Hal.

'Father was a trustee of the Association for Psychical Research,' said Sophie. 'The spirit world was very real to him. A great comfort.'

Hal imagined the man must have been a regular at his mother's séances. 'Let's join the others in the kitchen. We have a great deal to sort out.'

'I forgot to tell you that old Beaumont's no longer with us,' Warren said.

'The Memory Man?' said Hal. 'Shame. He knew the estate inside out.'

'And the tenants man and boy,' said Warren. 'Sophie's

taken over the ledgers. We're transferring everything to the computer. Happy to say the cash flow is shipshape and Bristol fashion. Keep the wolves from the doors.'

A clock chimed dully. It should have struck **XII** but the chimes stopped abruptly at **IV**.

Smiling in wonder at the Christmas tree, Sophie said: 'Angels. The Wise Men. Shepherds. Oh, and Baby Jesus. Who made Baby Jesus?'

'I did,' Hal confessed.

'You must have a delicate touch with your fingers. And – Santa Claus. Haven't I seen him before somewhere?'

'I modelled him on Sir Glendower's statue by the entrance.'

'He doesn't look very merry.'

'Neither does Sir Glendower. By all accounts he was a miserable old boy.'

'And all your angels are dressed in white silk. Do you have a thing about white silk?'

'I suppose I must have.'

'I do too. Like Janet Leigh's nightdress in *Psycho*.'

They sat around the kitchen table. Hal at one end. Warren upright at the other. The others either side: Sophie. Teresa. And Francesca who poured coffee and offered cheese and biscuits. The two guests accepted Hal's offer of dry sherry.

'Like me to do the honours?' Warren asked and without waiting for a reply announced: 'This is really in the nature of an introductory meeting. One, I know, that Priscilla would've wanted. May I say . . .? May I say, she did say that she wanted me not, as it were, to *read* her Will; rather, to *inform* you, Hal, and you, Teresa, of certain facts and wishes as soon as comfortable after her passing. That's why, along with Sophie, I've invited myself here. Sophie being, how can one best put it? Sophie the trusted eyes and ears of common sense who will also oversee things, if you so wish of course . . . Basically one's here to keep you good people in the picture now that our dear Priscilla – rest her soul – is no more with us – and how we wish she were. My view is, in the interests of all, one should get straight on with the job of tying things up. Can we agree to sort things out?' He paused and tilted his empty glass towards Hal who filled it with more sherry.

Everyone gave a silent nod.

'Something one feels bound to say,' continued Warren, 'is that the Law requires one to comply precisely with certain requirements. I cannot, alas, allow execu-tors – namely in this instance, myself, Sophie and Hal, to distribute items of the deceased's estate against the terms of the Will. For example, I may say, "Priscilla always said I could have the Rubens." Actually that's true. But it's not in the Will, or her memorandum of wishes specifically noted elsewhere. So I cannot, as it were, be given the Rubens. Neither, in case you were wondering, will there be one of those mostly fictional moments when, with the executors and beneficiaries around this table, or any other, I solemnly list the contents of her Will. By the way, though, executors can be beneficiaries. I might add that beneficiaries, who in this instance include you Hal, you Teresa, and you too Francesca – cannot witness the signing of the Will as, indeed, one was careful to see you didn't. You will, at some stage, after probate has been achieved, be well advised to instruct accountants and stockbrokers and a solicitor and to pay for the expert advice needed.'

With scarcely a pause for breath, he took another gulp of sherry. 'May I ask—?' The smile returned to light up his face reminding Hal of a Halloween pumpkin's. 'May I ask whether or not you'd like us to act – that is, continue to act on your behalf?'

'Please do,' said Hal.

'The honour's ours,' Warren said automatically. 'I imagine it will take anything between a month – minimum – and nine months to wind things up. Timings depend on probate and so on. Is there anything else you'd like to ask either of us?'

'Is this the appropriate time to discuss fees?' Hal asked.

'Why not,' said Warren, 'Sophie, my dear?'

'I won't bore you with technicalities,' she said. 'We normally charge around two to three per cent of the value of the Estate—'

Teresa let out an audible sigh.

'It's negotiable,' said Warren quickly.

Hal looked at Teresa and wondered quite why she'd reacted with a sigh. What did she know of the value of The Towers, its contents and its Estate or, even, the contents of his mother's Will?

Sophie continued in her quiet voice: 'As of today, the value of the Estate is very considerable. After payment of debts and any gifts to charity, Inheritance Tax may be payable at a rate of forty per cent. As to probate, I can't offer you a fixed quotation. The process is too complex to do so, as it were, speculatively. Monies will be held securely in your accounts and our compensation fund protects them—'

Warren interrupted her. 'The good news is, that you have financial security and peace of mind. Any questions? No? Good. Then I think that's that. My office will circulate the minutes. May I declare the meeting closed?' He paused a moment. 'Agreed? Good. As dear Priscilla used to say: "The Spirit of Yuletide be with you."'

Hal was drawn to look at Sophie. Fleetingly she held his gaze, then quickly lowered her eyes.

Hal walked the visitors to their car. 'Sophie,' he asked. 'Please – d'you mind doing me a small favour? I've mislaid my mobile phone, our landline's on the blink. Could you get on the internet and see if anyone's got Jack Russell pups for sale in the Carlisle area – and what they're asking?'

'My pleasure. How many do you want?'

'One will do.'

'How lovely,' she said. 'It's your lucky day. I have two friends in Carlisle who have Jack Russell puppies for sale. I'll call them.'

'Better walk out down the drive a bit,' said Hal. 'To make sure of a signal.'

'Lovely creature,' Warren said. 'We're lucky to have her. Funny she mentioned Janet Leigh. Ever see *Psycho*? Great picture. You know, it's Janet Leigh she reminds me of.'

Once she was out of earshot Hal turned to Warren:

'I have one or two questions.'

'About what?'

'About the immediate future. Can I, for example, sell off any of the land to raise capital?'

'I can't give you an immediate affirmative, d'you follow me?'

Hal gave a general wave in the direction of the house as if he were bidding it farewell. 'It's going to need a fortune spending on it.'

'Responsibility's in your hands, old thing,' said Warren. 'What makes you think otherwise?'

'I couldn't help noticing Sister Vale's reaction to the mention of your fees as a percentage of the estate's worth.'

'Really?'

'I had the feeling that she might very well be expecting to receive a bequest.'

'There isn't much to say.'

'Or, to put it another way, that *I need to know*?'

'Strictly between ourselves, Priscilla was anxious that both mother and daughter remain here *pro tem*. Her idea was that they should care for you, old thing. No one could have seen the outcome of Afghanistan. Teresa tells me she's in touch with your doctors about your recovery regime. I can tell you that your mother has made substantial financial provision for whatever services you may require the nurses to perform. There's also another matter . . .'

Sophie was smiling and taking a short cut through the snow, her open fur-collared Russian-style coat flapping, leather boots ankle deep in snow, her breath on the air.

'This is private – I'll have to be quick,' said Warren. 'In brief, should you die without an heir or a spouse The Towers and the estate pass jointly to them in their entirety.'

'To Teresa and Francesca?'

'Priscilla said it was your father's wish.'

'What the hell has he to do with it? He's been dead for years.'

'He spoke to your mother. That's what she told me.' Warren's voice was subdued with reverence. 'Face to face. Just as we're standing here.'

'When?'

'I don't know when the old chap spoke to her. Maybe, a week or two ago before she altered her Will.'

'A week or two ago? She can't have been of sound mind.'

'Oh, I rather thought the same. Matter of fact, I happened, very discreetly mind, to mention my concern to the GP. His diagnosis was *sharp as a tack with all her marbles. The old girl's as sharp as a tack with all her marbles. And several other people's into the bargain."* That's exactly what he said. I suppose by citing "several other people" he was referring to your parents' friends in The World Beyond. It's a bit of a difficult one. Just because one can't, as it were, *see* God – doesn't prevent one from *believing* in Him. As my adorable wife says, it's a matter of faith – you believe in Him, He exists. You believe in the voices – they exist . . .' He hesitated a moment.

Cheeks glowing, Sophie was now within earshot.

'We haven't had this conversation,' Warren added quickly.

'My friends in Carlisle have a Jack Russell pup,' Sophie announced. 'Two hundred and fifty pounds in cash if you collect it this afternoon.'

She wrote the address and telephone number down, tore the page from her notebook and handed it to Hal with a look of triumph. 'Fearless Jack Russell,' she said. 'Jack Russells, mind, feel fear. Take care. Biting is the JR defence mechanism. God knows, I've seen it. I saw an Alsatian threatening a JR and the JR went bananas and bit the Alsatian's owner in the hand. Almost bit his thumb off.'

'There you are, old thing,' Warren said. As if it were a compliment of the season, he added, 'Don't say you weren't warned.'

Over lunch Teresa announced that she and Francesca would drive to the Stonsey supermarket to stock up on provisions. Hal told her he had some business to do in Carlisle. He'd do the shopping in Carlisle himself and be back later in the afternoon.

Almost at once, as if she knew what was on his mind, Teresa told him there was no sign of the missing mobile phone and its charger. 'You must have been very tired,' she said. 'The weary mind plays tricks. So does Velamorphine.'

'Not in this instance,' he said. 'I definitely had it with me.'

'Then it must be somewhere,' Teresa said, handing him the shopping list. 'Perhaps you put it down. Forgot where . . .?'

'Perhaps.'

'You must get proper sleep.'

'Easier said than done. I'm thinking of getting a TV for us.'

'Your mother,' Teresa warned. 'She said there'd only be a TV here over her dead body.'

'Then no one need worry if we get one.'

'I'd like it,' said Francesca. 'I would—'

'Like *what*?' Teresa snapped.

'A TV.'

'You'll like what I tell you to like, young lady.'

'I've never seen *The Sound of Music*.'

Hal walked to the door. 'Two against one, Teresa,' he said over his shoulder.

'I've never seen *The Sound of Music*, Mam,' Francesca said.

'I heard you the first time,' Teresa said. She called after Hal: 'Mind the ice. Be worse after dark. Wouldn't want an accident.'

The snow had ceased. Gazing at the sky Hal felt this was a winter afternoon to be free, to relish the drive to Carlisle. His mother hadn't driven the Range Rover in years. Neither had Hal who'd always preferred to use hire cars and had never owned a car himself. According to Teresa, Ryker MacCullum had driven it irregularly and had it serviced, cleaned and polished till it gleamed – just, so Teresa said, just as if it were his own.

He accelerated down the drive, careered and shuddered over the bump of the old and narrow balustraded Glendower Bridge. Glancing sideways he saw the Moster River in full spate.

The river banks were beleaguered. His attention momentarily diverted by the raging water, he felt the steering wheel loosen in his hands.

The Range Rover skidded on ice the other side. Its tyres thumped against the verge, bounced off, and the lurching vehicle sped on. A wonder, he thought, the ancient bridge has survived so long.

The roads across the moorlands had been cleared and newly covered with salt, grit and watery sand. Dirty melted snow splattered across the windscreen and the sweeps of the wipers left smears.

Children were building snowmen in Stonsey; beyond Moster Lees the snow, purplish, sometimes crimson, covered the humps of heather and bracken.

In Gretan and Warely, Christmas lights flickered in the windows of the houses, in the few shops and in each pub. His heart lifted. He drove steadily, his spirits raised still higher by the reds of the fading sun.

Lowering across Carlisle, the sky began to turn a shade of indigo.

The radio weather forecast suggested heavier snow-falls might be on the way. *And now the Shipping Forecast, issued by the Met Office on behalf of the Maritime and Coastguard Agency: South-east Iceland. North 7 to severe gale 9. Heavy snow showers.*

He slowed to let two women horse riders pass by in the opposite direction. Pretty brightly-coloured Christmas-card figures; they waved with good cheer, perhaps recognizing the Range Rover. He drove on fast into Carlisle.

Judging from Teresa's lengthy Tesco shopping list she didn't like to spend time in the kitchen.

The majority of the Christmas treats she wanted were pre-cooked.

In House of Fraser he bought the TV: a Panasonic.

WAS £949.9 NOW £599.99; he told the assistant to wrap the whole box in brown paper. 'It's a surprise.'

On to WH Smith for Francesca's *The Sound of Music*.

He negotiated a deal on a new mobile telephone at the O2 store and called the woman with the Jack Russell puppy to confirm his appointment.

She would see him straight away at her house on Arnside Road, not far from the industrial estate. He followed her directions to the letter.

By the time he drew up outside the semi-detached house darkness had fallen. He rang the bell and a light went on behind the door's frosted glass.

The woman who opened the door was dressed in black and wore a kitchen apron and oven gloves.

She called out: 'Minti – the fella for Bertrand . . . Come on in, love, before you catch your death.'

In the hallway was a Zodiac chart poster advertising the services of Madame Schadzi's Psychic Readings.

'I'm Schadzi. And you're Hal – for Bertrand.'

'For the Jack Russell.'

'*Bertrand*. We call our pups after Russells. Bertrand. Jane. Rosalind. Crowe. You don't have a dog, then?'

'No, I don't. It's a gift. For Christmas.'

'You should give yourself a consultation with Madame Schadzi. When's your birthday?'

'Twentieth January.'

'Give him a cup of tea!' Minti shouted from upstairs. 'Won't be long!'

'Let's sit in the kitchen,' Schadzi said. 'Make yourself comfy. Minti takes her time putting on her face but when she does it's worth it.' Everywhere Hal saw the photos of an Anglo-Thai girl staring into the camera lens.

Schadzi opened a plastic bag of Police Dog Brand Thai Tea Dust. 'The magic dust. Minti and me like it hot . . .' She continued with tea making. 'What with you being born on the cusp of Capricorn and Aquarius you're mentally well equipped but not understood by others. You're a Reasoner-Thinker. Successful in military, police, scientific or government work. Capricorn's the thrusting Cardinal Earth sign. Saturn the planet of adversity rules it. Am I right?'

'You tell me.'

'I'm right. You're high-minded and independent. Hate being under the control of others. You're an outsider. The man alone. You don't fit in. Your concern is for others. You make enemies. You're unforgiving. You may seem cold. You smash the obstacles getting in your way. The leader. Serious. Reserved. Sensitive. If you need a shoulder to cry on you need another Capricorn. You don't have an easy family life. You have to be kind to yourself. Your life's an extreme of good and evil. Your girl – you have a girl, what's her name?'

'Sumiko.'

'Bertrand's for her?'

'For her daughter.'

She filled two cups with the tea and Minti, the Anglo-Thai in the photographs, drifted into the kitchen and kissed Schadzi on both cheeks.

'I've got Bertrand all ready for you,' Minti said. 'D'you want to see him?'

'Please.'

'Schadzi. Do us the honours, love.'

Minti sat down next to Hal and crossed her legs. She smelled strongly of Dioressence. 'I've assembled a package for you.' Her long and painted fingernails dabbed at a typed list. 'Collar. Retractable lead. Stainless-steel food and water bowls. Pillow. Hottie – hot-water bottle for snuggling. Blanket. Crate. Good supply of foods such as I've been feeding him. Chew toys. Ball. Plush toys. I've given you a copy of *Minti's Training Tips*. Take the first few days off at home to attend to him. Can you do that?'

'Sure.'

'Make sure he gets several short periods of stimulating exercise every day. Walks, fetching toys, tugs-of-war. Tell everyone at home that he needs to adjust to his new surroundings. Home sweet home. He'll have to be in someone's care most times. Don't leave him outside or anywhere parasites and dirty things can get to him. You've got a new baby, Hal. His immune system isn't strong. Leave him alone when he's in his crate

97

or sleeping. And you have a Minti Car Crate. Twin doors on one side with an up-and-over on the other. Perfect for the car.' She turned round. 'And – here we are . . .'

The three-month-old pup was peering out of the Minti Car Crate.

'Quite the little gentleman,' said Minti. 'Pretty eyes for a boy.'

'He loves you already,' said Schadzi. 'Let me help you take him to your car.'

'I have to settle up with you. For the pup – and my astrological reading. It was remarkably astute.'

Schadzi purred.

'All taken care of, Captain Stirling,' Minti said. 'No bill.'

'Sorry?'

'Bertrand's a Christmas gift. A surprise. Here—' Minti handed him a card. It was a Marks & Spencer card covered with iridescent glitter. The message inside said: *Friend for Life. Sophie Peach XXX*

'We think Sophie may be a little smitten with you, Captain,' Schadzi said. 'She's a lovely girl. Your sort we think, don't we Minti?'

Minti fluttered her eyelashes.

'And, guess what?'

'A Capricorn?'

'You guessed.'

'I told you. I'm spoken for.'

Minti gave him a studiously sultry look. 'Don't you go breaking her achy breaky heart.'

'I'm going to give her back her money.'

'You mustn't. Anyhow, she's no need of money. Her family set her right in spades when she left home. She's free as air.' Minti brought a long finger to her lips. 'Sssh. Forget I told you. All she needs is love.'

'Like Bertrand,' said Schadzi.

'Like everyone,' said Minti with a look of pity.

They helped him set the pup's crate in the back of the Range Rover. 'Keep in touch,' said Schadzi. 'Happy Christmas.'

'Hal to Bertrand. How you doing back there? Over.'

No reply.

It was after six o'clock and he couldn't wait to tell Sumiko about the Christmas present he'd got for Yukio. It was Yukio who'd have to be persuaded first to come up to The Towers for Christmas. Snow of course permitting.

He reached Carlisle to find a starlight lantern procession winding its way from the castle, across Castle Way to Castle Street and on into the city centre.

Here were the Three Wise Men mounted on camels, the Christmas carnival band: Flemish bagpipes, tabors, glockenspiel, reedy shawms, woodblocks, bells, the works. Lanterns were being held aloft. Here was the sparkling thirty-five-foot-high Christmas tree from Grizedale Forest.

For old times' sake, he drove to the Hallmark Hotel on Court Square near the railway station. He bought a double brandy in the bar and made his call to Sumiko.

No reply from her mobile so he called her landline.

Yukio answered: 'Mummy's out.'

'When will she be back?'

'Soon. Do you want me to give her a message?'

'Actually, Yukio, I've got a message for you. It's about Father Christmas.'

'My Christmas wishes?'

'Yes. Have you written to him?'

'Yes.'

'Can you tell me what your bestest present might be?'

'A puppy.'

'Well. I have news for you. I have seen Father Christmas—'

'Have you told him about me?'

'Yes. And—'

'He has to be a Jack Russell.'

'That's what Santa said.'

'But he hasn't seen my letter yet.'

'He has a way of knowing. Not everything. But he knows about bestest presents.'

'Where is he?'

'He's on his way.'

'To me?'

'To you.'

'Yes. Yes. YES.'

'Please ask Mummy to call me. I have a new number. Can you write it down and give it to her?'

'Wait. I'll get a pencil . . .'

So far so good.

Yukio asked him to repeat the number twice. 'I'll tell her to call you. What's the puppy's name?'

'He hasn't got one yet,' Hal lied. 'He's still small. You'll have to think of one.'

'Akitoki,' she said. 'Akitoki. It's beautiful. It's the bestest thing that's ever happened in my whole-whole life. And I want to see him and you at Christmas. Can we come to your house?'

'I hope so—' A movement in the small mirror above the telephone distracted him. No more was he listening to Yukio's excited voice.

In the mirror he could see two people leaving the lift across the foyer. If he wasn't much mistaken – Teresa and Warren. Arm in arm, deep in conversation, they were crossing the hall bound for the exit. Teresa, looking demure and furtive at the same time. In a mackintosh. Headscarf. Carrying a small bouquet of red roses. Warren, shoulders back, Man of Law, jaw set, Man of Trust, Family Solicitor. 'Old thing.' And now Ladies' Man? Teresa his bit on the side?

'Hello?' Yukio was saying.

He stiffened. Teresa *and* Warren. Well, well. Warren *and* Teresa.

'Hal – can you hear me?'

'Sorry. Yes. Mummy ... it depends on where ... on where you two want to spend Christmas.'

'With you, Hal. And Akitoki. I'll tell her we've *got* to.'

'And give her my new mobile phone number. Don't forget. Ask her to call me. Promise?'

'Promise.'

He went to the reception desk and asked if they had any sort of afternoon rate for rooms. 'Only for a few hours, you understand? For a couple of friends of mine who want to break their onward journey north?'

'When would that be for, Sir?' the woman asked.

'Later this evening.'

'Bear with me a moment.'

While the receptionist was peering at her computer screen, tapping the keyboard with a single finger, Hal lifted a slim brochure, *Romantic Lakeland Breaks*, crumpled it in his fist, and edged round the desk and dropped it in the wastepaper basket. He stayed there a moment looking at the screen. There they were: had to be: *16.00–18.00 Mr and Mrs Peach.*

'Forgive me,' he said. 'I've made a mistake. Couldn't help noticing my friends have already booked. Mr and Mrs Peach. Damn it. I'm supposed to have paid the bill.'

'No problem,' the receptionist said. 'Mr Peach settled it beforehand,' adding with approval, 'they're regulars, always pay in cash – with a tenner for little me.'

'Then we've nothing to worry about,' Hal said. 'Sorry to have wasted your time.'

'You're welcome. Will that be all, Sir?'

'That's all, thanks. Happy Christmas.'

*

Over the car radio the weatherman was now predicting 'severe conditions in Greater Manchester and East Lancashire, over the Pennines and across Cumbria where snowfalls will be the heaviest ...' Snow was already falling again in Carlisle.

He parked the Range Rover near Marks & Spencer.

'You stay put, young man,' he told the puppy.

He bought cold-weather clothes: Blue Harbour Outdoor Jacket, Leather Round-Toe Lace-Up Boots, Lightweight Long-Sleeve Crew Thermal Vests, Long Wool-Blend Thermal Socks. Then he headed home.

The snow covered the roads and verges. The roads ahead began to disappear and his headlights hit amorphous flurries of swirling white. The north-east wind buffeted the Range Rover; snowflakes surged across the windscreen and the wipers began to squeal.

'Get you home as soon as possible,' he told Arotiki.

Apart from the humming engine, the air was white: the noise white, a distant ominous hiss: the sort of noise, he imagined, you might hear in outer space: the noise of your own breathing, the sound of weightlessness ... s ... s ... s.

Warely and Gretan assumed the look of Arctic outposts. No more could Christmas lights be seen. The hillocks and sloping heather and bracken near Moster Lees had disappeared; and the children's roadside snowmen were fantastical North Pole sarcophagi.

A quiet voice was speaking to him. *I am Fear. I am waiting for you. Come home.*

He activated the self-locking doors device. The click became an alien squeal. *You're not getting into this cage.* His crouch over the steering wheel became a cower of desperation. *Keep going. Don't stop.*

The blizzard forced him to reduce speed to a snail's pace. *Where am I? Five miles from The Towers minimum. Make a plan for being stranded. Spend the night in the Range Rover with the puppy. Dog-food dinner for two. Use the mobile.*

He settled it on his lap.

Wrap up in the Blue Harbour outdoor jacket, boots, thermal vests and long wool-blend thermal socks. Alert the emergency services in Carlisle. Or freeze to death alone.

The headlights were powerful: they illuminated the snow as if it were a barrier. He lowered them, flicked them up and down. It made no difference. During these brief moments of experimentation he twice turned the headlights off altogether. He was aware of other lights; lights of a car approaching. He came to a stop and started pressing the horn. *Stop*: he was trying to signal. The car came towards him slowly. He waved to the driver. *Stop.*

It did stop, only for a brief moment, parallel to the Range Rover. He could make out the car, but couldn't see either the driver's or the passenger's face. The car was a silver Mercedes. Warren's car.

'*Warren. Warren,*' he heard himself shout.

The Mercedes didn't stop.

He heard a small cry from the back. There was something urgent in Arotiki's cry. *That makes two of us who're goddamn miserable.*

And bugger you, Warren. 'It's all right, Arotiki. We're going home, boy. Don't you worry.'

His face felt numb. The inside of his mouth dried; he kept swallowing; but the saliva dribbled from his lips. He felt the road dip.

'We're almost there, Arotiki.'

The Range Rover was crawling downwards and he quickly glanced back at the dog's crate. Arotiki had a half-transparent piece of cord in his mouth.

Too late – the front of Range Rover struck the stone parapet of the Glendower Bridge.

– the disconnection, the bite of the wire will kill its nervous system. Waterproofed.

– command wire seems to be a tripwire.

– I'm looking for a battery, a wire. The point at which I can break the circuit to the shiny detonators.

Arotiki gave a howl of pain.

The wire is tightening around his scrotum.

The eyes stared directly at Hal: its pupils dilated, teeth bared, ready to attack.

He struggled to open the door, unlocked it and jumped out, aware that something had slipped from his lap and banged his knee, falling heavily, up to his knees in snow.

– the mobile. The mobile was in my lap. He dropped to his knees clawing the snow.

Call me, Sumiko. Tell me, tell me where it is.

She didn't call.

He could hear a voice though. And his father's laugh: *'Fear of Fear is Everything.'*

I am Fear. I am waiting for you. Come home.

Get back to The Towers. One more hill to climb. The headlights blinded him. Disoriented, he was choking on the snow, his breaths whistling in his throat.

I am waiting for you and little bleeding Arotiki. Arotiki will hate you for what you've done. You have a dead neuter on your frozen hands. I am Fear and I too have cold hands.

He climbed back into the Range River and peered at the dog's crate. He could see no movement. Arotiki was motionless. 'Dog,' he whispered. 'Dog. Don't you die on me.'

Arotiki was silent as the grave.

He reversed the Range Rover and bumped very slowly across the Glendower Bridge imagining the fury of the river beneath.

'Arotiki?'

Not a sound.

He stopped the Range Rover and looked into the back. The pup was staring up at him: tongue pink, nose wet, ears soft, crouching well clear from a pool of piss.

He took a deep breath and drove up the final hundred metres to The Towers. Lights were shining in the windows. Darts of unearthly lights in the snow.

The entrance door opened slowly and he saw the phosphorescent silhouette of a woman's figure.

15

She stood in the doorway wrapped in an overcoat, scarf and black shawl.

Hal began to unload the provisions.

'Can I help?' Francesca offered.

'Please.'

She carried some of the carrier bags inside and then returned to help him with the box wrapped in brown paper containing the TV.

'Is this what I think it is?'

'No guessing. Santa Claus doesn't like nosey Parkers.'

'Do you believe in Santa?'

'What d'you think?'

'I do, Hal.'

'He'll be pleased to know.'

Then Arotiki's crate.

'Oooh,' said Francesca. 'What've you brought home?'

'There'll be four of us here from now on.'

'Look at her . . .'

'It's a him.'

'Is it? I never know with dogs. He's beautiful. What's his name?'

'Arotiki.'

She heaved the huge doors shut against the blizzard and bolted them.

'Everything okay here?' Hal asked.

'Fine enough. I was worried, mind. What with you late in getting home. The snow. It's frightening. Being alone here, you know, I mean, it's, well—'

'Your mother not here, then?'

'She isn't, no. She's away for the night. Gone to Haydon Bridge.'

'In this weather?'

'She's helping Ryker out tomorrow. His wife's poorly. Got a funeral at St Cuthbert's. Widow's an invalid and Mam's gone to see she'll be okay. Are the roads terrible?'

'Diabolical. By the way, I think I saw Mr Warren's car going the other way. Has he been back up here again?'

'No.'

'Let's find some warmth. Oh, and I saw your mama in Carlisle.'

'Mam?'

'Earlier this evening.'

'Mam. Carlisle? Your eyes must have been playing tricks. Mam went with Ryker to Moster. Been with Ryker ever since. She had to – well, don't you ever say I told you this. She had to help refurbish a used coffin. The satin lining needed patching. Ryker's run out of new ones so they used one that ought really to have gone in the oven at the crem but, well, it didn't. You know, Ryker sometimes does a little fiddle with the coffins. I've got a nice supper waiting for you in the kitchen. And the pup can share it, if he likes. Can't tell you how relieved I am you're back. I hate being here alone.'

Once in the kitchen, she donned an apron and busied herself with the preparation of the meal. Hal settled the contented Arotiki near a window seat and opened a bottle of claret.

Francesca's gulps prompted chattering: ' . . . this is . . . can't believe it, the last week before Christmas . . . what d'you want for Christmas? . . . What I want is a great big bottle of Miracle perfume. Lancôme. Can you guess what's the book I've got for Mam? *The Human Aura. Astral Colors and Thought Forms* by Swami Panchadasi-something.'

She wiped her hands against the front of her thighs. With her back to Hal she straightened the tight black cotton leggings, the pale blue tops underscoring the line of her small behind; then she shuffled back and forth from the oven range dancing absent-mindedly with pleasure.

'How are we feeling, Hal – bit better . . . are we? Mam said to remind you to take your medication.'

'I haven't forgotten.'

'We'll have a lovely Christmas, won't we? Just the three of us. Me. Mam. You.'

'About Christmas. We need to get some extra rooms ready.'

She turned sharply. 'Why?'

'Guests.'

'*Guests?*'

'I'm keen to have two guests stay here for Christmas.'

'Who?'

He sensed the hostile curiosity in her voice.

'I'll tell you later,' he said. 'How long till supper?'

'Twenty minutes and everything will be hunky-dory . . .'

'Are we eating at the table here, then?'

'No. I've been busy in the Library. There's a nice fire lit. Table's laid for two. I braved the snow to get in some holly and ivy. Even got us a sprig of mistletoe. I found an old apple tree in one of the kitchen gardens. Hey presto. Holly and mistletoe – and ivy – symbol of us sticking together no matter what . . .'

'Call when you're ready,' he said. 'I've got a surprise in store for you.'

'Oooh. What is little Francesca to be surprised by?'

'You'll see. Don't come in till I tell you to.'

'Hal won't tell?' The wine was going to his head. 'Naughty.' She chuckled. 'Naughty Hal . . .'

'And don't you come looking.'

'Just a peep?'

'If you do you may wish you hadn't. The Library's full of scary things.'

'I know.'

'You do?'

'Of course I do. Priscilla told me, when you were a little boy, you used to spend hours and hours alone in there. You looked at things a child shouldn't know about, didn't you?'

'Like what?'

'I promised her I wouldn't tell you. Your mother knew everything. What she didn't see with her eyes she saw with her mind. She said you frightened yourself in the Library and that you'd bear the scars of looking at what you shouldn't have for the rest of your life.'

'What was it I shouldn't have looked at, Francesca?'

'You father's business for one . . . you know what I'm talking about. Some things should be kept out of reach of boys.'

'Like what?'

'Never you mind. Now you – here – leave that bottle of vino with Francesca – so Francesca can work a miracle with the casserole.'

As he walked unsteadily to the Library, footsteps clacking in the gloom, The Towers began to commandeer his consciousness.

A slit of light from beneath a door induced a sense of sudden safety. Inevitably, it was extinguished accompanied by the sound of a switch's metallic click.

The faintest creak of a loose nail in a floorboard

moaned, a picture wire whined, straining on its hook. The embracing aura was tightening; slowly suffocating him with half-memories, winding around him like a succubus.

He stood still listening to the noise of silence, the hissing, the rushing liquid in his ears.

16

The Gothic Library was a rectangular musty room with high shuttered arched windows at each end. In summer it smelled of varnish and old carpet; in winter, of damp, mildew and dead mice.

Rows of rosewood bookcases contained the assembly of the Stirlings' unread books bound in many varieties of gilt and leather. Strips of cloth pinned to the edge of each shelf protected the most regularly used volumes from dust and dirt carried on The Towers' cold draughts, moulds, decomposing bugs and insects, mites and their excreta and human skin flakes.

The uppermost shelves were within reach and for any of the rare visitors who couldn't reach them wooden library steps were readily to hand. The lower bookcases contained alphabetically arranged statuettes and busts of Aristotle, Maynard Arcus, Darwin, Galileo, Machiavelli, Thomas Paine, Plato, Socrates, Adam Smith, Spinoza and Voltaire.

Hal's forebears had filled the bookcases with no apparent discrimination or logic of arrangement. This was a heart of learning where uninterrupted reading might take place for those seeking to polish their graduation from the university of life, and the Library had played its silent role in establishing the reputation of the Stirlings as men of literary, scientific and philosophical bent.

This was the rich man's display of learning he didn't possess, the education he'd never had. One or other of them used to tell suitably impressed visitors that his offspring would realize there was a universe of learning to be found in the volumes, ready to be perused as the fancy took you.

Here was where Stirlings had read *The Times*, *Sporting Life*, *Country Life* and *Picture Post* or browsed or dozed off in peace and quiet after dinner. Here too were the remains of his mother's favoured reading: the College of Psychic Studies' quarterly *Light*; the newsletters of the International Institute for the Study of Death, Pembroke Pines, Florida; *The Mercury*, magazine of the British Astrological and Psychic Society; and the quarterly *Circle of Light* from Ryde in the Isle of Wight. She had designated a table for these papers and journals with notices on top of each pile written in copperplate: DO NOT DISTURB.

One separate case was packed with the collected works of Maynard Arcus, disciple of Aleister Crowley.

Above it was a framed text:

The Revelation appeared in a cloud of incense. Imbibe the juice of mandrake root! Yield to the rasp of psychic orgasm and the intercourse of creation. Seek ye the Womb of Man and ye shall be God. Now and in life everlasting crowned in glory. For all is you. You are all. For evermore.

Maynard Arcus

He flipped through the pages of the Adventist magazine *Youth's Instructor*, finding that someone had inserted a handwritten note: 'Abuse not any that are departed, for to wrong their memory is to rob their ghosts of their winding sheets.' The scuffed *Child's Guide to Knowledge* of 1828 had been thumbed through to near destruction.

He was drawn to the novels of his fellow asthmatic Ann Radcliffe, known variously as 'The Great Enchantress' and 'Mother of the Gothic', who, finally insane, is said to have been incarcerated in a Derbyshire lunatic asylum. The young Hal, briefly an aspiring poet of fear, pored over Radcliffe's *On the Supernatural in Poetry*.

The Library was also where he'd done his school revision in the holidays seated at the cloth-covered solid table with its sliding drawers and cushioned chairs, his feet on a mangy sheepskin rug beneath the table.

Once he was tall enough he wrote at the standing desk, swaying and jiggling about to avoid cramp in his legs.

Beyond the Library, to the left side of the fireplace, where Francesca had built the glowing fire, were the doors to what was effectively a separate and self-contained study: his father's firmly locked and secluded 'workshop of the spirit' with its recessed entrance doors suffused with a Miltonic deep religious light.

Salvaged from a church in Mallerstang, the arched doors were of varnished English oak with decorative iron hinges painted black.

Above them was a hand-painted sign with Milton's lines from *Comus* asking: 'What need a man forestall his date of grief / And run to meet what he would most avoid?'

Milton's question had summoned Hal long ago.

FOUR

Hard is it to die, because our delicate flesh doth shrink back from the worm it will not feel, and from that unknown which the winding-sheet doth curtain from our view. But harder still, to my fancy, would it be to live on, green in the leaf and fair, but dead and rotten at the core, and feel that other secret worm of recollection gnawing ever at the heart.

H. RIDER HAGGARD
She

17

Soon after his tenth birthday, Hal convinced himself that The Towers was possessed of an evil core, by phantoms, and wizards, and certain madness.

He discovered that his father had played a part in fomenting disturbance of the soul by beckoning evil and dangerous spirits.

Later still Hal would discover that the world of the spirits flew in the face of the conclusions reached by more reliable modern scientific minds.

The map of his father's spirit world was vast, its lands uncharted. His father was the cartographer of territories populated by apparitions, hags and crones, hobgoblins and wraiths.

This first physical exploration of his father's workshop of the spirit showed young Hal the evidence of what the man was about. At the time, of course, the innocent meddler was unaware of its implications.

What lay behind the locked arched doors of oak? What was drawing him to find out? He decided or, more likely, some malignant fear stirring in his glands decided him to undertake a secret reconnaissance of the locked workshop of the spirit.

Torrential rains had fallen almost nonstop for two days across the north. His father and mother had gone to Carlisle and wouldn't return until early that evening.

The affable if somewhat deaf woman cleaner, Crabtree, was at work far off in the upstairs bedrooms. Apart from Crabtree, pillar of the Ebenezer Church in Gretton, Hal was alone at The Towers. Crabtree wouldn't hear a thing.

The mission excited him. He thought briefly of taking apart some of his old fireworks, Standard Sky Rockets, and using their explosive to blast the oak doors open. Questions would be asked. No good. There had to be a way of getting in and getting out without anyone being any the wiser.

Reconnaissance revealed the type of modern lock to be attacked. Taking a similar door lock apart he determined its mechanism. Easy. Release the pins; disable the cylinder enough and the thing would give way to his steady touch. Burglary seemed easy. A fine challenge. Thing was, you had to avoid getting caught. And this wasn't actually burglary. He wasn't going to steal anything. All he wanted to do was have a poke about.

He made a pick out of a hacksaw blade and bent it a full ninety-degree angle, then found a thin-tipped flathead screwdriver in the garage: each implement fine enough so he could get both into the door lock.

Face to face with the arched oak doors, he felt his apprehension turning into fear. It was a pleasurable sense of fear, the sense of heady danger like a moment free of restraint when you ready yourself to kill a quarry, an aggressive prey: the lock, the silent enemy. Hal began to live.

Inserting the pick in the keyhole, he pressed it gently upwards feeling each lock pin with the tip. As he delicately pushed them up he could feel them shift then slip back down as he decreased the pressure.

One or two of the pins proved obdurate. This is where the tension wrench, the screwdriver, came in. He eased the torque, the twist or turning force, and up they went. Another of the pins was very awkward indeed; so he pressed it just enough to keep the spring from relaxing. He was trying to push – push the upper pin out of the cylinder cleanly. He paused to listen; heard the upper pin click and fall. He repeated the process: then the cylinder and the lock opened. Presto chango. He was in.

The secret sanctum's bay window framed the blurred view of the rainstorm, the blue-green woods and distant moorland. He could see the black weathercock on the end of the old stable buildings strained and buffeted by the storm.

To the right was another window, small and narrow, set deep in the stone wall with a wooden shutter. Like the main window it had a stone transom across its top.

High above it, just beneath the ceiling, was a sixteenth-century wooden carving – a succubus – looking down at the Turkish rugs spread across the parquet floor. Yellowed elephant tusks stood each side of the fireplace of Sienna marble, its Indian red, burnt sienna and Prussian blue shot through with violet veins. Across the sanctum, set in shadow, a second door led through to the Billiard Salon.

The workshop of the spirit boasted an early nine-teenth-century Winterhalder & Hofmeier UhrenFabrik chiming clock. The clock was cased in solid oak with ormolu trim, wide brass urns on its top and a central dial. Hal had always loved the chimes: St Mary's on its eight tuned bells or Westminster on its four deep gongs. The clock chimed the quarter-hours and struck the hour on the hour.

Near the fireplace was a Victorian walnut upholstered daybed or chaise longue with a scrolled arm. It stood on four turned feet of walnut with porcelain castors. The centrepiece of the room was his father's imposing Edwardian mahogany partners desk. In front of it, matching the red of the desk's leather top, was a red leather swivel chair.

Beside the desk, two large faded black-and-white photographs confronted him. Mounted on card and propped up for display on an artist's wooden easel, they showed a pretty, smiling oriental woman in a V-necked kimono.

In the photograph on the left the four men surrounding her were grinning; in the one on the right, the two men by her side looked serious. One seemed to be wearing a military or police uniform.

A small card beneath them bore the mysterious inscription –

阿部 定

Who was this beautiful woman from the East?

He tiptoed across the rugs to the desk and eagerly leafed through the ledgers, innumerable piles of manuscripts, reports, scattered index cards, sheaves and scraps of paper covered with his father's notes in the familiar permanent red ink with emerald-green ink underlining.

To begin with the crowd of words in red, almost as baffling as those of a foreign language, were beyond his understanding:

SKOPTSY [скопцы]
Christian sect. Imperial Russia. *See*: Ritual Castration.

He memorized castration and sexual organs with a view

to seeking out the meanings in whatever dictionaries and encyclopedias would explain them.

His father was also apparently engaged in the close study of books, interleaved with index cards, their entries in red ink such as CAVEN, John. *Post-Mortem Examinations Methods and Technique.*

He sensed the hidden meaning was strange, unpleasant even. It wasn't anything he could put his finger on, or ask his mother to explain; let alone his father.

He heard the twelve noon Westminster chimes of the Winterhalder & Hofmeier clock. Crabtree would soon be knocking off for lunch.

As if to confirm her present whereabouts he heard distant footsteps, walked back to the door and took one last glance at the workshop of the spirit.

It was then he noticed the file on the upholstered daybed. It was a white file tied with a bow of red satin ribbon. In large and bold black ink was the inscription –

阿部 定

– the sign that revealed the file obviously held the key to the woman's identity. He felt a fierce attraction to her. *Open me.* She induced a pleasure he didn't recognize. *Let me tell you my story. You'll never forget it. Be my friend. Touch me. Open me. That you may follow my way. Do what I do.*

Crossing the room he heard his voice saying louder and louder: *I've read your secret in this file before.* **One day I will marry a woman like you in your kimono**.

He untied the red satin bow, opened the file and read what his father had written.

Two hours after midnight at an inn in Tokyo, on Monday, 18th May 1936, Sada Abe, sometimes known as Abe Sada, quondam author, actress, geisha, maid, prostitute and waitress, strangled her lover, Kichizo Ishida, with her obi or sash. Wishing to die while achieving orgasm, Ishida had invited Sada to strangle him. She wrapped her obi round his neck twice and tightened it.

Using a kitchen knife, Sada then cut off her lover's penis at its root, then his testicles and slipped the genitalia inside her kimono.

She cuddled Ishida's bloodied corpse for some hours and at some time during the morning she carved her name 定 into his left arm.

For the next three days, wearing Ishida's underpants, she carried his genitalia around Tokyo in her handbag. Finally, she handed them in at a Takanawa police station confessing to what she'd done. When the interviewing officer asked her why she'd castrated her lover, she is reported to have replied:

'Because I couldn't take his head or body with me. I wanted to take the part of him that brought back the most vivid memories. I felt attached to Ishida's penis and thought that only after taking leave from it quietly could I then die.

'I unwrapped the paper holding them and gazed at his penis and scrotum. I put his penis in my mouth and even tried to insert it inside me—

'Then, I decided that I'd flee to Osaka, staying with Ishida's penis all the while.

'I loved him so much; I wanted him all to myself. But since we were not husband and wife, as long as he lived other women could embrace him.

'I knew that if I killed him no other woman could ever touch him again, so I killed him.

'In the end, I would jump from a cliff near the cherry blossoms on Mount Ikoma while holding on to his penis.'

It was a lie.

Sada was adorable.

I relieve and release your hurt that you may be set free.

'I will always love you,' he whispered with ferocious innocence. 'Always—'

– haunted

– By woman wailing for her demon-lover!

'HAL?'

'Coming, Crabtree,' he yelled, the shout echoing the length of the Great Hall.

Still he hesitated, his curiosity aroused by a small

velvet-curtained mahogany and brass cabinet against the wall.

There was a black eyepiece at the cabinet's front, beside it a small light switch. Perhaps it contained another photograph of the exquisite Sada Abe.

Longing to see more of her, he knelt on the floor before the cabinet, flicked the switch and peered inside.

The small electric bulb illuminated a miniature stage, above it a banner, no more than an ivory strip engraved: L'INFERNO DI GIOTTO DI BONDONE.

He heard a curious scratching and, from a puncture above the large hand to the left, for a brief moment, narrow watery bloodshot rats' eyes appeared, blinked and vanished.

Had he imagined the eyes, or were they real? He leaned away from the eyepiece; turned off the light switch and let the velvet curtain fall back into place.

The view of L'INFERNO DI GIOTTO DI BONDONE, the vast hand clutching the dead or alive naked figure between the legs and the flickering appearance of the rat intrigued him. Could there be a link to Sada Abe: what did these things add up to?

With the vivid image of Sada Abe in his mind he left the workshop of the spirit just as he'd found it, relocked the door and danced towards the kitchen.

'You're LATE.'

'I'm late,' he called to Crabtree. 'I'm late . . .'

Alice: But I don't want to go among mad people.

The Cat: Oh, you can't help that. We're all mad here. I'm mad. You're mad.

Alice: How do you know I'm mad?

The Cat: You must be. Or you wouldn't have come here—

– the kitchen

– where Crabtree was fussing over a pan of mulligatawny soup, two plates of cold meat and a large baked potato. 'Enough for two,' she said. 'And what has Hal been up to?'

'Curiosity killed the cat.'

'Lily Crabtree brought it back . . .'

18

Years after what he thought of as his pioneering exploration of the workshop of the spirit, he sought to get
his mother to tell him quite where his father's private
researches in the sanctum had led him. What, in other
words, were the subjects of his father's obsessions? What
had he achieved worth sharing with the world beyond
The Towers?

With a tone of wistful admiration she told him his
father had uncovered 'remarkable matters of
psychology, natural sciences, the regions of the dead,
the mind, the spirit; the world beyond, the infinite.
The Truth.'

He asked her whether she'd ever regretted that these
remarkable matters had received no public recognition.

'There will,' she said, 'be a prophet among us who
will speak the truth your father found as if in a dream.'

By then, of course, Hal had long since worked out
that his father's interests in these matters were, frankly,
best buried and forgotten. And yet, how far, he
wondered, did his mother go along with whatever The
Truth might be?

'His papers and research materials,' his mother told him, 'are under lock and key safe from the profanity of sceptics.'

'Where?'

'The Skoptsismic sect's vows are secret. They will live on.'

'For how long?'

'For eternity. For as long as The Towers stands.'

Long after his father's death, at home on leave from Sandhurst, he again asked her to explain this eternal truth his father had, as she put it, touched upon.

She was, when he put the question, standing at the edge of one of the lawns that had gone to seed, vainly trying to breathe some life into the mouth of a dying raven.

'Hal,' she whispered, her brow furrowed, settling the dying bird on a windowsill and then pressing her hands against her temples, whispering so softly he could barely hear her. 'You have no acceptance of the spirit world, do you?'

He smiled and said regretfully she knew the answer: of course he didn't.

She closed her eyes: 'Please, I beg you, learn, please, to accept our living dead and their spirits as they are. You must welcome the feminine, the anima, into your soul.'

With her untidy white hair swept back and her white

dress buttoned to her throat, her eyes raised to the heavens, he noticed her striking resemblance to the painting in the Chapel of Hildegard von Bingen, the twelfth-century Benedictine nun, composer of hypnotic Gregorian chants. And, as if some psychic message passed between them about the resemblance, she began to chant:

'He shall wipe away all tears from our eyes. And He will hold out in His right hand – seven stars: and out of His mouth will come a two-edged sword – and His countenance will shine as the sun shineth in His strength – and when we see His sign, we will fall at His feet as dead.'

With great suddenness her face changed from softness to a mask of heated accusation. 'You've explored the recesses of the house?'

'What d'you mean?'

'You've found your way to the basement. To the storage vaults and crypt?'

'Never.'

She assumed the attitude of an inquisitorial Unholy Sister. 'You know what the workshop of the spirit is?'

'Never heard of it.'

'You're lying, Hal. Please – don't lie to your mother ...'

'What on earth are you talking about?'

'Earth? This is about more than earth. Your father is with the dead and the buried. He is the cartographer of the descent into hell. His is the route of the vertiginous rise from the dead. The ascent to the other side. From thence shall come the judgment of the quick and the dead. We believe in the life everlasting.'

They stood facing each other in silence broken only by the caw-caw of the crows. Presently she continued: 'When I pass over, everything will be yours. Everything. As I'm responsible for your soul and body, Hal, I'm responsible for your future. You should know it by now. You're mature enough to know. Your father, rest his spirit, according to the precepts of the Skoptsy ... I will always be with you. In the spirit and in the flesh – protect me.'

He looked into her eyes and fear held him, unable to speak, sensing she wanted him to shield her and he had no earthly idea how to give her the protection she craved. Stooping almost double like a crone, she stared into the eyes of the dead raven, symbol of the spirit of King Arthur, and following his gaze she whispered: 'The bird lives ... its soul ascends.' And her shoulders began to shake.

'You go inside, Mother, and I'll dispose of it.'

She wasn't taking her eyes off the raven. 'How?'

'In the rubbish bin.'

'No,' she whined. 'Leave it be ... Amen ...' Quite out of control, the words tumbled from her mouth. 'Mist ... eternal night clouds the closing eyes. So the wings of freedom perish. . . here, where the spirit lives with us. Amen.'

'Mother – stop it.'

'We are one in flesh and blood. Do not abhor my womb. You are my beloved son in whom I am well pleased.'

'You're not yourself. Please – come indoors ...'

'I absolve you from your sins.'

'Mother ...'

She drew away from him. '*Ego te absolvo a peccatis tuis.*'

There was no point reasoning with her. She was both pitiable and frightening. And, there was no escaping from it, he loved her. It was unbearable.

He never again raised with her the subject of his father's workshop of the spirit or its contents. It was, he imagined, as if he'd discovered a cache of love letters from the pair of them containing passages of an indelicate nature.

One day, he decided to put paid to the insufferable caw-caw chorus of the crows. Their tree roosts were filthy, their droppings shrouded leaves and bark. There were solitary soaring ravens out there too calling gronk-gronk.

He found the key to the Gun Room where his father had stored some ancient pistols and rifles, family relics from the Second Anglo-Boer War. A German Mauser automatic pistol, a Lee-Metford and two Lee-Enfield rifles. And among these museum pieces was the shotgun his mother had uncharacteristically been persuaded to buy for a temporary gamekeeper who'd insisted upon wiping out the crows and ravens. The weapon was a Holland & Holland Badminton double-barrelled shotgun. It would serve to put paid to the crows. He might even bag a raven.

Before he removed the shotgun he opened a box marked THE NAVY KAMAKURA TENSHOZAN FORGING WORKSHOP. The box measured some twenty inches long. Inside it he found an original Second World War Japanese naval dagger and scabbard in mint condition. The blade was razor sharp.

A note in his father's handwriting said that his father had bought the lethal-looking dagger in Osaka from a Mr Zenjiro Hattori, dealer in swords. A further note read:

'*Used in at least three recorded instances of disembowelment or evisceration: the removal of the gastrointestinal tract with a horizontal incision.*'

Coated with images of cherry blossom, the dagger's handle was wrapped in polished rayskin or shagreen, a popular finish for the handles of Japanese swords and daggers. Dyed bright green, the rayskin was bumpy, the protuberances like tiny pearls.

He did succeed in killing several dozen crows though no ravens.

Perhaps the ravens were *sui generis* and protected by numinous dread, the awe-fullness generated by the innermost chambers of the workshop of the spirit and he cursed.

'Let their spirits rot and perish, eat themselves away like some malignant, festering, legless larvae in the damp dark of the mouldering bowels of The Towers.'

19

The wood fire Francesca had made crackled in the grate. Small sparks rose up the chimney. She had created a touching romantic corner in the Library taking pains to lay the table for two elaborately with the family silver cutlery, two silver candelabra, a centre-piece of holly in a low vase and white linen table napkins embroidered with the Stirling family crest.

He began to unpack the television. His plan was to have it up and running by the time Francesca brought dinner to the table. The television would create an air of normality. Neither the subterranean waters in the cellars nor the effects of polluted air would disturb the entertainment and diversions it had to offer.

Assembling the equipment made a comforting change from dismantling IEDs. The whole thing might have been something of the size of two ammunition boxes; the TV had no steel cylinders filled with plastic explosive: nitroglycerin with a stabilizing agent.

He skimmed the manual. INFORMATION FOR YOUR SAFETY INSTALLATION REMOTE CONTROL OPERATION

His fingers quivered. Optional Equipment Connections Main Menu Feature Chart Special Features Lock

He reminded himself sharply that he was here in the Stirling Library, for God's sake, unpacking a Christmas present of a TV for a ditsy nurse. A normal thing to do. Why was the Library so oppressive? *Why are my hands shaking?*

He shivered and straightened the loops of wires. He found himself looking quickly at the window. Something moved across the darkened glass.

He looked compulsively into the room's darker recesses. *What's moving in the gloom?*

He raised his head and listened to the low sounds coming from within the room that was the workshop of the spirit. Was that monstrous shrine to Sada Abe, after all these years, still there with the sickening image of Giotto's, and any surviving descendant of that repulsive rat?

Had his mother dismantled the records of his father's secret collection of amputated genitalia and morbid memorabilia?

He fought to control the twitching in his fingers and heard his mother pleading: '*Won't someone help me? I'm dying. Does no one understand? We are one in flesh and blood, my son … My beloved son in whom I am well pleased …*'

Another voice called out: 'Is anybody there?' *Is that my father speaking?* He heard his own voice plead: 'Father, *are you there?*'

The pages of the instruction manual floated in front of his eyes: their pages raised by a sudden gust of cold air, the manual's bland guidance followed across the world by millions of eager Panasonic customers.

This very ordinariness, the sheer reasonableness of explanation terrified him.

V-Chip Operation: Remote Control

Familiar, condescending, patient, free.

Come not to sojourn, but abide with me.

Buttons

What but Thy grace can foil the tempter's power?

DVD Operation

And, though rebellious and perverse meanwhile,

Thou hast not left me, oft as I left Thee –

DVD Setup Menus

Shine through the gloom and point me to the skies.

Heaven's morning breaks, and earth's vain shadows flee –

In life, in death, O Lord, abide with me.

Language Code List

Then he saw the line of buttons: dwarf IEDs dancing as lighted figures on a Christmas tree, actually, silent grinning toothless tombstones ... in a war cemetery, and they sang: '*Captain Hal Stirling. Come to Mummy, Hal. In life in death, the man who calls himself the bomb disposal expert.*'

The two strange women finished undressing. Mother called: '*Is anybody there?*'

– whimpering

on and on. 'Is anybody there?'

TROUBLESHOOTING CHART – TV

I see the blinding light. The explosion. Darkness. I actually see the pain.

THE KALEIDOSCOPE OF HORRIFIC FRAGMENTED IMAGES

TROUBLESHOOTING CHART – DVD

'Dinner's ready,' Francesca was trilling. 'Can I come in now?'

'Just a second. Hold on.'

Captain Von Trapp's Austrian family home is restrictive and harshly disciplinarian. Maria soon finds that the children need love and singing and music. Maria and Captain Von Trapp fall hopelessly in love. Unfortunately, the Captain is engaged to another and Maria is a nun.

PRESS **PLAY** FOR MOVIE

PLAY starts but then stops immediately. Make sure disc is installed with label side up.

He flipped over the disc. Pressed **PLAY**. Fast-forwarded to the Overture.

'You can come in now.'

She wheeled in the trolley. 'Hal . . . I can't believe this.'

'Good, isn't it?'

He froze the frame at the start of 'The Hills are Alive . . .'

'Good?' she said. 'It's *fantastic*.'

'D'you want to watch it during or after supper?'

'After. Let's eat before everything gets cold.'

She lifted the tray from the trolley, on it two dark candles, a dish of crushed herbs and a bowl of water, lit the candles and handed one to Hal. 'Hold it and keep silence. Let your anger flow into it. If you feel tears coming let them fall. Together now . . .'

They sat in silence for several moments.

Then she said: 'Lower your candle slowly into the water.' She sprinkled the herbs. 'Watch it flow around the candles anticlockwise. Now repeat after me: "By fire's power, we banish anger and all fear and hatred. We turn evil into love. For one another. Hal and Francesca here tonight. Harming none of the Living Dead. We protect each other in soul and body. One being. One love. So the Living Dead will harm not us. We light the Ylang Ylang candles and part the moist lips of our psychic centres. Our wormwood and sandal-wood scents summon eternal spirits to our mansion. Ylang Ylang now opens our bodies that they may receive each other and be united. Two souls in one. One in two. Two in One. In spirit and in flesh. Hal in whom I am much pleased.'

She remained silent awhile and then said softly: 'You're much better, Hal. Ours is a symbol perfected in the eternity of death. And all shall be well; all manner of things shall be well by the purification of the motive in the ground of our beseeching. Let us break bread.'

She turned out to be a better cook than her mother. 'You've got your appetite back. It's a good sign.'

'The casserole is good, very good.'

'Shame Mam isn't here. Tell you what, though. The snow won't beat Ryker. He'll get through, you see. I heard him talking with Mam about it and the days he had a job up the Moster gravel pits. They'd get through in all sorts of weather. And there are the back roads too. Tracks and that sort of thing. Ryker's good in emergencies and he'd do anything for Mam. Don't you think Mam's beautiful? Touchy-feely too. I sometimes think it's a pity Ryker's married. They look good together. He makes her laugh. That's the way to a woman's heart.'

'How long have they known each other?'

'Since they were kids. And Mr Warren has an eye for her. What with the séances they hold together. In Carlisle. At The Hallmark.'

Was that the explanation for the tryst he'd witnessed?

'One thing leads to another,' Francesca said. 'That's what séances are all about, isn't it? Everyone knows everyone. Especially in these parts. You should know. I mean, even out here, you must've got to know everyone in your time.'

'Our family kept itself to itself. What with being away at school, the Army and things, I seem to have spent most of my life away.'

'That'll change now, won't it? With you taking the place over. I daresay a lot will change.'

'I want to keep things running smoothly. Mr Warren's people will see to that.'

'He knows the place inside out, doesn't he? And so does that assistant of his. Sophie. Miss Peach. She was up here most days when you were down south.'

'She was?'

'Busy-busy-busy. Drawing up plans. Making lists. Taking photographs. She inspected all the towers. Up and down the stairs. Round and round. Up the ladders. All the attics. She'd come back down filthy. Covered in dust. She and Ryker even went out on the roofs. Ryker said they're in a terrible state of repair. What will you do, Hal, if you have to sell all of this?'

'I don't intend to sell a thing.'

She smiled. 'Reckon the ghosts know that?'

He laughed. 'Do you think that ghosts ever ask the owners of the house they haunt whether they intend to sell? I don't think so.'

'But you believe in ghosts, don't you? The spirits and all?'

'Do you?'

'Of course I do. So does Mam. Like Priscilla. We've all of us seen them.'

'Where?'

She pointed at the ceiling. 'Up there.'

'What did they look like?'

'It was a she when I saw her. Mostly this woman. Barefoot. Looked to me like an oriental. Wearing a kimono. A silk kimono tied with a band around the waist. Very white face and red lips. There was quite a strong smell around her. Patchouli incense. Mam said it was definitely Patchouli. She smelled it too. But she wasn't there with me. She saw the same woman the next Monday. I'd seen her on the Monday previous, like I said, the week before. On the Monday when Mam saw her, I'd gone down to the pub in Moster Lees. Except for Priscilla, Mam was here on her own. She wasn't scared though. Not like I was. Mam asked Priscilla about it next day and Priscilla perked up and said the woman often appears. Always of a Monday. Except one day in the year – even if it isn't a Monday – and that's May the eighteenth. May the eighteenth's some sort of special day for her, so Priscilla said. And your father knew about a very special anniversary of something or other for the woman. She's a spirit your father took a great interest in all his life. She didn't just come here unannounced.'

'What do you mean?'

'I mean your father, you know, he asked her here, didn't he? He'd communicated with her in séances and she spoke to him. Then she came here at Christmas. I mean she was a special Christmas visitor. You know, the regular Christmas visitor. That's what your mam said. "It brings back memories," Priscilla said. "My wonderful husband adored her to distraction. They achieved an ecstasy of Platonic love. They were insepa-rable." See, your dad . . . well, I shouldn't be telling you this.'

'Telling me what?'

'Well, you know, there were two women in his life. Seems the Stirling men – they all had two women in their lives, didn't they? Anyways, when your dad and his woman . . . when they left this world . . . each became a dove. You know why? See, the gods what they call *transubstantiated* the willow pattern lovers into doves and the two of them stay up in the sky flying for eternity.'

Hal was searching his memory to find the significance of the eighteenth of May. 1936? It rang a bell. Had it been a Monday? There was, however, an error of sorts in Francesca's bizarre account. She had the origin of the Willow Pattern legend wrong.

'It's so lovely,' she said and tears formed in her eyes.

They both heard the sound at the same time. Someone, something was tapping at the window.

FIVE

Alone upon the housetops to the North
I turn and watch the lightning in the sky –
The glamour of thy footsteps in the North.
Come back to me, Beloved, or I die.

RUDYARD KIPLING
'THE LOVE SONG OF HAR DYAL'

20

'What is it?' Francesca said.

'The wind.'

'It's at the window.'

There it was again.

'What is it?' Francesca said.

This time the tapping was louder.

'There's someone out there,' she said.

He walked to the window and looked out.

There was blackness, not simply darkness, blackness. Then whiteness. And in the window's glass, his own face staring at him. His eyes wide. 'There's something there.'

'What is it?'

'I don't know.'

'Please – *don't leave me*.'

'I'm going outside.'

'You can't.'

'I want to see who's there.'

'I can hear it. Listen: "*Won't someone help me?*" Please. Don't leave me.'

He sat down beside her and held her shaking hand.

'Listen . . .'

They listened to the silence.

'There's nothing there. It's okay. Now, where was I? That Willow Pattern legend. It's a Chinese legend. Not Japanese. Some people believe it was even invented by British pottery manufacturers as a sales gimmick. Be that as it may, did my mother say who the woman is?'

'Someone your father loved. Someone he knew . . .'

'Francesca, tell me the truth. You're quite sure she was Japanese?'

'Yes. Japanese. I saw her with my own eyes, Hal.'

'What sort of age?'

'In her thirties, maybe. Your mother said she's a murderess who your father offered sanctuary to – right here, at The Towers. Did she never tell you? She stabbed her lover to death in 1936 in Japan. Same year as your mother was born.'

'When was it you say you last saw her?'

'About a month ago.'

'What time?'

'Night-time. Be about eleven-thirty.'

'Were you on your own?'

'Yes. Priscilla was asleep. Mam had gone off to bed.'

'You're certain it wasn't Teresa you saw?'

'I know my mother when I see her. And she's not oriental, is she?'

'I know that. Did she say anything?'

'The spirit? "*Won't someone help me?*" And then she started speaking in a language I didn't know. She just stood there, very still, whispering. . .'

She shook her head and nudged her plate of unfinished casserole to one side. 'I asked her who she was. "Who are you?" I said. "What do you want? I won't hurt you." She was holding a handbag and very slowly she reached out.'

Francesca raised her arm parallel to the table. 'She stretched out her arm, see? As if, you know, she wanted to show me what was in the handbag. I backed off as far as I could, mind. I mean, I didn't want her touching me. I was petrified.'

'You didn't run away?'

He poured more wine. 'Francesca, tell me, why were you wandering about the house at that time of night?'

She shrugged. 'Mam takes night-time strolls. She's trouble sleeping. Sometimes she takes a serious knock-out sedative for insomnia. Other nights she prefers to go down to the Chapel and sit there and light a candle.'

'Why did you leave your room?'

'I was lonely. I wanted a chat. I wasn't going to wake Priscilla. So I went to see Mam and she wasn't in her room or in the Chapel. At least that's what I thought. But after I walked away from the woman in the kimono I went back to Mam's room and there she was. Mam, I mean, tucked up and sound asleep. I said to myself: "Francesca, get real. You're seeing things."' She gave a frightened laugh. 'And I had been seeing things. Right in the face. You don't want to hear the rest.'

'I do want to hear the rest. What sort of movements did she make?'

'Only her eyes moved. She blinked a lot. Like a newborn child or, you know, how an old woman blinks at a bright light; maybe because my being there in the first place baffled her. I felt she was as scared of me as I was of her. She shook her head side to side if she meant Yes. Shook it up and down if she meant No. I couldn't tell what was going on inside her head. Hal, you don't want to be hearing all this. We should cosy up and put on *The Sound of Music*.'

'In a minute. Tell me, it must have been hard for you to make out the woman's face. I mean, the landings above are poorly lit. How was the landing lit?'

'There was this faint glow like, as if it was coming from behind a church altar. It looked to me that the light was sort of coming out of her head. Or coming from a lantern.'

'What sort of lantern?'

'Well, you know that painting of Jesus that's up in the gallery. *The Light of the World*. Mam worships it. She's got this postcard of it by her bedside leaning against a crown of thorns she made herself. That's the sort of lantern she was holding. Who did the painting then?'

'William Holman Hunt. The one in the gallery we

have is a study for the versions in St Paul's Cathedral, an Oxford College and the Manchester City Art Gallery.'

'Yes, well, Mam says Jesus is about to open a long-closed door and he's saying: "Behold, I stand at the door and knock; if any man hear my voice, and open the door, I will come in to him." That's what the woman looked like a bit. Like a woman Jesus standing by a locked door.'

'You say your mother saw the woman too?'

'She saw her. Cross my heart. So help me God.'

'Where did she see her?'

'By the entrance. When it was locked. As if she was trying to get in through the door. Mind, I thought, if she were a spirit she'd have no need to open it. She'd just, like, go *through* it. Mam says that the woman wanted her to open the door. So Mam unlocked it, heaved it open, and these sort of shafts of sun came in and when she turned the woman had vanished. Mam said the weirdest thing was that the sunshine was nice and warm but the woman left behind this eerie space of cold, cold, cold: where she'd stood like, there was a tomb of cold. Same thing happened another day, this time, by the doors to the Chapel and then again, by the doors down to the Turkish baths. And not just inside the house – outside too, in the gardens.'

'What did you mother do?'

'She mentioned it to Ryker and he wanted us to have an exorcism. Mam said she wasn't having anything to do with exorcists. She said you couldn't exorcise a real thing.'

Momentarily the blood seemed to drain from Francesca's cheeks. 'Between these four walls – Mam and I held one or two séances with Priscilla, that's before your mam grew too weak. Did you ever take part in a séance with your mother?'

'No. I don't like tampering with mechanisms I don't understand.'

'You don't believe in the spirit world, do you?'

'Let's be straight. It's not a matter of belief, Francesca. Put it like this – I don't jump off a fence unless I can see that I'll land safely on the ground. I don't dive off a rock by the seaside unless I know how deep the water is. The risks I take in life are calculated risks. Ones that involve getting my fingers in contact with real things, not ghosts.'

He leaned back in his chair. 'Watch out for people who think they can explain them. Ghosts can frighten but they can't harm.'

'But Mam and I have a psychic aspect to our natures. Your father spoke to us.'

'And what did he actually say to you?'

'He said he was looking forward to being closer to Priscilla. It was very beautiful. Mam burst into tears. And Priscilla wanted her to communicate with my father.'

'Did she?'

'No. My dad died at sea, off of Africa's Atlantic coast.

He was a seaman with A. P. Moller-Maersk. They buried him at sea. That's what he wanted. Mam didn't want me to know about him. Things were bad between them. He could be abusive towards her, very violent. To me too. It was boiling cooking fat. Across my legs.'

Hal flinched. 'I'm sorry.'

'She'd always known he could be an animal. Perhaps it was what attracted her to him. She can be pretty strong herself. I've seen her restrain a paranoid schizophrenic. A bloody great unmedicated railway worker with rolling eyes to match. Mind, Mam does like to think she's, you know, a bit grand. The main thing is we're very close.' She crossed her fingers. 'Tight as a knot – see? I know what's she's thinking in that head of hers even before she thinks it. Same goes for her with me. It's strange but true. And the truth is often too hard to stomach. You must know that, Hal.'

'Perhaps. The truth always hurts. When people say they're going to tell you the truth what they mean is that they're going to hurt you. That's truth.'

'Mam and I can deal with it – that's what we do twenty-four-seven, we handle hurt. Not like the people who've died hereabouts. Ryker says this place has a history of distress and hurt and misery and madness and demons. They've brought pain here each time there's been building works, even minor repairs to old pipes and electric wiring. You tell me why the workmen don't want to come up here. Are they telling the truth?'

'You should ask them yourself.'

'I have, Hal. And this place scares grown men shit-less. They hate coming here. Too many people have died here. And the last one, just a day or two ago . . . your mam, right? Upstairs in her bed. D'you want to know the details, like what it was like when she died?'

'Another time perhaps. But I meant to ask – what happened to her things . . . in her room?'

'Mam and I cleared it out.'

'But what happened to her clothes and personal things?'

'We burned her clothes. To save you the pain. The Vicar advised us. Said you wouldn't want to handle your mother's intimate clothes, nighties, knickers and girdles and hats and stuff.'

'And her necklaces, bracelets, rings, her watches?'

'Mr Warren made an arrangement with a security storage firm.'

'Including the wristwatch she always wore?'

'What watch?'

'Her platinum and diamond watch with blue steel hands. A cocktail watch with a solid platinum case. What about her engagement ring?'

'I never saw a watch or an engagement ring.'

'She wore them all the time, Francesca. Don't lie to me.'

'*Excuse me?* I'm *not* lying.'

'You couldn't have missed the ring.'

'What's it like, then?'

'A fourteen-diamond cluster ring made by Cartier. The gemstone: a 3.96-carat maroon-red Burmese star ruby.'

'How would I know? Mr Warren saw to everything. He discussed things with the Vicar. Always particular about doing the right thing. If you're so worried about your mother's old stuff you should ask them. It gave off forces. You don't wear a dead woman's shoes. You cuddle the dead. Like Mary in the statue in the gallery. By Michelangelo, isn't it?'

'It's a copy.'

'Same thing, though. Tell me about it.'

'The Pietà. The original's in the Vatican, in St Peter's. Mary holds the body of Jesus in her lap after the Crucifixion.'

'Mam says it's cursed. People have tried to obliterate it. Like the brave and sainted man who belted it with a hammer forty years ago shouting, "*I'm Jesus Christ. I'm risen from the dead.*" Mam says he was right to break the Pietà. He didn't like what the Pope was doing about Our Lady of Fátima. She'd seen the truth. Demons and souls in fire in clouds of smoke. Like they'd been struck by a bomb in the desert. Crying out in pain. Like animals. Dead dogs and cats. So Mother had me cradle and cuddle Priscilla in her lap. Like she was Jesus. And she says there needs to be another death, another hanging from the bell. The Bell Tower being a place of execution. It's prophesied. It's Holy Writ. There'll be a sacrifice to rid the demons here.'

'It's bullshit.'

'Pardon? It's *not*.' She wrinkled her nose. 'Mam believes in poltergeists as well. She's heard these rattlings, knockings, felt them mucking about with the telephone and light switches. Unexplained puddles in the corridors. Lingering smells. It's like they're feeding on our fear and dread. That's why she keeps *The Light of the World* next to her bed and her crown of thorns and lights a candle before she goes to bed. She used to keep the BBC World Service going on the radio through the night. Now the signal's gone crappy. You must have felt, when you were stressed, I mean stressed right out, that fear was crippling you. Haven't you ever felt that?'

'Perhaps.' He got to his feet. 'You make yourself comfortable, keep warm, and settle down and watch *The Sound of Music*.'

'Aren't you going to watch it with me?'

'I'm going to wash up, make a few telephone calls.'

'I thought you said you'd lost your mobile,' Francesca said shortly. 'And the main phone's still down.'

He slid the DVD into the TV set and started *The Sound of Music* for her.

'You know what, Hal? I feel safe with you. Now ...' She wiped the palms of her hands on her apron, took hold of his hand and led him coquettishly to the door. 'Look up, handsome,' she said. 'Mistletoe.'

She raised her hand to his chin and turned his mouth to hers. Her tongue lingered in his mouth. She was stroking it against his teeth.

'Merry Christmas,' she sang. 'Nothing Francesca need worry about now she's got TV.'

21

He left her in the Library, pushing the trolley along the darkened corridors in the direction of the kitchen.

He lifted the telephone handset.

Dead.

He took it from its usual position on the largest of the kitchen dressers and set it on the table.

The instrument was an ivory-coloured touch-tone, one of the models BT used to allow subscribers to buy outright. Hal took the assembly apart. He reflected, ruefully, this was the first device of any kind he'd investigated since Helmand. It was, as it were, a device that wouldn't blow up in his face and he wanted to put it to peaceful use. Even so, he couldn't help himself searching for any telltale signs that Terry Taliban might have paid a visit to this neck of the Cumbrian woods and put together a dirty little booby-trap.

He found that both the dialling and transmission circuitry were on the same microchip. The wiring was simplicity itself. Nothing had been damaged. Damaged: No. Disabled: Yes. Someone's fingers had disconnected the wiring.

Outside the entrance to the kitchen was a high cupboard, its shelves filled with old newspapers, shoe-cleaning equipment, small cardboard boxes containing a variety of nails and screws, pliers, screw-drivers and blunted chisels. He removed a battered Quality Street Christmas tin filled with still more screw-drivers, old plugs, fuses and balls of string, some PVC insulation tape, a pair of electrician's pliers, and took it back to the kitchen.

A chill had replaced the warmth generated by the kitchen range since Francesca had finished cooking dinner. The wind had risen and there was a whistling in the chimney breast.

He closed the kitchen door in case she made an unwanted reconnaissance and returned to the makeshift workbench, reconnected the telephone, and dialled.

Sumiko picked up. 'I've been trying to reach you,' she said.

'Same up here. Guess why I'm ringing? Yukio's Jack Russell is fast asleep here in a special box and badly wants to meet his new owner.'

'Ha! She'll be thrilled.'

'Only thing is that she's got to come up here and collect him and she has to bring you with her.'

'Are you sure?'

'Of course I'm sure. Will you get here in time for Christmas?'

'We'll do our best. If we have to ... we'll break the journey in Leeds.'

'If the snow puts paid to the trains, then I'll drive down overnight and bring you here.'

'We'll make it somehow. Expect me when you see me.'

The dilemma remained.

He didn't want Teresa or Francesca to know he knew that anonymous hands had tampered with the telephone's wiring. The knowledge gave him a certain power. All in good time, circumstance would doubtless reveal the guilty party.

He left the kitchen and returned to the cupboard to put the tin back where he'd found it. As he placed it on the shelf he felt it nudge an envelope. It was addressed to Captain H. Stirling, Stirling Towers, Moster Lees, Cumbria.

Originally it had contained an issue of *The Sapper*, the Corps of Royal Engineers' bi-monthly magazine dispatched to him from the Regimental Headquarters Royal Engineers.

He recognized it at once as the envelope containing the photographs of Sumiko both dressed and naked. The envelope had been removed from his room and placed here. *By whom?*

He hurriedly wrapped the envelope in an old copy of the *Cumberland News*, took off his jacket and wrapped the whole thing inside it. *Who was the snoop? The same person who'd disabled the telephone?*

He returned to the kitchen, to the dirty dishes and the sink.

'Hal?'

He spun round. 'How long have you been standing there?'

'I heard voices.'

'You're imagining things.'

'You were speaking to someone on the phone.'

'Well, I hate to say it, but it's none of your business.'

'You're my patient. You'll do what's good for you.'

He considered her order for a moment. Then feeling a rising spasm of anger, with a tone of pointed reasonableness, he said: 'I don't want to quarrel with you. Why don't you just go back to the movie – or has it finished?'

'No,' she said, 'it hasn't finished. I'm tired. I'm going to bed. First I want to know who you were talking to?'

'Go to bed.'

'But the phone. It doesn't work.' She stomped to the telephone and lifted the receiver. 'Dead.'

'I know it's bloody dead. Now for God's sake go to bed.'

She made to lift up his jacket from the chair.

'Leave it,' he snapped.

'You should hang it up properly.'

'Is that so, nurse?'

She stared at the jacket, then at Hal. 'You'd better know something – I couldn't help hearing your conversation. Mam isn't going to let you have a visitor at Christmas. *No way José.* Oh, no. Not that Japanese friend of yours.'

'What the hell are you saying?'

'Mam promised Priscilla that Japanese woman of yours would never set foot in this house ever again.'

'Did she just? Well, you – and your mother – better remind yourselves who pays your wages and if things aren't done my way it's the one-two-out-you-go.'

'You wouldn't dare. You'd have to deal with Mr Warren.'

'Get this straight in your head. Warren deals with me. You can tell Mister bloody Warren, you can tell Lord God Almighty what you like. *Listen* to me.'

Arotiki began to whimper.

'*Listen* to me,' he said.

'Don't you raise your voice at me. You've upset the puppy. You've upset both of us.'

'For Christ's sake go to bed.'

The wine glass in her hand was shaking. 'Why—' she said, 'why was the phone working?'

They were both staring at the telephone as if it were possessed of a malignant force.

'Why was it working?' he said. 'Because your damned poltergeist mended the bloody thing, that's why. And then he came back and buggered it up again. You ask him what he was doing with the telephone.'

Francesca winced. 'It's bust.'

'Too right it's bust. And I'm telling you the telephone won't be the only thing bust round here if you don't get yourself to bed. And fast. You're dreaming things, Francesca. Go to bed.'

She stared at him, her eyes narrowed.

'And there are no ghosts here,' he continued. 'Understand? No ghosts. No Japanese woman wandering about pulling faces. No ghosts, right? I know. I've lived here all my life. Nobody on earth knows The Towers like I do.'

Her mouth began to twitch.

'And don't pull faces at me. And I do not, I say again, I don't want rumours flying about that The Towers is haunted. I don't want stories like that in the papers or coach loads of spotty anoraks with pony tails and spliffs turning up here wandering about stoned in the mud like Glastonbury twats. And stop biting your nails. You'll bite your fingers off.'

'*STOP IT*.' She put her hand over her mouth. 'You're frightening me.'

'Okay, okay. I'm sorry. Now – did you remember to turn off the TV?'

'Yes. It made me sad.'

'Well, it wasn't meant to make you sad. Thanks for the supper. You're a fine cook.'

Her face seemed to darken. 'You're welcome,' she said tartly.

'And please . . . wipe that sour look from your face.'

She clutched her elbows. 'I thought I could trust you,' she said.

'Takes two.'

'You don't trust me, d'you?'

'The problem is, Francesca – you don't trust yourself.'

'*Problem*,' she yelled. 'I haven't got a problem. You have.'

'I'm sorry, Francesca. Don't get me wrong. I know what you're feeling.'

'*You don't*,' she shouted. 'You don't know anything about my feelings.' She began to chew her thumbnail. 'There's something I want to say to you.'

She stood very still, her eyes transfixed with a look of fear and anger that said *you're evil*.

'What do you want to say to me?' he asked.

She was about to suck the tip of her thumb, then thought better of it. 'I dream about you,' she said.

'C'mon. You don't.'

She shook her head as if to say I-give-up-and-nothing's-any-use-now.

He looked at her gently. 'Don't dream about me. I'm not worth dreaming about.'

'You don't know what happens in my head. Who d'you dream about then – that Sumiko?'

'It's none of your business. I dream about myself.'

'Everyone dreams about themselves. I dream about you.'

'Then try not to.'

'And just you don't keep on telling me what to do.'

He smiled. 'I could say the same to you.'

'You don't understand, d'you?'

'For God's sake, Francesca. Understand what?'

'I'm going to visit *The Light of the World* and then I'm going to bed.'

'Better take a torch with you.'

'I can manage,' she said.

'Goodnight then. See you in the morning. When the day is dawning.'

'I hope so, Hal. Ours is a symbol perfected in death. And all shall be well and all manner of thing shall be well.'

Her eyes drifted away towards the shuttered windows. Then she turned her back on him and left the kitchen to walk into the gloom.

He listened to her steady footfall on the stone floor towards the foot of the balustraded Gothic staircase.

It was as if a cold black mouth had opened to swallow her.

22

He hoped he hadn't made an enemy of Francesca.

Perhaps it was a slight sense of guilt that persuaded him to feed the puppy, wash the dishes and finish clearing up the kitchen. To put it mildly, winning over the nurses to the idea of Sumiko's arrival at The Towers looked like being an uphill struggle.

He imagined a scenario in which mother and daughter made their separate Christmas at The Towers while he, Sumiko, Yukio and the pup enjoyed theirs. He was damned if the nurses would make life difficult and began to contrive some plan whereby he would make them a generous gift from the residue of his mother's estate. He would discuss it with Warren. Such a gift would, he felt, be a pay-off. Something they could take and stay away from The Towers. It was his mother who'd sanctioned their appointment. Now she was gone there was no longer any need for them to assume any further role in his life.

He felt no inclination to watch the TV light entertainment on offer; and instead decided to make a brief investigation of his symptoms, to gain a second opinion, to look up *delirium* in *The Encyclopædia Hippocratica*, 1938 Edition, Volume VI, *pp.* 275–6.

Delirium. This is what Mother suffered. Is delirium in the Stirling genes?

DELIRIUM. Transient disorder of the brain (cerebrum) frequently occurring during acute fever, the result of diseases and injury to the brain, fatigue and toxins; e.g., alcohol, apocynum cannabinum (Indian hemp), belladonna, chloroform, fittonia albivenis (Nerve Plant) and opium. It is characterized by abnormality of expression and incoherence, mania and delusion leading to unconsciousness.

Prior symptoms include insomnia, nightmares, hyper-activity and rage; hyperhidrosis (heavy perspiration), twisted facial expressions, rapidity of heartbeat.

Mental confusion surrounds the patient, who may talk incessantly, grow distressed and see visions particularly imagining he is pursued by daemons, plagued by ghosts and spirits who will injure or destroy him. The delusions are often temporary. Yet the patient's visual hallucinations are real. Though frequently experienced in quietude, the visions and his fear are real to the patient. He sees them. They invariably produce phobias.

In most cases the symptoms lessen within a week. The patient may then have periods of sleep and awaken with his mind seemingly restored. He may be unaware of his sickness and strongly deny its existence.

Treatment. – Withdraw medication, follow a healthy diet. Tranquillity and sympathetic nursing will be required. Strict medical supervision of the administration of drugs is mandatory. Electro-convulsive therapy (ECT) is recommended for patients who have developed intolerance to anti-depressant medicines.

Leafed into the next page he found a carbon copy of a letter. It was undated. Headed THE DARK HEART OF DELIRIUM & MADNESS it began: 'To the Light of the World My Beloved Priscilla.'

23

THE DARK HEART OF DELIRIUM & MADNESS

To the Light of the World My Beloved Priscilla.

The Towers is the Dark Heart of Madness. The Dwelling Place of the Possessed and Dispossessed.

Beyond the bounds of consciousness; its madness is contagious. You must always remain here.

The routines of community established by my family had once been smooth and regular; the Stirlings presided over a community of souls in which the gulf between staff and inmates was unbridgeable.

Sympathy and friendship between these two classes was non-existent, The Towers occupied by Them and Us or Us and Them, depending on which side of the gulf you stood.

This is our world.

In the early years of its existence The Towers, stolid in spirit, exclusive and gloomy as any British isolated country house, confined the wilder shores of insanity within its walls.

The Stirlings prayed to the Almighty to forgive us our trespasses but they were disingenuous when they added *as we forgive those who trespass against us*.

KEEP OUT, said the notices on the boundary walls: TRESPASSERS WILL BE PROSECUTED. BY ORDER.

The Almighty heard them ask: *lead us not into temptation* ignoring the quid pro quo when they asked Him to deliver us from evil. Enemy forces delivered it in spades.

Year in, year out, The Towers' platoons of kitchen gardeners grew abundant healthy produce; butlers and housekeepers saw to it that the cellars stocked ample quantities of the greatest wines Europe had to offer. Laundry maids kept everyone spick and span, shipshape and Bristol fashion. The cooks saw to it that good food was enjoyed in the both the family and servants' dining rooms.

During the appropriate seasons, Stirlings rode to hounds, and shot and fished; attended concerts and recitals in the Music Room; played billiards in the Billiard Salon; tennis, croquet, even clock golf on the lawns. The servant class remained and buried its discontents; the Stirlings enjoyed the fruits of the family's fortunes.

When signs of mania, psychotic obsession, solipsism and hallucination revealed themselves, they were swept beneath the carpet. Within the sanctuary provided by The Towers, Us could be as mad as Us liked so long as Them didn't report things to the Cumberland and Westmorland Constabulary.

It is not surprising that, like its sisters, the lunatic asylums, The Towers boasts its own Chapel and Crypt. Stirlings know where their earthly remains end up.

Towards the end of the nineteenth century, indeed for years into the twentieth, The Towers, this asylum for the sane and not so sane, fell into disrepair and neglect. The rot set in. Paralleled by the gradual deterioration of its fabric, this asylum for the sane sank gradually into its present lonely wretchedness, country house squalor, and has latterly evinced its own peculiar degree of sadism.

> Sunk in the caverns of insanity and pain
> You howling creatures lay;
> Sans sense to smile again,
> Condemned to Satan's prey.

Fair Treatment for the Mad has rarely if ever been an efficacious political slogan. Fair Treatment for The Towers has never even been one. Remember Arcus.

> Breathe in the breath of the Dead.
> Taste the juice of love.
> We are kindred.
> It is written in the Infinity above.

Remember Browning. 'Love Among the Ruins'.

When I do come, she will speak not, she will stand,
    Either hand
On my shoulder, give her eyes the first embrace
    Of my face,
Ere we rush, ere we extinguish sight and speech
    Each on each.

The Towers is the Dark Heart of Madness. Dwelling place of the Possessed and Dispossessed. It's beyond the control of consciousness; its delirium contagious.

WE MUST FIGHT ON, BELOVED. DO WHAT THY WILT SHALL BE THE WHOLE OF THE LAW. UNTIL HELL FREEZES.

24

There was neither sound nor sight of Francesca. She must have paid her visit to *The Light of the World* and gone upstairs to her room. He sought better news on the TV.

The newsman was reporting the death of a thirty-three-year-old Royal Engineers Lieutenant. Serving with the Counter-Improvised Explosive Device Task Force, he'd died from his wounds: '... the victim of a roadside Improvised Explosive Device at Nahr-e Saraj in the north of Helmand.'

He saw the face of the smiling young officer in a still portrait photograph on the TV screen. The newsman said the dead man had been in Helmand for two months. Hal hadn't known him.

The dead man's Commanding Officer spoke of '... a confident enthusiastic officer held in the highest affection and respect by all ranks ... The regiment is profoundly saddened ...'

The newsman continued:

'Speaking from his constituency this afternoon ...'

The Secretary of State was droning: 'I offer my deepest sympathy to his family and loved ones.'

Hal leaned back in the deep armchair, resting his head against the cracked leather.

'British troops,' the Secretary of State maundered on, 'are in Afghanistan with those of more than forty-five other nations. And let me remind you, when it comes to our Armed Forces, we don't want them in Afghanistan for a minute longer than is vital to our purpose.'

The fire had burned down to a mound of light greyish ash and flickering glows peered out of it like watchful pink albino eyes.

The silence offered him its eldritch warnings. *Seek your father and your mother, only son,* he heard them say. *'We invite you to join us among the dead. How long will you keep your silence?'*

'As long as I wish,' he said aloud.

'*Wissssh,*' echoed back. '*Weer-issh ...*' and became an irregular whining.

A rat?

The puppy far off in the kitchen?

He fiddled with the torch. Its light probed the dusty air sending long and shaking diagonal beams like continuous tracer shells into the towering bookshelves. Twisting the torch so it shone upwards across the ceiling, the tip of the beam became invisible as if its power had exhausted itself in infinity.

He heard his voice say: 'I am coming to you, Father, into the workshop of the spirit.'

– *spirittt*

'Is that you, Hal?'

– *lllll*

'That you, Francesca?'

– *ttttyyy*?

He heaved himself out of the leather chair, his movement stirring the old springs. Twang.

– *twaaaaanger*

and marched towards the door to the workshop of the spirit.

It was unlocked. When he flicked the switch one solitary light came on: a dim light bulb at the end of a cord of fabric-covered wire hanging above his father's Edwardian mahogany partners' desk.

There was enough light to see what was there in the secret sanctum but he was gripped by what wasn't there. The sixteenth-century carved wooden succubus no longer looked down at the Turkish rugs spread across the parquet floor.

Gone also were the yellowed elephant tusks from either side of the fireplace. But the early Winterhalder & Hofmeier UhrenFabrik chiming clock remained and to his delight the mechanism still functioned. He wound it, set the chimes and let it play Westminster on its four deep gongs.

Near the fireplace a white dust sheet covered the Victorian walnut upholstered daybed or chaise longue with a scrolled arm. The centrepiece of the room remained: his father's imposing desk with its worn red leather surface, and, still in front of it, the matching leather swivel chair. There was something else that had drawn him here again.

The pair of large faded black-and-white photographs that years ago had been displayed on the artist's easel. The dusty wooden easel was still there.

There was no sign of the pretty smiling oriental woman in the V-necked kimono surrounded by the four men one of whom had seemed to be wearing a military or police uniform.

Gone too were those ledgers, innumerable piles of manuscripts, reports, scattered index cards, sheaves and scraps of paper covered with his father's notes in the familiar permanent red ink and emerald-green ink underlining. All gone. Presumably dead and buried along with SKOPTSY [скопцы] Christian sect et cetera.

Might they conceivably have been removed and stored in the basement?

He remembered – Second Levels, Rack 5 and that sign or ideogram 阿部定 – the sign that had revealed the file held the key to Sada Abe's identity and again he felt that fierce attraction to it. Beckoning. *Open me.* The pleasure he didn't recognize.

Let me tell you my story. You'll never forget it. Be my friend. Touch me. Open me. That you may follow my way. Do what I do.

He stood there thinking of his father, mother and Crabtree – knowing he wasn't supposed to be here.

He heard his voice saying louder: *I've read your secret in this file before.* **One day I will marry a woman like you in your kimono.**

He remembered the first time he'd set eyes on Sumiko: how intensely he had wanted her. Certain they would be lovers.

Another image like a slide beamed from an old-fashioned projector. Here was the copy of John Collier's *Lilith*, and the black eyepiece at the front of the cabinet, now gone. The miniature stage and above it a banner, now no more than an ivory strip engraved: L'INFERNO DI GIOTTO DI BONDONE. The narrow watery bloodshot rats' eyes, long gone.

He walked to the window and parted the shutters. The snow had turned into a fine misty rain. Good. Tomorrow surely the roads would be opened. Sumiko and Yukio would get through as the thaw set in.

A low *whoosh* over the lintel of the alcove alerted him. The noise of dripping water followed it, a dull pulsing plink from across the room and he saw water dripping from the light fixture above his father's desk.

He turned off the light and went out into the hall.

Here there were noises of water hitting the floor and a small continuous stream of water was striking the stone staircase.

More of it dribbled from the balustrades of scrolling acanthus.

The leak seemed to be coming from the high ceiling designed to give the impression of a dome.

Approaching the foot of the staircase, his head tilted, he fixed his stare on the dome imagining it might imminently cave in. He had a vision of the ceiling trapping him beneath the rubble.

There was a faint strip of light beyond the top of the staircase. He heard the plinking of the water leak and a noise, the squeak of a rubber sole on stone coming from the direction of the first floor gallery and he heard a low voice: '*Let the Light of Your Presence guide us—*'

'Francesca?'

'*— for in Your Light do we see light.*' It wasn't Francesca's voice.

Steadying his balance on the handrail, he began to climb the staircase, lowering a foot squarely on each step, waiting in case it squeaked before setting his full weight on it.

At the top of the stairs he paused to stare at the source of the narrow ray of light from the gallery slanting across the floor to his feet.

Very slowly, the light was drawn down as if from the

wick stub of a paraffin storm lamp, its flickers elongating shadows of a crouching jungle predator ready to leap at his throat.

He blinked and then, from his right, a new and savage light pierced his eyes and he opened his mouth in a silent scream.

25

He felt his breath sucked out of his lungs, his throat tightening, a violent pressure around his neck, his eyes pulled open forcing him to confront the travesty of a human face deformed by putrefaction.

Hemispherical plastic cones with grated surfaces hid the oozing eyes in the ocular cavities. A thin trail of bloodied adhesive gel had been applied to the edge of the hanging eyelids. Its cheeks and lips had contracted; the membranous whiskered facial tissue scarred taut.

Surgical thread had been stitched in a criss-cross pattern through the base of the purple-and-black gums fastening the shrunken mouth open, fixing it in a monstrous grin that revealed teeth pared back to the roots of the protruding jaw, its point glistening with streaming mucus.

He fought to control the spasms in his chest. His mind never did reveal exactly from which direction the wailing rose in chorus or the source of the immensely powerful light.

The kaleidoscope of searing lightning slashed his eyes; its electric forks illuminating two women

– in nurse's cardigans: one bright red; one pale lilac

– their short-sleeved dresses cut below the knee

– with waist belts fastened by sparkling nickel-plated clasps

– one dress bright white; one pale blue

– both wore nurse's shoes.

Their eyes were wide open with looks of familiarity and knowing innocence.

He fled the wailing, his knuckles striking the walls, oblivious to the grazes and the bruising, his legs leaden.

The grating chorus grew louder, chasing him through the maze of twisting landings and passageways that became narrower until he reached the vertiginous and slippery flights of the backstairs that would take him to his room.

Darkness faced him like a steel curtain. He was lost; held back by unresponsive muscles, restrained from escaping that hideous face and the demonic figures in close pursuit. He felt he'd spent all his energy.

Dim light flickered across the bars of a grille ahead. He saw the nooses of padlocked ropes dangling from the diamond-patterned grille of the disused Waygood water hydraulic lift. Suddenly, to his left and right, a pile of rusted bed frames blocked the corridor.

He tried to heave them aside but the moment he

gripped the nearest frame he overbalanced and his head crashed against the wall.

Face-high a window hung open, the wind whipping melted snow across his face. He clutched the bars of the lift doors in a desperate attempt to yank them open, to put the bars between him and the creature baying in the darkness like a hound excited by the scent of quarry, his arms shaking with such violence that the vibration dislodged a startled rat. The squirming creature spiralled squealing and kicking to the floor and vanished.

26

From a black hole, some gap of no return in deep space, torchlight shone down the passage.

Francesca hurried towards him.

'You saw her?' she said.

'I saw Teresa. I saw you.'

'Mam's not there, Hal. I wasn't there either.'

'I saw her. I saw you. A white dress, a red top . . . You were there . . . I saw both of you . . . and that vile, hideous thing. You were there. What the hell were you doing?'

She stared at him with bewilderment. 'I wasn't *doing* anything. Please – let's get out of here.'

'You went to the gallery, Francesca.'

'Only for a minute. Then I went to my room.'

'Hand me your torch.'

He shone it up and down her body. She was wearing a long-sleeved velour shirt over black pyjamas. 'When did you dress for bed?'

'Just now. Then I heard you call out, went downstairs. The dog was yelping, wailing. It knows there's something evil happening. I went through the hall and went up the staircase and, just for a second, I saw Priscilla

– then I heard running footsteps. I thought it had to be you. But you'd vanished and I went round looking for you. Then I heard you screaming and shouting. Hal – please, do you mind? Stop your shaking. Stop holding your breath. Come back to the warmth.'

'We'll go to the kitchen,' he said.

The whole way there she held on to him for dear life.

'Shouldn't we take a second look,' she said. 'Shouldn't we go back – put your mind at rest?'

'Not too fast, Francesca. There are things I need to get straight with you.'

'Stop it. I can't stand this madness much longer.'

'You're not the only one.'

'The stress, Hal. It's bad for you. I've got a whole lot of tranquillizers in our medicine cupboard. Stuff that'll make you happier. Whatever.'

'Brandy will do.'

'One of us is . . . both of us are . . . seeing things.'

He lowered his voice: 'Before someone gets hurt, I want you to help me.'

'You've only to ask. You see, I know things I can do to help you. Like Mam, I'm psychic.'

'Then explain one or two things.' He nodded in the direction of the sideboard. 'Tell me who tampered with that telephone.'

'Who would do such a thing?'

'I've no idea. It was someone who could take the

thing apart and then reassemble it. Who could do it surreptitiously so you and your mother wouldn't know. Someone who could get in the house on their own without anyone knowing. Who has keys?'

'Me. Mam. Mr Warren. Perhaps Sophie Peach. Ryker. Perhaps his wife, Betsy. Dr Mackle has a key. But I think he gave it back to Mam. Must have by now.'

'Who would know whether he did or he didn't?'

'Mam. And Dr Mackle would know, wouldn't he? There may be others I don't know of. People come and go, Hal. Don't they?'

'Think hard, Francesca. Can you remember when the telephone stopped working?'

'The day before yesterday. Perhaps the day before that even. I don't remember. It has to have been a poltergeist. Or just a fault on the line to do with the snow and stuff.'

'Someone disconnected it deliberately.'

She sat rigid in her chair, then raised her hands in resignation. 'I don't know. Mam has a telepathic link she shares with spirits. You should ask her.'

'Bloody right I'll ask her. There's another thing. Outside the kitchen here is a cupboard full of old news-papers, shoe-cleaning gear and do-it-yourself junk. I took a look inside it and found an envelope addressed to me. A brown envelope – you know what I'm talking about?'

'No.'

'I think you do.'

'Please. I don't.'

He remembered that he'd been carrying his jacket with the envelope inside it when he'd climbed the Gothic staircase. He must have dropped it there.

'Spirits move things,' she said. 'They can help you find things. They can tell you where things are. They must have been trying to help you find the photographs.'

Photographs? So she knew the envelope contained photographs. She must have either seen them herself or Teresa had told her about the contents.

However tempting it was to ask her straight, he decided not to point out her slip of the tongue. She might, or might not, know what was in the envelope. She must surely have been party to its removal from his room. 'I have to tell you, Francesca that I never found my mobile phone or its charger. I left it in here.'

'So you said and I don't know what happened to it.'

'You're as white as a sheet. Are you feeling all right?'

She shook her head.

'I don't blame you for feeling terrible. I do too. Are you up to talking about it a bit more?'

'About what?'

'About the face.'

'Your mother's face?'

'It wasn't my mother's face, Francesca. She's dead and buried. That was an apparition, a delusion, phantom. Hallucination. Spirit. Call it what you like. My mother's dead.'

'Listen to me, Hal. What I know is that The Towers has been taken over by tragedies. Your mother said she and your father fought a bloody war for years against the evil. They sacrificed themselves. They gave up their lives for the struggle with demons. It was in their blood to be soldiers of the spirit. People don't come here voluntarily.'

'You did.'

'Because Mam and me are shielded from the spirits. Otherwise Priscilla would never have employed us in a month of Sundays. There were plenty of other applicants for the job of caring for her. Not one of them would take it. Your mother said they went away fearful. Don't tell me you aren't haunted by the memories that live here. You've heard the noises, you saw your mother's face and she's not the only one stalking the darkness. The spirits live and breathe in the empty rooms, imprisoned with locks and keys and chains. In the basements. In the attics. In the Great Bell Tower. In the Turkish baths. The Chapel and the Crypt. Everywhere. They possess the place and no one's disturbed them in years. Not until now, Hal. Not until you came here to take possession of The Towers.

Up until you arrived here everything was peace and quiet. Everything was in control. And now Priscilla's passed over there's no one to control them except you. The power is in your genes and blood and in your mind.'

'Then tell me, frankly, why on earth *did* you agree to come here? . . . Surely the atmosphere alone must have chilled you from the very start?'

'Why do people do anything? For the money, Hal. And because Mam and I can deal with what's happening here. You have to understand why. The spirits respect us. That's what it's about, Hal. Respect. All they need is to feel somebody wants to communicate with them. That there's someone on earth who will love and understand. And that, if you don't already know it, is what life's about, isn't it? Loving and understanding our fellow beings.'

'Then how do you explain that monstrous thing at the top of the stairs?'

'What we saw together, you and me, explains itself. Nightmares spring from evil truth within us, see? Priscilla, God rest her, appeared to you because *you* don't respect her spirit. Listen to me, you may think she isn't your mother. You and me, we *know* she is, don't we? If you refuse to admit her in your head and heart . . . then she'll come at you again and again, until you respect her living soul. So don't you resist her any more. Work through it. And, swear to God, you'll find the peace you crave.'

'Why are you talking to me like this?'

'Because it's my job. You must share your innermost feelings. You aren't alone, Hal. You've a long walk ahead of you and I'll be with you always. And something else. You've grown too used to telling others what to do in the Army and all. To having everything your own way. It's time you listened to your inner voices. Time you tuned in to others and yourself. If you don't, the pain will get much worse. Look at you. Your face . . . all twisted up. You're so . . . taut, I mean, you're taut in mind and body. You're grieving. You're hurting. Grief's an extreme emotion . . . and extreme emotion causes us to hallucinate and lose our fragile hold on real life. That's why you need nursing. Professional nursing and tender loving care. You need pampering. Cosseting. By Mam and by me.' She rose to her feet slowly and looked at him with tenderness. 'I'll see you to your room. Make you comfy.'

'I want to go back to the staircase.'

'And say goodnight to Mother?'

'To see if that thing's still there, Francesca.'

'She'll have gone.'

'Let's check. I'm going to take a look—'

The sound of the Hofmeier UhrenFabrik chiming clock banging out XII startled him.

She shook her head. 'You want to go there alone?'

'I'd rather you came too.'

'Aren't you frightened about what you might see?'

'It's what I can't see that scares me.'

'You mean what's in your head.'

'I mean what's out there waiting for us.'

27

Beams from his torch sparkled across the puddles of grimy melted sleet. All gone. Vanished into thin air. Neither his mother nor his jacket with the photographs was there. Their absence reinforced the terror he'd felt standing on the staircase so short a time ago.

'Here,' he said. 'This is where I saw it.'

'Me too. She's only gone because you've returned to bear witness.'

'She's gone, Francesca, because she was never here in the first place.'

'She's here, Hal. Almighty God didn't give us eyes so that we might be deceived. He gave us eyes that we might see. You and me. We're no different from anyone else.'

'Where's my jacket, then?'

'God knows. How do I know what you did with it?'

'I know what I did with it, for Christ's sake. I dropped it. It's here somewhere.'

'But it isn't now, is it, Hal?'

She was right. The jacket had vanished.

'C'mon, Francesca. You took it, didn't you?'

'Of course I didn't take it. Why would I? I never saw it here. I last saw it in the kitchen, didn't I? What is it you want to hear me say?'

'I want to hear you tell me everything you did after you left the kitchen. You went to the gallery—'

'I've told you,' she broke in. 'I went to see *The Light of the World*.'

He took her by the hand. 'Show me the route you took.'

She pointed at the Gothic staircase behind them, its long sweep curving into the darkness across the hall below. 'I came up the stairs to where we're standing now,' she said. 'Then I turned left — here. Follow me and I'll show you . . .'

They walked along the passage, through a heavy wooden doorway and entered the main gallery, passing picture after picture: darkened Stirling ancestral portraits: a poor Franz Xaver Winterhalter of Queen Victoria and another, its companion piece, of Prince Albert; minor Pre-Raphaelites: Leighton, Windus, Hughes and Sandys, Waterhouse and Alma-Tadema.

She suddenly let his hand drop, walked ahead of him and broke into a run.

He heard her let out a strangled sob.

'No. I knew it. *LOOK* . . .'

*

The beam from her torch shone directly into the face of Christ. Rivulets of water were running down His face.

'Look,' she said. 'He's weeping,'

'It's only gutter water running down the glass.'

'Jesus is weeping. Jesus wept . . . it's written.'

'Yes. Yes. Yes. The shortest verse in the Bible. "Jesus wept." Now come away.'

'Don't you believe your eyes?'

'It's cold, Francesca. And there's a whole lot of nasty water on the roofs. And the attic's waterlogged. The ceiling plaster's sodden. It could collapse any moment. So let's just get away before things gets worse.'

Far below his bedroom, the Hofmeier UhrenFabrik clock chimed I.

Francesca had brought candles to his room and they sat watching the contorted shadows play across the walls. She sat on his bed curled up in the silk eider-down. Hal paced slowly around the room.

'Your Japanese woman,' she said, 'she isn't going to come here, is she?'

'She has a name. *Sumiko*. And she's coming with her daughter Yukio.'

Francesca looked pained.

'I'm going to make the place as comfortable as I can for them,' he said. 'And I'd like you to help me.'

'They mustn't come here.'

'You try and stop them.'

'You must stop them. I've told you – you need peace and quiet and loving care.'

'Which is what they'll give me. Neither you nor Teresa has any right to make me change my mind.'

'Your mind is what we care about. You must let us heal it. Think of what the future has in store for you.'

'I've no idea.'

'You do, Hal, The Towers. The Towers is your future. It's your past, your present and your future. Without you – it's nothing, is it? What might happen to this place if you weren't here to love and care for it? If you were to—?'

'– die? If and when I die, you mean – what then?'

'What then?' she echoed quietly.

And he remembered what Warren had said. Word for word: '... *should you die without an heir or a spouse The Towers and the estate pass jointly to them in their entirety ...*'

'What do you imagine,' he asked, 'will happen then?'

'Who knows?' she said.

'Has your mother ever discussed your future with you?' he asked.

'I'm an adult. I can see the future. God may have wounded me but He's merciful. He allows me to see the path of life ahead. You must let me teach you how to trust in Him. You will see His way. Come to me, Hal. Come to Francesca. Let me massage your neck.'

'Some other time. You'd better get to bed.'

'I can't.'

'Can't what?'

'Can't be alone. Please, Hal. Mam will be back here in the morning. Then everything will be back to normal. Be gentle with me. If you don't mind, please, I'd like to stay here with you, just for tonight. Please.'

'If you must. I'll stay up.'

'You need your beauty sleep too.'

'I need to find out what's going on. I'm not sleeping until it's daylight.'

'I'll stay awake with you.'

'You do what you like.'

'You need your medication. It helps you sleep.'

'I know. That's why I'll take it later. Look, I've told you, I'm staying on sentry watch. You sleep if you like.'

'I know I can help you. I'll keep watch over you.'

'I'm fine. Just let me get on with my life, okay?'

He took three spare blankets and a pair of pillows from the wardrobe and turned the largest bedroom chair into a makeshift bed.

Francesca fell silent. Once asleep, she breathed audibly.

His brain teemed with plans to fight the spirits and rid The Towers of their insidious aura. Why not employ a full-time caretaker? Nightwatchmen? Install security CCTV cameras and a bank of monitors? Round-the-clock surveillance?

He wanted to reconnect the telephone to establish

normal life when morning came and he wanted to retrieve the photographs. Fired up with loathing for the horror at the top of the Gothic staircase that had temporarily destabilized him, he grew the more determined to begin the pressing business of doing battle to save The Towers from self-destruction.

He'd present a plan for an altogether speedier programme of restoration to Warren and Sophie Peach:

The immediate reconstruction of the living quarters. A resurrection, no less. A proper modern kitchen. A comfortable living room, sensible dining room, modern baths, new boiler, an altogether new and efficient hot-water system, new wiring and a powerful, albeit limited, central heating plant.

He thought of all this as the creation of a house within a house. An immediate sale of some of the paintings would provide the necessary capital to start work immediately after Christmas. If the local builders refused to work in January then he'd import a team of Polish builders from London or nearer home if he could find any.

A new look, the new broom, an altogether new atmosphere of lightness would soon persuade the spirits to pack their bags and bugger off to some other unwitting place of dereliction and insanity offering sanctuary to the living dead and their perverse disciples.

*

The chair was uncomfortable and, even though he was fully dressed, his clothes and the heavy blankets offered little warmth.

Francesca had dropped into a noiseless sleep and the only sounds were of the sleet beating against the windows, the rattling of the shutters, a low mumbling in the chimney breast and the deadened chimes of the clock below.

It was shortly after the clock chimed IV that he heard the noise.

28

It was hard and sharp: *crack-thwack-crack* of grit against the window.

At first he dismissed it as a freakish gust of wind.

When he heard it the second time, then a third, he could think of no logical explanation other than that human hands had lobbed grit against the glass.

Without disturbing Francesca he used his shielded torch-light to find his way across the room and drew the shutters open.

The light was adequate enough for him to see the figure in the driving sleet standing on the gravelled terrace below.

Hollow eyes flashed him a look of recognition. The signal from one eye, a pointed glint; the figure's tortured stance and the stillness of it, in spite of the heaving wind, suggested supernatural strength in the skeletal frame. Obviously alive, it was a deathly figure.

The mask of putrid flesh he'd seen at the top of the Gothic staircase was summoning him.

He held the torch as steady as his shaking hand allowed, projecting its beam straight into the sockets of the sunken eyes, challenging it to make some comprehensible gesture.

The figure must have understood his challenge because it raised an arm from its white shroud, gestured at the walls and then began to tap a claw against its breast to signify All-This-Is-Mine.

Every spirit is original; its disgusting carapace bears its signature. Each spirit is in a different place. I think of it as warfare hand to hand: one false move and the enemy's hands will seize me.

He pointed towards the gravel, the gesture the command: *Stay-Where-You-Are-Don't-Move-I'm-Coming.*

The amorphous creature looked up into his eyes and slowly gave a willing nod:

I'm-Waiting-For-You.

He fled the bedroom, running along the corridors, down the stairs and careered across the slippery stone to the Gun Room.

29

By his calculation the ground-floor window nearest to where the figure stood was in an anteroom adjoining the Billiard Salon.

He fed a cartridge into the chamber, checked the safety catch and telescopic sights and walked silently along the passage to the darkened anteroom.

Taking his time to part the shutters, he removed the horizontal locking bar and lowered it sideways against the wall.

The windows were blurred with a fine film of ice, though not blurred enough to prevent him seeing the figure had changed position in the storm.

Good, he had time to ease the window open to the sleet and wait for its inevitable reappearance.

He held the gun in his right hand, behind the trigger's guard. His left hand was further down the shotgun, under the barrel.

He raised the gun, settling it comfortably against his shoulder. With his dominant eye, his right, he peered into the telescopic sights, taking careful aim at the space where he'd last seen the spectre. He kept his right eye a short distance from the aperture, the crosshairs of the sights centred on the target's general position, then released the safety catch and waited, his finger ready to squeeze the trigger.

30

Fewer than forty metres distant, he saw the shroud. The very moment he set eyes on it triggered the signal: CHIP OPERATION: REMOTE CONTROL FAMILIAR, condescending, patient, free. Come not to sojourn, but abide with me.

– light cut into the anteroom and he twisted round to face the beam.

– a still small voice behind it said: '*Don't.*'

Francesca stood in the doorway, erect and very still.

'Get out,' he yelled.

She was tight-lipped and unmoving.

Then, with great suddenness, she hurled her torch across the room at him. It struck the wall beside the window, crashed against the floor, and rolled a short way along the skirting board.

'Don't move,' he ordered, jerking round to face the window again, and as he peered into the sights, his eyes were filled with a far stronger light from outside, as if the storm had exploded behind his eyeballs.

Instantaneously, he squeezed the trigger.

The gun recoiled, throwing him off his aim. He prepared to take a second shot but the residue of the dazzling light from within the turmoil of the sleet played havoc with his eyesight.

– for a moment he was blinded.

– the big N as in nada nil zero zippo Nothin' = N = big 0e0. Nothing.

The light from outside dimmed, then went out altogether leaving the beam of the torch Francesca had thrown shining feebly across the floor.

'I saw,' she said. 'You were trying to kill her.'

'Bloody right.'

'Do as I say. Put that gun down. I said, put it down.'

'Not before I get another shot.'

'Let me see her.'

She walked across the room and stood close beside him in the gloom.

Setting the shotgun carefully aside, he never saw the syringe she was clutching behind her back.

She drew close to where he was seated at an angle in the alcove.

Head tilted, she smiled at him. 'Oh, Hal, what *are* we going to do with you? Let me make you a nice hot drink. Close the window.'

He shifted his position in the alcove, slightly off balance, steadied himself on the window-seat cushion, and stretched out his hands to lift and refasten the heavy bar across the shutters. His arms were fully extended when the needle found the *vastus lateralis* muscle on the outer edge of his thigh between his knee and hip bone.

The heavy shutter bar thudded against the wall.

With her free hand she gripped him round his neck, the bone of her forearm tightened against his larynx as if she intended to asphyxiate him.

'There-there,' she said softly.

He clutched his throat.

'Didn't hurt, did it?' she said.

He felt blood seeping inside his trouser leg; his thigh had become sticky and he looked at her in disbelief.

She said: 'No worries, my love.' She was folding a paper tissue carefully around the needle. 'Given my love a little something to make him happy.' She stepped away from him as he struggled to his feet.

He said: 'What the hell have you done . . . what is it you've—?'

'—what is it Francesca's given you? An advance Christmas present from Santa's little helper.' There was the edge of warning in her banter. 'You're coming up to bed.'

He reached out for the shotgun.

'Leave it,' she said, setting it out of reach.

He tried to snatch the ball of tissue containing the syringe away from her and failed. A deep lavender liquid oozed through the tissue in her fingers.

He swung his arm at her frantically – *trying to hit the*

viper very hard with his fist, stab her with fingernails in the softness of her throat—

'Stand up carefully now,' she was saying.

Her hair brushed his cheeks and he sensed her warmth and the scent of jasmine oil. She drew a wristband of white silk thread towards his eyes so he was forced to look at the small ornament dangling from it. His thigh began to throb. *No doubt about it – definitely a Levantine viper.* Or, was he looking at the image of an Indian cobra's head, a *Naja Naja's* severed head? *Kill. Kill it.*

'Girls in white kimonos; with white silk ... I want you,' she whispered with an intimacy that said I've-Got-You. 'Now I'm your Sumiko.' Then she drew his lips towards her open mouth and rubbed her tongue slowly across his teeth.

Possessed of a natural gift for physical seduction, she was *disponible* and generous and wanted to pleasure him.

Naked, they slept in each other's arms oblivious of the raging storm.

And no one would've been any the wiser had the storm not run out of energy.

MacCullum delivered Teresa to The Towers as it weakened.

SIX

I came into the world naked, man.
That's how I'm a-leavin' it.

KEN D.J. MOSES

31

At about ten o'clock in the morning, finding no sign of Francesca in the kitchen or her bedroom, Teresa opened the door of Hal's room to be confronted with the sight of her daughter and Hal naked in each other's arms. Her reaction to this discovery was to remain silent.

She didn't raise her hands in horror; neither did she walk out of her daughter's room in a huff. She undressed without ceremony, lifted aside the eiderdown, and drew Hal to her.

They took their time.

Francesca offered no protest.

She showed neither shame, guilt, nor embarrassment, as Hal and her mother became lovers beside her.

When finally they lay still, Francesca stroked his lips and then kissed him gently.

He heard her saying:

'He's sleeping like a king.'

Teresa whispered: 'Don't wake him, love.'

They were standing by the window.

Hal stirred and listened.

'I'll come down for coffee, Mam.'

'I'll make the coffee,' Teresa said. 'Run a nice hot bath for him.' She sounded remarkably matter-of-fact. 'We must get on with what's left of the day.'

'It's not that late, Mam.'

'There's lots to do.'

'Busy. Busy. Busy. Are you all right, Mam?'

'I'm fine, love. Fine. Yes. Just fine.'

'Ryker all right?'

'Everyone's all right, Francesca. Don't keep on about everyone being all right.'

'I'm only thinking of others.'

'Then you freshen up, girl. Make yourself nice. I'll be in the kitchen. I've got to clear up the mess that puppy's making. It's shat itself.'

'It's only tiny.'

'It's still shite.'

'Roads clear, are they?'

'Yes, yes, yes. Main roads anyway. There's a likelihood of floods. More snow too. I can feel it in my bones.'

'Me too. We had a bad time of it here in the night.'

'Tell me about it.'

'That storm. And worse things besides . . . I thought it'd be the death of us.'

'You don't have to tell me, sweetheart. Ryker's had a

look-see at the damage. There's a whole lot of muck and water in the picture galleries. He says we should be careful the plaster doesn't fall in on us.'

'There's more than water that came in last night.'

'You had a visitation, didn't you?'

'You know?'

'Of course I know.'

'She was as clear as daylight.'

'I know she was. I knew she was with you two. It was Monday yesterday, wasn't it? You should've been warned. Monday. Monday. That's what your father used to sing. Idle bastard. *Monday Monday ... Monday morning ...*'

Francesca joined in: '*... Oh, Monday Monday ...*'

'Don't need to remind me, girl.'

'Monday always turns out bad.'

'Turned out all right for you though, didn't it? I might've guessed what you two'd be up to.'

'Speak for yourself.'

'He's nice,' said Teresa.

'You don't mind, Mam?'

'I was young once.'

'You're still young, Mam.'

'I think so. Others mightn't.'

'You won't tell anyone, Mam?'

'Tell who?'

'Priscilla.'

'Priscilla? She'll be happy.'

'Think she knows?' Francesca said with pleasure.

'What d'you think, love? 'Course, dear. Of course she *knows*. There's nothing she doesn't know. You're a good girl.'

'Take after you, don't I, Mam?'

'So Ryker says. He's right about most things. At least someone's got a brain in that bloody village. Some old yob was saying last night we must be mad to stay out here. Going on and on and on about how Christmas is the cruellest season. That old man Stirling should've been up on a charge of serial murder. How he was a pervert. Kept Priscilla his prisoner. Believed in the Great Beast. Had 666 tattooed on his chest. How Priscilla was a witch. That the Vicar should step in. The police should carry out a search. Leave no stone unturned.'

'What did you say?'

'Nothing. Kept mum. Ryker says that madness is normal around these moors. Inbreeding and all that. Incest. How everyone's related and everywhere blood's turned sour. Livestock wouldn't be diseased otherwise, would it? Foot-and-mouth disease. Mastitis. Brucellosis. TB . . .'

He heard the bedroom door open, then close, and their voices fading as they went downstairs:

'Swine vesicular disease. You name it. The country-side's sick and dying on its feet. No one wants to know . . .'

32

His arms had stiffened. The sweat in his eyes was sometimes hot, sometimes cold.

What happened in bed was one thing. The appearance of the spectre at the top of the Gothic staircase
was another. So was the violence of his reaction
to it.

Similarly, the figure in the storm he'd attempted to
annihilate. By definition, he reasoned, the thing would
anyway have been impervious to gunshot wounds.

The first advice he gave himself was to discover what
Francesca had injected into his bloodstream. True, he
was taking his Velamorphine, but quite what else she'd
injected he'd no idea.

Two things were for sure. At best, if best it was, the
revenants, the wandering souls back from the dead,
were bent on persecution. At worst, the sighting, the
physicality of the dread and horror had shot unadulterated fear into his bloodstream as if it had been venom
from Francesca's syringe. To prescribe an antidote was
as difficult as prescribing a catch-all antidote for the
toxins of real life.

In Afghanistan the 'real life' vacuum had been filled with the singular arousal of warfare only men and women on active service experience. Civilians prefer not to be reminded of it because military combat embodies violence at its most intense.

It's animal versus animal, creatures slaughtering other living things. To understand it fully you have actually to do it and keep on doing it. Once it's over all you find is simplicity itself: living proof you've survived. Soldiering, for Hal, meant getting the job done or the big N.

Then, always lurking in the ether, was the worst, the greatest threat of all: someone somewhere, one day, might whisper: 'He's a coward.' Fighting men may confess to many things. Cowardice most definitely isn't one of them. Fear of it attaching to you ranks on a par with incest – not something to talk about over the family dinner.

A confusion of guilt and shame decided him to visit Dr Mackle, the local GP who'd attended his mother's death.

Successfully avoiding Teresa and Francesca, he let himself out of the house and drove straight to Mackle's surgery.

The receptionist said the doctor would see him in half an hour.

*

What would he say?

'*Whenever I feel the likelihood of the things appearing my throat and mouth tighten, so does my chest, I feel nauseous. My legs turn leaden. It's getting worse. Is it connected with the Velamorphine?*'

That was something the GP could easily determine.

The paunch and smoker's cough identified Mackle as an old-fashioned doctor.

Hal recited what he'd rehearsed, told him about the apparitions, and added: 'I don't want it getting round the village.'

'That you're off-colour?'

'I'm one hundred per cent fit. I'm not off-colour. I've never been fitter. That's what's so bloody weird about these things defeating me.'

'They won't defeat you.'

'Then how do I deal with them?'

'By realizing that fear's a protection. It's one of the most normal things in the world.'

'I've no control. I can't take those things – those spirits – apart. I can't defuse them. It's fear. It's a psychosis.'

'Only if you let it lead to panic.'

'It's worse than panic. Don't you understand?'

'I understand.'

'What I want to know is – am I . . . am I losing my mind?'

'I wouldn't say so. It's only fear that's handicapping you.'

'Are these things in my head?'

'Of course they're in your head.'

'That's not what I mean. I mean – are they real?'

'Obviously real to you.'

'What?'

'I said they're obviously real to you.'

'Will they harm me?'

'It depends on you. If you believe them to be real and you set out to harm them then I've no doubt you'll succeed. I'm sure they'll be as terrified of you as you are of them.'

'You believe in them?'

'I believe in you.'

'Then answer my question. I want to know. Do you or do you not believe in them. Yes or No?'

'I believe in you.'

'Which means you do believe in them.'

'If you say so. Yes, I do.'

'Answer me this – there's something else.'

He told him about the injection Francesca had administered.

Dr Mackle was silent for a while. Then he said slowly: 'Well, perhaps the silly girl needs reminding she's responsible for the administration of some powerful drugs. There are professional standards to be observed. She may even have a problem with drug abuse herself.

And there's the matter of that gun you have. I hope I'm right in assuming it's properly licensed?'

'As a matter of fact it isn't.'

'Then you of all people don't need me to tell you that possession of an unauthorized firearm is a pretty serious offence. Best surrender it to the police. Make sure it doesn't fall into unwelcome hands. Meanwhile, it'll be for the best if you give up alcohol. I know it'll be hard work, what with Christmas in the offing.'

33

Hal did not set off immediately for Carlisle nor did he abandon alcohol. The useless consultation with Mackle was, he felt, cause for a solitary diversion: one he awarded himself in the bar at the pub in Moster Lees.

The Moster Inn doubled as a bed and breakfast guest-house and also offered a single-storey annexe for hire as a venue variously for weddings, funerals, birthday celebrations and meetings. The ageing Anglo-German licensees, Mr (Smitty) and Mrs (Cilla) Schmidt-Kingsley, had spared no expense to fill the pub with overblown Christmas decorations.

Hal's parents had rarely, if ever, visited the pub. His mother shared his father's view that the pub was strictly for non-commissioned officers and Smitty wasn't officer material. The portly man was anyway Bavarian and this was an additional reason for the Stirlings to give the Moster Inn and the Schmidt-Kingsleys a wide berth.

Moreover, Priscilla Stirling abhorred animal sports. For her, the Moster Inn was a repository of sickening evil, a D.E.I. — a Den of Extreme Iniquity. Worse still,

Smitty and his wife were apostles of the Countryside Alliance and Smitty was also, into the bargain, the sole pillar of the Moster Lees branch of the Carlisle Angling Association.

To anyone who would listen Priscilla muttered darkly about Smitty's crimes against the Animal Kingdom, threatening to report the atrocities to the International Court of Justice in The Hague.

He ordered lunch and found himself a small table in the lounge bar near the open fire. He settled down alone with cod and chips, a vodka tonic and Campari, and skimmed through yesterday's *News and Star*, *Cumbria: Lakeland's Favourite Magazine* and *Cumbria Life*.

Shortly after lunch, a group of some dozen people came into the lounge bar.

Among them were the familiar faces of MacCullum and Betsy MacCullum; the Vicar; Smitty and Cilla Schmidt-Kingsley; Dr and Mrs Mackle and WPC Dee MacQuillan of the Carlisle Constabulary. Hal was on nodding terms with all of them. Without exception, they showed surprise to see him.

'Trust you enjoyed our vittles,' Smitty said. 'Sorry about Afghanistan.'

'The Royal Scots Borderers are out there presently,' said Mackle's wife. 'Are they not, Captain Stirling? My father was in what the family calls the Kosbies. You know who they are, I daresay?'

'Kings Own Scottish Borderers,' said Hal. 'Fine regiment.'

They had just finished the Christmas meeting of the Parish Council in the annexe over lunch. 'And when it came to me,' said the Vicar, 'I said I hoped you'd agree to read the lesson at Morning Service on Christmas Day. St Luke 2: 1 to 20. And perhaps lead us in prayer for our boys overseas. *Ecclesiastes*. "A time to love, and a time to hate; a time of war, and a time of peace." Mention them by name if you like. A roll of honour.'

'Fine,' Hal said. 'It'll mean mentioning a lot of servicemen by name.'

'How many lads and lasses is there overseas, then?' asked MacCullum.

'As of now?' said Hal. 'I don't know ... thousands.'

'Make a good question for the New Year's Quiz,' said Dr Mackle.

'Difficult one to answer,' Hal said. 'It's always a changing number.'

'Go on,' said Betsy. 'Tell us.'

'Let's say, give or take eight to ten thousand in Afghanistan. Eight hundred in the Balkans. Fifteen hundred in Northern Ireland. Three thousand in Cyprus. And we have men in Gibraltar, Diego Garcia and Ascension Island and maybe a few hundred more elsewhere.'

'How are things out at The Towers?' asked the woman police officer, MacQuillan.

'Very quiet.'

'You'll be well looked after by Teresa and Francesca,' MacCullum said.

'Don't know what I'd do without them,' said Hal.

'Teresa's got things buttoned up,' Betsy said. 'Puts the rest of us to shame. If you need a hand with the Christmas dinner we can help.'

'That's very kind of you.'

'And the Help for Heroes' carol singers will be calling on you,' the Vicar said.

'Not, I trust, putting themselves out on my account?' Hal said.

'It's a multi-ethnic children's choir,' said the Vicar. 'The Choir of Lakeland Angels. They'll be calling on all servicepersons' families in the area.'

'First time in years angels will be up at The Towers,' Betsy said. 'Kids used to be too scared to go there. Christmastime being the season for the spirits. Am I right, Vicar?'

The Vicar said: 'The light of the body is the eye: if therefore thine eye be single, thy whole body shall be full of light. But if thine eye be evil, thy whole body shall be full of darkness. If therefore the light that is in thee be darkness, how great is that darkness.'

'There's nothing *at-all-at-all* to be frightened of,' said Mrs Mackle.

Smitty puffed out his chest like a Regimental Sergeant Major about to bring the parade to order. 'It's a bit of luck you're here, Captain. We've had a visitor from down south, Ghost Holidays Limited of—'

'*Guildford*,' prompted Cilla. 'In Surrey.'

Cilla's interruption appeared to sting her husband. Purple veins on his forehead protruded. His jowls wobbled, his roseate mouth twitched. He fiddled with the band of white silk thread around his wrist from which a small ornament dangled.

'– on a reconnaissance,' he continued, 'with the aim of making bookings. The young man had a tip-off that there are major hauntings in the area and he's got access to a list of punters who are what they call paranormal investigators. They hold these ten-day vigils. Seems that plenty of people will part with good money for day and night trips of scientific interest and need local catering and accommodation. The Parish Council has no objection to them happening here. Am I right, Vicar?'

'They'd inject some much needed resources and new spirit into the community,' the Vicar said. 'Help The Aged has shown an interest ...'

'So this being Christmas,' said Smitty, 'seems a propitious moment to sound you out about it, Captain – good idea?'

Hal shrugged. 'Do these poor deluded souls pay for these tours of theirs – vigils, or whatever they are?'

'*Pay* for them?' said Dr Mackle. 'They certainly do. If The Towers is to be the hub for tours it will generate a welcome boost to local tourism here and across Cumbria in general.'

'Thanks for mentioning it,' said Hal. 'I'll mull it over and have a word with Mr Warren. Let's see what we can come up with.'

'You've got a healthy supply of hauntings up there, Captain,' said MacCullum. 'Been there for generations.'

'I've never been a witness to them,' Hal said quickly.

'Your mother saw them,' said Betsy. 'Any road, that's what she told me.'

Hal gave a hollow laugh. 'I'm afraid we can no longer call upon her services as tour guide.'

'You can follow in her footsteps,' put in Cilla. 'When the heart is willing the spirit follows. Like mother like son.'

'And you, Captain ... you're following in your mother's footsteps,' said Dr Mackle. 'The Stirlings are deep in the heart of Moster. A place of holy spirit.'

'More power to your elbow,' Smitty said. 'Things will never change in these parts. Not while there's an England.'

His wife broke into song:

> '*There'll always be an England,*
> *And England shall be free*
> *If England means as much to you—*'

The others joined in: '*As England means to me.*'

A murmuring of goodwill and approval followed the brief singsong.

And if you people believe this claptrap, Hal thought, impatient to escape, you'll believe anything. The idea of these paranormal investigators swanning about The Towers filled him with the sort of hostility and suspicion he imagined his mother must have entertained for the villagers.

'Trouble the ghosts,' said MacCullum, 'and they'll trouble you. They won't disturb us, or your good self, Captain. That's what I believe.'

'No need to take a vote,' said Smitty.

All of them raised their glasses. 'Cheers,' they said as one.

Hal sensed the bonhomie was intended as a taunt. He felt his fingernails press into his palms. Little wonder the younger and marginally less insane in the community had fled for urban street-lit pastures where malignant spirits might be less inclined to graze. A small patch of redness had formed in his palms, unholy stigmata, the brand for a slave or livestock, the proof of possession by another . . .

'You'll be finishing your Christmas shopping in Carlisle, then?' asked Betsy MacCullum.

'I have a lot to do,' Hal told her.

'You're most welcome to join us here for the Moster Inn Christmas Feast,' said Smitty. 'If it'll make life easier.'

'And bring Teresa and Francesca along with you,' said Cilla. 'That's all right, love, isn't it?'

Smitty paid her no attention. 'Will you be having Christmas guests over the festive season?' he asked.

'I hope so.'

'Your lovely oriental lady perhaps?' Cilla asked. 'Smitty called her Madam Butterfly, didn't you, love. What's her name, Yoko?'

Hal looked at his watch and got to his feet. 'Sumiko – Forgive me – I must get going for Carlisle.'

WPC MacQuillan said: 'Can you give me a lift?'

'I was going to take Dee back to Police HQ,' said MacCullum, 'wasn't I, Dee? Brought you here, was going to take you back. Assisting the police with their enquiries. Do it all the time.'

'Our Ryker's always up to something,' said Smitty.

'I can drop you off,' Hal suggested to the police officer. 'Headquarters. Out at Duranhill nowadays, isn't it?' He smiled at Smitty. 'Thank you for lunch.'

The Vicar said: 'I'll come up to The Towers with the text of your Christmas Day reading.'

'No need,' said Hal, heading for the exit. 'My father made me learn it. I know it off by heart.'

He felt their eyes following him all the way outside.

'There's more snow forecast,' MacQuillan said. 'The sky looks heavy.'

Hal opened the door of the Range Rover for her.

'I wouldn't want to answer an emergency call out here after dark. Have to be a job for the Army.'

'The Army's already here.'

'Oh yes, so it is,' she said. 'You think that makes me feel safe? This is the beat of the Living Dead.'

WPC MacQuillan was what his mother would have called A Handful.

34

'Have I been rabbiting on too much?' she said as they neared Carlisle.

She'd talked ceaselessly about wanting to take a year's leave from police duty to backpack around India and end up kneeling at the feet of guru Sri Sathya Sai Baba. She'd 'chill out' at Sai's ashram Prasanthi Nilayam, the Abode of Supreme Peace at Puttaparthi in Andhra Pradesh, not too far from Bangalore. She said she intended to avail herself of two darshans or daily meetings with the guru.

'Cool,' she said. 'Beats being a copper in Carlisle ... I'm really grateful for the lift. Two minutes – and we'll be at Vernons Tea Rooms. Tell you what; if you've time to spare, I've half an hour to kill. I'll treat you. Nice hot cup of tea? Or are you in a hurry?'

'No. Matter of fact there are things I'd like to ask your advice about.'

'About Ghost Holidays and things—?'

'Things at The Towers in general.'

VERNONS TEA ROOMS
WISHES ALL OUR CUSTOMERS
A MERRY CHRISTMAS

MacQuillan said: 'If I were you, I wouldn't touch Ghost Holidays with a bargepole.'

Their voices competing against the repeating tape of Robbie Williams's 'Misunderstood', they continued their conversation over mugs of tea next to the XXL plastic Christmas tree.

'Your mother was a one-off,' said MacQuillan, leaning across the Formica tabletop. 'A special soul. A light in the darkness. I'm sad she's passed. You must miss her. I know I miss my mum. Think of her every day . . . D'you think of yours like that? You can't get some people out of your head. Loved ones are always with us. You can be sitting quite still and peaceful and you hear this whisper and the hairs stand up on the back of your head. I think it's out-of-body electricity. And you can feel them there, can't you. I always know it's Mum speaking to me. She was the only person who ever called me Deidre. "Deidre killed herself on her lover's grave to join him in a better world." Never tired of telling me. You only have one mum.'

'True enough.'

'In this life, true, isn't it?' she said. 'Mine was single. Lived in a world of her own. No other way for single mothers. Yours wasn't always the easiest of people to get on with, I heard. Not everyone's cup of Tetley's.'

'Who told you?'

'It's what the tenant farmers say about her. Only they put it a bit stronger.'

'What did they say about her?'

'Best not go there. We don't want to upset her soul. The tenants would curse her, wouldn't they? And now you. No man loves his landlord. Mind, it's not as though the rent your mum charged the buggers was all that much. She hadn't increased it in years. Nicer you are, the worse you get treated. Those peasant muck-spreaders don't know how bloody lucky they are.'

'Life would've been easier for all of us if she'd acted more realistically when it came to money.'

'She must have left you comfortable – moneywise, I mean.'

'My mother's philosophy was that you can't take it with you. Just so long as there was enough to preserve The Towers. That's what mattered to her most.'

'You . . . her only son, you must have mattered most to her.'

'I like to think so. My mother believed the tenants owed it to her to pay for the benefits of making a living from the estate – her estate, not that any of them benefit a great deal. Anyhow, she never did herself. And she preferred to have as few dealings with them as possible. And vice versa. So Warren does the donkey work and I can't say I envy him his job.'

'What will happen when the teenagers have all gone, I don't know. None of them wants to stay here a moment longer than's necessary. Most have them have left already. Leaving behind a bunch of surly bastards.'

'I don't entirely blame the younger ones, do you – I mean for clearing off? That's more or less what I did.'

'Can't say I blame them. Main reason is that the mad families don't like Mr Warren.'

'Warren – what's he done to make them leave?'

'Accused them of poaching, vandalism, flogging off the lead from barn roofs. He suspects they're using explosives to kill salmon. The kids nick the explosives from the quarries. God knows why it's still there. Some arsehole locked the stuff in a strongroom and threw away the bloody keys. So the kids bust in and nicked it, didn't they?'

'Which quarries?'

'Cramfell and Howlbeck. Poaching's one thing. Possessing high-explosives is something else. Didn't you hear about the high-explosives at Gretan? These hikers found an abandoned backpack on Gretan Moor. Midsummer. You'd have been in Afghanistan. You know what was in the backpack? Seven sticks of very nasty Army-issue PE4 plastic high-explosive.'

'Who was responsible?'

'We've never found out. Daresay kids. Hoodies involved in poaching. Dropped it in a panic maybe. Kids involved in petty crime: Breaking and entering.

Farmhouses. Weekend cottages. Medical centres. Nursing homes. Old people's residential accommodation. Even BBC Cumbria in Annetwell Street. Thieving cash, TVs, drugs, and any agricultural gear they can snitch, diesel and farm machinery, you name it, they nick it. Little scummy opportunistic bastards. They're dark and evil. The area's rotten with the Devil.'

'Local kids, are they?'

'Mostly. We have our suspicions. Poachers have been working commercially in organized gangs. There's some big money behind it. The water bailiffs have search-and-arrest powers. But you have to have a warrant from the Environment Agency. And chasing toe-rags across moorland's tough shite. The terrain around Cramfell and Howlbeck makes it tougher. You know the area?'

'Haven't been there in years.'

'Your mum used to have Ryker MacCullum drive her to Howlbeck. Right up to the end of her life she was begging him to take her there.'

'Why?'

'Show me your left wrist.'

She drew back the sleeve of Hal's coat above his wrist and glanced at the watch Sumiko had given him.

'No white wristband? Your mother wore the white silk wristband. Hasn't Teresa told you? She wears it too. And Francesca. This—' She showed him the band of white silk thread around her left wrist from which a small ornament dangled.

'What's it mean?'

'Our protection. Deliverance from Evil.'

'Have you been talking to Francesca?'

She laughed. 'What d'you mean – *"Have you been talking to Francesca?"* Course I have. We've no secrets from each other.'

He wondered what she'd make of Francesca's latest secret.

'This evil you're talking about. To do with The Towers, I suppose?'

'Wherever it finds you, Hal. The abyss. "And in those days men will seek death and will not find it; they will long to die, and death flees from them. And they besought him that he would not command them to go out into the abyss." It is written.'

'What's any of this to do with my mother's visits to the quarries?'

'She'd seen Howlbeck in a séance. She wanted to see it with her own eyes. Like face to face. She wanted to see the wrecked steel crane in the biggest Howlbeck opening. Beyond it there's the entrance to the tunnel with several chambers leading down to interconnected tunnels . . .'

She raised her wrist parallel to the Formica surface and allowed the ornament to dangle freely.

'Interconnected. Others are underwater. Abandoned. We had three divers drown there a few years back. Your mother said she spoke to them. She wanted to get as close as she could to the corpses.'

'Are the bodies still down there?'

'Only one. The next of kin said he should be left there where he'd been happiest, doing what he loved best – diving below Earth's surface. Underwater in the dark. In the end, well, there we are, it did for him, didn't it? Drowning's a terrible way to go. I've seen it too bloody often. Haunts my dreams. Lad lying in the water, mouth open, hyperventilating. No focus. Glassy eyes. You know ... it's fast. And asphyxiating victims don't shout for help because they bloody can't. That poor bloke at Howlbeck. Imagine what it must have been like for him.'

'They should've got his body out.'

'Why?'

'Because it's the humane thing to do.'

'There was closure.'

'Closure?' Hal said.

'Closure – knowing he lives.'

'But he doesn't live,' he said. 'The man's dead.'

'There was closure.'

'Listen, closure is New Age shite. You accept death; you find ways of living with death. Closure is Death, Death is Death. The big N as in nada nil zero zippo Nothin' = N = big 0e0. Nothing.'

'Death is Life.'

'Look, my friend—'

'– *Dee*. Do you mind?' she said, adding very slowly, 'I have a name, right? Do you mind not talking to me like I'm a man? Call me *Dee*.'

'*Dee* – I hate to have to disagree with you. You *close* doors in rooms or wardrobes, a fridge or lavatory, Dee. You don't *close* doors on loved ones.'

'You don't believe this, d'you?' she said. 'You don't think there's an atom of truth in all this? Truth is painful.'

'Not as painful as lies.'

'Tell me – what d'you believe? Tell. What does Hal believe in?'

He looked at her in silence.

'God?' she said. 'You do seem to be a man possessed of deep thoughts. What man isn't, eh? I can see it in your eyes. You can see depth. Most good-looking men don't, do they?'

'I wouldn't know. What makes you think I have deep thoughts?'

'Because it's what you *think* that matters. Whether you listen. Men hear; they less often *listen* unless it's to the sound of their own voices.'

'Is that what the Sri Sathya thing tells you?'

'Haven't seen him yet, have I? You weren't listening to me. Look. Here—' She leaned her face to his. 'Look into my eyes, Hal. What d'you see?'

'Myself.'

'No. You're looking but you're not *seeing*. You *see* into my soul.'

'I *see* my reflection, Dee.'

'The eyes are the gateway to the soul. You know who's supposed to have said that?'

'Yes, as a matter of fact, I do. Herman Melville. And you know what he came up with? *Moby Dick*. And I think this idea of there being ghosts at The Towers is bullshit. If I were you, I'd stay out of it.'

'And you – I think, I think you're frightened of what you don't understand. There's fear in your eyes. I can see it, Hal. And I have to tell you. You must accept it. Like Death. And don't you be angry with me. I know what I'm talking about.'

'Listen, Dee. I'm frightened of what I *do* understand. I am not frightened of death. I am frightened of dying. I am frightened of a lonely incapacitated old age. I am shit-scared of losing my mind like my mother did and that happened too bloody long before her allotted time ran out.'

'But you are not going to die, Hal.'

'Oh, come off it. Listen. I've stared death in the face. Have you?'

'I've told you. I've been as near death as I am to you here and now.'

'Then we have that in common, don't we? I've disabled bombs to prevent more death. Disabled IEDs. Have you heard about IEDs?'

'Is that what you did in Afghanistan?'

'Never mind what I did in Afghanistan.'

'It's a bloody silly war.'

'Maybe it is. Maybe it isn't.'

'Well, it is.'

'If you say so. I know what happens when people die. To pretend, like you people do, that we wander about after death like white phantoms is finally a waste of time – in your case, a waste of police time. Tell it to the Marines. And, you know what, Dee? To try and convince people of the existence of evil spirits, daemons, poltergeists, rampant disembodied perverts and all the rest is finally cruel, abusive, vicious – call it what you like. You're preying on troubled minds like bent priests, high-falutin' intellectuals – and I don't like it. You understand? In fact, I despise and loathe it. If you believe in that "closure" balls then close the door on it. Close it. In fact, slam the bloody thing.'

She smiled, impervious to his outburst, and went on smiling.

'Well?' he said.

'Well what?'

'You look as if you're about to issue a warning to me.'

'You could be right. You're talking to a police officer.'

'You don't say? Are you going to arrest me?'

She rested her hand on his. 'I might. If you don't hand in that shotgun of yours I can bang you to rights. It's up at The Towers. In the Gun Room, right? Along with a whole lot more guns from the Boer War?'

'How would you know?'

'It's my bloody job to know. *Section 2 Firearms under the 1968 Act as amended.* Unless you want to keep it. But, between these four walls, Hal – bearing in mind what Dr Mackle has to say about you – and Teresa and Francesca – remember this: "*persons applying for licences with recent, serious mental health issues will be refused a certificate. The penalty for possession of a prohibited firearm without a certificate is a maximum of ten years in prison and an uncapped fine. Unauthorized possession of firearms attracts a mandatory minimum of five years.*"'

'Then you can take the bloody thing.'

'Know what? I think I might.' She got to her feet. 'I have to go. I'll pay. Remember what I've told you.'

'Think I'll forget it?'

'No, Hal. Somehow – No. I don't. And you won't forget all the rest I've said to you. Be a good boy now ... go do your shopping.' She peered out of the windows. 'See? It's cold and dark outside. You watch out for the snow tonight. There's going to be another blizzard. A bloody Christmas white-out.' She raised a finger to her lips. 'You heard it here first. In Vernons Tea Rooms.'

'And you remember that those people raising the spirits of the dead are evil. Criminal. Maybe even homicidal.'

'You remember that you commit an offence if you make me falsely think there's a real danger to the safety of a person or a property. You also commit an offence if you pretend you have relevant information in relation to a police enquiry. It's governed by section 5 of the Criminal Law Act.'

'Do me a favour, Dee. Take a look at abuse and harassment at The Towers. Prosecute the Living Dead.'

'It's takes a brave man to laugh at the Living Dead.'

'Don't you worry. My job's with the Living.'

'Same as mine – with a little difference. Happy Christmas.'

'Same to you.'

35

It was in the bitter wind outside Vernons Tea Rooms, as he was unlocking the Range Rover, that he saw the warning light.

He was still cursing Francesca for having confided in the police – presumably, he reasoned, she was the person who'd told MacQuillan about the shotgun – and he felt sickened by the thought that Francesca might soon boast to the police officer, even unintentionally, about what had happened between her sheets.

But the warning originated from the glare of a lorry's powerful headlights. The lorry was a nondescript removals vehicle and its dazzle overpowered him so that for a few moments he stood, blinded and part paralysed, like a rabbit hoping against hope that if he remained motionless he might be as invisible as the predator behind the vicious beam.

In spite of the warmth afforded by his Ski Wear Store overcoat, he shivered uncontrollably: possessed by the powerful reality that *he was remembering the future*; places, events and faces, familiar and unfamiliar, that he *had* seen, but *not yet*.

He stretched his gloved hands out, his arms apart, leaned against the Range Rover. Still, his irregular breaths collected on the air like a shroud.

He heard his own voice as though from a gradually increasing distance: *Buy mobile phone. Collect Velamorphine as per the prescription from VJK Pharmacy.*

Where am I?

I am standing here.

True, he was standing there. But what he perceived did not originate from within him.

His senses were constructing another realm with great rapidity. It was a sort of dream in which half-familiar people and places emerged illogically, yet with far greater vividness and indeed much more slowly than any he encountered in nocturnal dreaming.

His sense of Time felt utterly perverse. For this was the future. He was, with strange certainty, *remembering the future*. His mind was telling him: this is not present time; this is not the past; it isn't even the future.

The sensation was extraordinarily powerful. *I AM REMEMBERING THE FUTURE.*

— and there was another voice, his father's: a whisper:

Two girls in silk kimonos, both beautiful, one a gazelle—

Two beautiful women's faces peered at him through veils of bloodied mist.

*

Sumiko was standing there in her white silk kimono. The other woman was also wearing white silk, not a kimono but a silken robe. Then the bloodied mist parted and another woman appeared.

One of the women was struggling to take his pulse; someone else was trying to get a cannula into him to deliver an intravenous drip of saline fluid. He was telling them in a matter-of-fact way: 'If I am about to die the odds are on my doing so within the next thirty to forty minutes.'

The reality was that painted fingernails were drawing out his eyes, literally pulling them out, tugging at his irises, the smooth muscles of his pupils capable of contraction were being stretched from his face like elastic bands.

It was a warning, an admonition, the alien pulling and yanking and tugging at his contorted face; malignancy invading his soul, sucking out his bloodstream, numbing nerve ends, making contact through his eyes with a supernatural and evil electricity: a *mysterium tremendum*, pumping into his heart, the very seat of conscience, the heart of fear: 'you stiffened your neck, and hardened your heart from turning unto the Lord God ...'

He had heard this, without a shred of doubt; he'd heard it, not before, but in the future:

And I have seen faces forming in flakes of snow and glit-
tering on the mist in front of my eyes: I have seen this
shroud of death.

I have felt the claw of squirming fingers at my bleeding
eyelids; then moist lips pressing against my ear and I hear
its morbid whisper:

'And behold, and, lo, in the midst of the throne and
of the four beasts, and in the midst of the elders, stands
a Lamb as it has been slain, having seven horns and seven
eyes, which are the seven Spirits of God sent forth into all
the earth. And I saw when the Lamb opened one of the
seals, and I heard, as it were the noise of thunder, one of
the four beasts saying: Come. Come. Come and see.'

Whose voice . . . other than—?

Sada Abe's

– lost in the tumult of The Towers' bell booming with
neither rhyme nor reason.

Sa-da-Sa-da-Sa-da: the booming thundered from The
Towers across the desolation of the moorland—

'And from far off, above the moors, at the place called
Howlbeck, I heard an angel scream—'

'We are come unto a place called Golgotha, that is
to say, the place of the skull – They give me vinegar to
drink mingled with gall – And when I taste thereof, I
will not drink. I am drowning. My eyes will not, cannot
focus.'

For a moment Sumiko stood there, at his side, whispering beneath the booming of The Tower's bell: 'I believe in the unexpected ... fear of fear is devouring us.'

They said together: *I believe in God, the Father Almighty, Creator of Heaven and Earth.*

RUN!
The frantic urge overtook him.
RUN – to find the shotgun – to plead with Sumiko to run for dear life—

I believe in Jesus Christ, His only Son, our Lord. He was conceived by the power of the Holy Spirit and born of the Virgin Mary.
... Sumiko please – *be very careful* – the centre isn't holding ... *Chaos engulfs the world – He suffered under Pontius Pilate, was crucified, died, and buried. The blood-dimmed tide is loosed, and everywhere*
... The ceremony of innocence is burned ...
He descended to the dead—

And rose again—
– with the eyes in the Vernon Tea Rooms on him. The eyes of the cashier, the pair of cooks, the washer-up and two elderly women: one clutching a green-eyed cat to her breasts; the other saying: 'He's isn't dead.'
He ascended into Heaven,

and is seated at the right hand of the Father.

He will come again to judge the living and the dead.

– eyes of ordinary folk who'd seen a man stumble from the car park and collapse head first in the doorway, jamming open the swing doors, letting in the rush of cold, freezing them with unseasonal dread.

It's me, not them, who has sure and certain reason to dread the twisted future.

I believe in the Holy Spirit, the holy Catholic Church, the communion of saints, the forgiveness of sins, the resurrection of the body, and the life everlasting. Amen.

'Since we departed Nahr-e Saraj you've bloody died twice.' I don't think so. I mean, we'd been nowhere near Nahr-e Saraj. 'We won't let you die a third time.'

And for the third time you rose from the dead—

They lifted him onto a plastic chair and he sat protesting that he was all right. 'It's okay. I'm dehydrated. Thank you for the water. I'm much better.'

'We've called an ambulance,' the cashier said.

'Please ring them and cancel it.'

'Should you be driving in your condition?' someone asked. 'There's more snow coming. The ice is terrible.'

'I know,' he said, getting up from the chair and straightening his clothes. 'I'm used to it.'

They looked at him pityingly and gave a sort of collective shrug of bafflement. 'You should be careful,' said the woman, trying to kiss the cat on the mouth. 'You never know when something nasty's going to overtake you, Puss-Puss, do you – do you, Puss-Puss?' Puss-Puss dived for the floor.

'You're very right. Thank you for the advice. And thank all of you for helping. Yes. Happy Christmas. Just a dizzy spell.'

'Happy Christmas,' they said unhappily.

He left the tea rooms shutting his ears to Robbie Williams's 'Misunderstood'.

36

He bought the replacement mobile telephone, loaded the Range Rover with groceries, wines and spirits; then set off to the alleyway where VJK Pharmacy had its small premises.

Here he would collect the Velamorphine Teresa had ordered on his behalf. Dr Mackle had provided a repeat prescription and Dr Mackle was a VJK Pharmacy regular so it was simply a matter of collecting his drugs and leaving. Easy.

'Mr and Mrs Khan are very appreciative of Sister Vale's custom,' said the pharmacist's assistant. 'There's a Christmas bag here for her. A gift for Sister Vale and her daughter.'

She lifted a VJK Pharmacy carrier bag tied with Christmas ribbon across the counter. 'Sister Vale and her daughter like Lancôme's Miracle, don't they? Miracle. Scent for the sophisticated modern woman,' she read from the carton. 'A mix of freesia, lychee, magnolia and jasmine. And there's a little something Sister Vale asked Mr Khan to obtain.'

Hal looked inside the carrier bag.

The 'little something' was in a Jiffy bag sent AANGETEKEND (recorded delivery) from Amsterdam.

'This is very kind of you.'

'Don't thank me,' the girl said. 'Thank Mr Khan.'

'I'll make sure Sister Vale gets it.'

'And her daughter?'

'And Nurse Vale too.'

The assistant said: 'Sister Vale must be sure to check the therapeutic documentation care-plan for the type, route and dose of your medication.'

'What's the other item?'

'Additional medication for you, such as is unobtainable in the UK. Make sure it's correct. Please – have a quick look-see at it. Mr Khan won't like it if you haven't checked it in front of me.'

He opened the Jiffy bag and found four small vials in bubble-wrap, each containing deep lavender-coloured liquid. The very same colour he'd seen on Francesca's fingers.

He removed one of the printed leaflets and read:

VAN DER HECHTRITCEREN BESLOTEN VENOOTSCHAP
NULFAIL® MILLE DEBACTER SEXUAL ENHANCEMENT

Edging away from the main counter nearer to the racks of toothbrushes and toothpastes, he skimmed the rest of the leaflet.

His reading was interrupted – 'May I help you?'

He looked into the eyes of a neat figure sporting a fedora and voluminous black cashmere cloak. The man bore an uncanny resemblance to the President of Afghanistan.

The presidential person said: 'What's that you're holding?'

'My medication.'

'You must be Captain Stirling.' The man doffed his fedora with a flourish revealing a bald and shining head. 'V.J. Khan,' he announced with ingratiating formality. 'I regret we cannot allow you to take that.'

'It's my medication.'

'Sister Vale is the only one who can—'

Hal turned suddenly, knocked over a stand of umbrellas and pushed open the door out into the alleyway.

The pharmacist caught up with him and made a grab for the carrier bag.

Hal kept on walking.

'Give it to me.'

Passing headlights lit up the alleyway.

The pharmacist said. 'Keep your Velamorphine. Keep it. The packet's for Sister Vale. For me . . . to give her personally.' He fiddled with the chain at the collar of his cloak. 'Purely for recreational use.' He glanced nervously at the passing traffic. 'Are you alone?'

'Maybe.'

'You know what you've taken?'

'Yes.'

'It's harmless stuff.'

'Oh, yes?'

The pharmacist reached out his hand. 'Don't be a fool.'

'Then stop trying to grab it.'

'Do you want money?' the pharmacist asked.

'For what?'

The pharmacist tried to grab Hal's sleeve. 'I'll call the police.'

'And then?'

'Report you.'

'For what?'

'Having opiate analgesic medication in your possession – heroin – diacetylmorphine. People talk, you know. Word gets round. Diacetylmorphine has originated from The Towers. I have it on good authority.'

For a few moments they faced each other at the end of the alleyway.

'Of course,' the pharmacist continued, 'you can reseal the package and simply hand it over, can't you? Hand it over to Sister Vale. You need, as it were, to be none the wiser. It's a personal matter. Private and personal.'

'What you say about The Towers, the heroin – is that the truth?' Hal asked. 'Where's the evidence?'

'We're both in the same boat,' the pharmacist said. 'Trust me. Make no mention of this. For your own sake as well as mine. Tread carefully, my friend. You see, your mother was not entirely blameless.'

'What d'you mean?'

'Nurses and their patients develop unhealthy habits. Listen to me. Your mother ... no stranger to chronic pain. And the nurses, what do they do? They shield the suffering from pain. Only death relieves it. Death can be a mercy.'

'For God's sake.'

'*Please* – you mustn't allow your anger to get the better of you. We, all of us, have to do things unacceptable to ordinary folk.' He paused. '*Que sera, sera*. Why don't we have a talk ... private and personal, man to man?'

'That won't be necessary.'

'Then Sister Vale can tell you what I'm getting at.'

'What are you trying to tell me?'

'It isn't what *I can try to tell you*. It's an issue of what Sister Vale *must* tell you. Why not ask her in confidence who the father of her daughter is ... Tread carefully, Captain Stirling. As I say, people talk, you know. It's the business of little people to talk. As a pharmacist of long-standing one's privy to disagreeable confidences. The stain on the reputation and so forth.'

'What's it to do with my mother?'

'Ask Sister Vale. How many times do I have to tell you? Ask Sister Vale. They were very close.'

The pharmacist was shaking visibly. Hal read the fear in the deep-set eyes. 'I think you have no idea of the reality,' the pharmacist continued. 'You must allow me to help you.' His mirthless smile revealed a prominent gold tooth. 'You see,' he whispered, 'your mother is alive.'

A mouse darted from a discarded sandwich in the gutter.

'What?'

'Your mother is alive.'

Hal's throat contracted. 'Are you mad?'

The pharmacist inclined his head. 'Your mother is alive. Common decency requires me to tell you.'

'Where is she?'

The pharmacist retreated. 'Ask Sister Vale.'

'Where is she?'

Khan had already turned the corner as if he'd evaporated into thin air.

Back at the pharmacy he read the notice:

CLOSED

HAPPY CHRISTMAS & A MERRY NEW YEAR

A voice said: 'Chemist's gone to India for his holidays.' The informant was a ghoulish figure in a sleeping bag. 'Cup of tea for an old soldier?'

He gave the skeleton a handful of loose change.

'Hope you have a very Happy White Christmas,' said the veteran as if he'd been insulted. 'You know who I blame—?'

He didn't stay to hear the roll-call of the world's religious leaders.

There was a rattling of doors: the slam of steel shutters: the distorted voice from the Carlisle City Council's loudspeaker on a lamp post crooning 'Have Yourself a Merry Little Christmas'.

He needed Sophie.

37

She agreed to meet him in Carlisle Cathedral. She would wait for him in St Wilfrid's Chapel, near the sixteenth-century carved Flemish altarpiece, the Brougham Triptych. The cathedral choir was rehearsing 'O Little Town of Bethlehem'.

He gave her a garbled account of the testy conversation with MacQuillan, his collapse in the car park, and the encounter with the pharmacist.

'There are rumours he's peddling drugs,' Sophie said. 'The man's got good reason to be running scared.'

'So have I.'

'Not on account of your mother.'

'The idea of her . . . still alive—'

'Don't allow yourself to misled by some petty fraudster.'

'Do you think there's a germ of truth in it?'

'Do you?'

'I don't know.'

'Do you *want* to believe your mother's still alive?'

'Half of me does, the other half doesn't.'

'I think I can help you understand the situation. You

aren't going to like this. The truth is that the people in Moster Lees in the spirit circle devotedly believe in the force of the spirit world. They have done for generations. Your mother, and your father before her, inspired a messianic belief in the other world. Those Moster people, the pub landlord, his wife, the doctor and his Morningside wife; MacCullum and his wife, even the police officer MacQuillan – all wear the white wristbands of their faith, you must've noticed – so do Teresa and Francesca. So does Warren. To be perfectly honest, when the whole thing first dawned on me, I thought them pretty harmless. No more a nuisance than Rotarians or Freemasons. Now, well, I'm not quite so sure. You have to understand – for them, The Towers is the circle's heart. Your mother's death is generating real panic about its future. It's induced a crisis in their collective mind. Given your scepticism about their world, they're hostile to you. They'd honestly prefer it if you just cleared off. To be frank, life would've been easier for them had you not survived your accident in Afghanistan. They think it's taken a fatal toll on your state of mind. That finally you'll crack up. That's what they want.'

'They're going to be disappointed.'

'If you don't, then they'll lay siege to The Towers and make life too painful for you to stay.'

'This fucking circle. This was my father's doing?'

'And your mother's too.'

'What precisely is it?'

'The dead. The not-so-dead. The other world. Keep your head. Hold fast. Eventually they'll give up.'

'You're sure?'

'I'm not sure. As I say, they believe you're suffering from the damage inflicted in Afghanistan. They believe your wounds were inflicted by the spirits. That your psyche's dying. You're destined to die there. If the spirits in Afghanistan didn't finish the job then the ones at The Towers will. If they don't succeed, they can assist what's happening inside your head to kill you. Think Assisted Suicide. You can't prosecute a homicidal spirit. The spirit is entirely free to murder and commit conspiracy to murder. Voices inside your head may tell you to take your own life. If they succeed in convincing you then who's going to charge them with murder?'

'Has any of them said this in so many words?'

'Not to me directly. But from casual conversations I've overheard, you'll find I've got it right. Word gets out. Their firm belief is that all they need to do is sit back and let The Towers do its worst.'

'It's already started.'

'Then you have to fight it.'

'Alone?'

'Alone. No one can help you. I can't. No one can. You have to identify the boundary between your mind and the outside world. Only you can do it.'

They passed a woman in a pew. Her face was in shadow and she was praying fervently. She raised her eyes and stared at Sophie. Hal thought he saw a flicker of recognition.

Sophie walked faster and looked at her watch. 'I have to go.'

'Ladies and gentlemen,' the choirmaster trilled: 'Listen up. On Three, please. One. Two. And Three.'

O little town of Bethlehem
How still we see thee lie

'That woman seemed to recognize you,' Hal said.

'I know.'

'Who is she?'

'Warren's fucking wife.'

38

At the cathedral exit he asked her if there was anyone among the villagers he could approach with a view to getting trustworthy support. He mentioned the Vicar but Sophie said he was a naive and gentle soul who didn't seem to inhabit the real world.

'You're on your own,' she said. 'In enemy territory.'

'Without protection,' he said, 'and outnumbered.'

'Then numb that sixth sense of yours . . . the part of your brain that reveals sentient beings.'

'It's too late. I looked it up. Delirium's in the Stirling genes. My father reached the same conclusion years ago. He too was a law unto himself.'

'Such men are always dangerous, Hal. And I advise you against self-diagnosis.'

'How do you explain what happened to me outside Vernons Tea Rooms?'

'I can't. You're the only person who can disable the demons at The Towers. Given you don't hold with them it shouldn't be impossible.'

He felt he was reaching out to touch the senses of his soul: seeing them in a looking-glass. Looking at himself. Seeing someone else. A passage from *Through the Looking-Glass, and What Alice Found There* at once reformed itself in his head:

> 'So I wasn't dreaming, after all,' I said to myself, 'unless – unless we're all part of the same dream. Only I do hope it's my dream, and not Hal's! I don't like belonging to another person's dream,' I went on in a rather complaining tone: 'I've a great mind to go and wake him, and see what happens!'

'Sophie, wait . . .' he said. 'One more thing I need to tell you. You may not like it—'

He told her what had happened in Francesca's bed.

Sophie took the practical view.

That Francesca had administered drugs to him without his consent was a matter serious enough to have her nursing registration licence suspended, if not withdrawn. The Nursing and Midwifery Council might very well discipline her for the sexual harassment of a patient. Likewise Teresa.

But Hal would have to be a witness at the hearing. She asked if he was prepared to be put through the stress and humiliation this would inevitably involve. Teresa and Francesca Vale's lawyers would say that there was no proof he'd resisted their advances. Indeed, what evidence was there that sexual relations with both women at the same time in the same bed had actually taken place?

'Plainly,' she said, 'given your present state of mind, you'll prove a pretty unreliable witness. The nurses' careers are of relatively minor interest. Your duty is to regain enough stability to return to the military. To the Taliban and not two cunning nurses.'

As to the pharmacist, his professional future didn't greatly concern her. He was registered as a pharmacist with the General Pharmaceutical Council. She could approach the GPhC; it had the authority to issue a warning; impose conditions on his professional practice; suspend him, or remove him entirely from its Register.

'The GPhC could be asked to send in one of its inspectors who may take witness statements from Teresa and Francesca and you as well.'

The interviews would be undertaken in accordance with the provisions of the Police and Criminal Evidence Act.

'You'll be asked to attend a hearing in London in front of a QC and a two-man committee. Most likely the pharmacist will be shown the door and sooner or later face police prosecution. Let the Devil take the hindmost.'

Outside the cathedral she said: 'None of this needs go any further. I too have a secret, Hal.'

39

From where the incline was steepest, the Range Rover's headlights illuminated two vehicles parked by the entrance to The Towers. Warren's Mercedes was next to MacCullum's truck.

He got out of the Range Rover, steadying himself against its side and the effect of the sight confronting him.

Feathery snowflakes gusted across his eyes. Through the shifting veils he saw The Towers' face.

He squinted, jerked his head, and stretched his eyes wide open. He told himself it was a mirage. The house's shape had altered. Not an image from his remembrance of the future.

A section of the roof had collapsed. Broken stonework, splintered glass and timbers lay across the cobblestones of the forecourt.

The Towers had begun to disintegrate.

SEVEN

As fear increases into an agony of terror, we behold, as under all violent emotions, diversified results. The heart beats wildly, or may fail to act and faintness ensue; there is a death-like pallor; the breathing is laboured; the wings of the nostrils are wildly dilated; 'there is a gasping and convulsive motion of the lips, a tremor on the hollow cheek, a gulping and catching of the throat;' the uncovered and protruding eyeballs are fixed on the object of terror; or they may roll restlessly from side to side, *huc illuc volvens oculos totumque pererrat.*

CHARLES DARWIN
The Expression of Emotions in Man and Animals

40

MacCullum and Warren had brought portable lights, presumably intending to secure what reminded him of a scene devastated by an airborne high-explosive missile.

A Hyundai generator throbbed outside a side entrance. Following its orange power cable, Hal hurried into the building and down slimy stairs, wondering how far MacCullum and Warren had risked venturing beneath the damaged structure. Labyrinthine pipes gurgled above his head and a stench of sewage filled the chill and narrow passages.

Barely able to see the subterranean route ahead, he followed the cable on and on through the cellars to where the stone floors were drier and thick with putrefaction. Squealing rats tumbled across his shoes.

At the end of a low tunnel wavering lights and murmuring voices grew stronger. He made out the crouching figures of Warren and MacCullum.

MacCullum had one hand down a drain hole struggling with a wrench to isolate the rising main valves.

'Rats, fucking rats,' he chanted. 'Rats. It should go bloody clockwise – *rat piss, rats.*'

He struck out wildly at them with his wrench.

Both men wore waterproofs and fisherman's thigh-high rubber waders. Eyes glinting in the light, MacCullum glanced up at Hal: 'Seen it, have you? Tower's gone.'

Warren kept his torch beam pointed into the filthy water MacCullum had stirred up. 'Hurry,' he said. 'This is a bloody death trap.'

'What the fuck d'you think I'm doing,' MacCullum said. 'Piss. Fucking rats.'

'Take it easy,' Hal said. 'Have you secured the electricity supply?'

'What d'you bloody think?' MacCullum said.

'Circuit boards are addled with rot,' said Warren.

'How much more damage is there?' Hal asked.

'You're standing beneath the worst of it,' MacCullum said.

Hal asked: 'Are Teresa and Francesca okay?'

'Scared to death,' said Warren. 'They heard the thing come down as if it had been ripped apart by lightning.'

'The dog's out of its stupid mind,' MacCullum said. 'Howling like a witch. Teresa's had to tranquillize it.'

'There was an almighty rushing wind,' said Warren with the tone of an evangelist. 'Came out of nowhere with a chorus of rumbling. The Towers literally moved.

They thought it was an earthquake. Shuddering and banging, Teresa said. Francesca was hysterical. There's a desperate need to shore things up. This makes Sophie's survey imperative.'

'We'll worry about that later,' Hal said.

'I've asked her to get here fast,' Warren said. 'God knows where she's been. Someone said they'd seen her leave the cathedral. Did you see her, Hal?'

'Why should I have?'

'You were in Carlisle?'

'Things to do.'

'Not in the cathedral?'

'At the pharmacist's. Why d'you ask?'

'Never mind,' said Warren. 'We must get the survey done fast, old thing. Sophie will have to start work as soon as she gets here.'

'Tonight – what can she do to help tonight?'

'Help. That's what she can do. We must all help. With respect, including you. For your mother's sake. Do you have any objection to her staying here overnight?'

'Of course not,' said Hal. 'If she wants to. Have any of the farms been damaged?'

'How the hell would we know?' said MacCullum.

'I'm asking Mr Warren.'

'One thing at a time,' Warren said.

MacCullum levered himself to his feet and wiped

away the slime dripping from his gauntlets. 'Howlbeck and Cramfell were flooded this afternoon. Good job there was no sad bastard in the shafts.'

'Or for that matter,' Warren said, 'down here in this shit.'

41

They gathered in the kitchen's warmth. MacCullum and Warren went elsewhere to clean up. Pale with shock, Francesca offered to unload the groceries and wine from Hal's Range Rover.

Warren must have already told Teresa that Sophie was staying the night. The doorbell sounded and Teresa went to receive her.

'I've made up a room for you,' Teresa said. 'The suite next to Hal's. There's a fire and an electric heater. If you're frightened in the night you can leave your door open and the landing light on.'

'I don't mind the dark,' said Sophie.

Teresa gave her an unblinking stare. 'And,' she said, 'there's a nice fire in the Library for later if you wish to watch TV. I want Francesca to take her mind off things. I fear for her peace of mind.'

'I think she'll survive,' Sophie said.

'I feel it in my bones, don't you?'

'Perhaps.'

'Some things I know,' said Teresa shortly.

*

Teresa came into the kitchen and looked at Hal with a vacant smile. 'You'll be wanting to catch up with the news from Afghanistan. There's talk of our lads moving out of . . . where's it?'

'Helmand.'

'Yes,' she said. 'The TV said what with so many of our boys getting blown up there's a shortage of bomb disposal experts. I expect you'll back on duty there in the New Year.'

'We'll see. I have my hands full here.'

'And we'll be conducting a séance in your mother's bedroom. Tonight. At eleven. We need her help.'

'Does your séance have to be in her bedroom?'

'Why not? That's what she prefers. We wouldn't want to disappoint her, would we? I know her little foibles, Hal.'

'So do I,' he said glancing at Sophie.

She looked at the floor.

Teresa asked her: 'You'd like to join us, wouldn't you, dear? Priscilla will be able to answer questions for you.'

'How do you know?' Sophie asked.

'She told me.'

'Good for her. There's a lot I need to know about The Towers. Perhaps you can ask her some questions on my behalf?'

'No, I can't. Priscilla wants to talk to you, Sophie. It's you she wants to talk to.'

'Sister Vale – this isn't why I've come here.'

'The Towers asked you.'

'Think so?' said Sophie, disguising her incredulity.

Teresa looked wide-eyed at Hal. 'It's what your mother says, isn't it?'

'I've no idea, Teresa.'

'Sophie will show us the courtesy of attendance at our séance – can I rely on you?'

'If Sophie and I get through our business uninterrupted.'

'Your chairs will be at the table.'

Spruced up, yet still stinking of sewage, Warren and MacCullum rejoined them and gulped down Scotch before leaving. They disappointed Teresa by declining to stay for supper.

She announced that she and Francesca would have theirs in front of the TV in the Library and implied it would be best that Hal and Sophie finish their business on their own before the séance began promptly at eleven.

'Did you remember,' Teresa asked Hal as an afterthought, 'to get your medication from the pharmacy?'

Yes, he had.

It was in the Range Rover.

She told him not to forget to store it in the kitchen fridge.

42

Sophie's draft survey of The Towers was extensive.

'How long did this take you?' Hal asked her over supper and a second bottle of red wine in the kitchen. He lit a candle.

'Not long. My predecessor at Warrens, Beaumont the Memory Man, was a natural archivist. Right up until his death he was devoted to The Towers. He surveyed the roofs and upper floors. The photographic records and his written reports are here in detail. The East Wing's the one area where things have obviously changed for the worse since his day. As soon as the weather allows, the basic fabric needs securing. Some areas are problematic. Swimming pool. Turkish baths. Crypt and Chapel. Bell Tower. And the cellars. Everywhere's addled with wet rot and worse. The paintings, silverware, ceramics, the valuable rugs and furniture need properly storing off-site. Also, the rare books in the Library. The catalogues and inventories – hopelessly out of date. The last full-time librarian was employed fifty years ago. The entries are in copperplate. Hundreds are illegible. As to the problematic areas –

the doors are locked. No one seems to know who's got keys. Do you know who last had them?'

'I suppose my mother did.'

'Unfortunately, Teresa can't lay hands on them.'

'It was never her job to do so.'

'That's not what she thinks,' said Sophie, adding without a trace of humour, 'maybe we can raise the matter at the séance. She said she thought your mother kept them in her bedroom desk. But they're not there. Don't you really have any idea where they are?'

'No idea. Along with a lot of other stuff . . . You have to understand there's a great deal I don't know about the family possessions. It wouldn't surprise me if the nurses have been scuttling around for valuables.'

Sophie doodled rats' faces on a notepad. 'My father used to say The Towers is a repository of hidden riches. He told me your mother said one day you'd be the guardian of national treasures.'

'She was prone to exaggeration.'

'So was my father. Pour me some more wine – mostly he exaggerated the achievements of the Association for Psychical Research. He was obsessed with the idea that the Stirlings might endow professorial chairs for the encouragement of Psychical Research at Oxford and Cambridge. Both Vice-Chancellors chucked the idea in the bin. Your mother invested an inordinate degree of trust in my father's schemes, just as she trusted Teresa's obsession with the life beyond. I hope you don't mind me saying this, Hal, but your mother's trust in Teresa was misplaced.'

'You don't need to tell me.'

'Whatever. It's not for me to judge – but sometimes Teresa seems seriously unhinged. This addiction to the spirit world . . . it's sickly. Minti and Schadzi think she's dangerously possessed. A bomb waiting to go off.'

Hal thought: IED.

'And Warren,' he said. 'What does your boss think?'

'He's a solicitor. What isn't down on paper on his desk staring him in the eyes doesn't exist.'

'What about him and Teresa? Afternoons in Carlisle, at the Hallmark? I saw them there. They're an item, aren't they?'

'They are. He's frightened of her. The fear excites him. They've been lovers since Teresa first came here. She gives him sexual favours in lieu of fees. Francesca's let him have his way with her too. He's spellbound by them, mostly Teresa. All three can be violent. There's S & M abuse involved.'

'How do you know?'

'Because he made a vague proposal to me – to see if I might be interested. He keeps a supply of sex enhancement drugs in the firm's safe. Along with photographs of him with Teresa.'

'That means there's a third person in on the sessions?'

'Of course. Warren and Teresa like Francesca to watch what goes on.'

'Does Warren's wife know?'

'Not as far as I know. She's a magistrate. Pillar of the church. In and out of the cathedral every day. You saw her. Runs a choir. The Choir of Lakeland Angels. She's blind to her husband's weaknesses. Her preference is for the Holy Spirit. The other spirits are her husband's business.'

'She must know he's a member of the circle.'

'You don't need to tell me. He spends a fortune on painkillers at Carlisle's favourite pharmacy. Guess which. For Warren the law of the land's one thing, the law of the spirit world's another. Didn't you understand me? The spirits aren't registered citizens of the United Kingdom. They aren't answerable to the criminal justice system.'

'Warren is. I seem to remember he had sets of duplicate keys.'

'So did Beaumont. The firm still has them in the safe. They're out of date. Any number of locks were changed before your mother died.'

'By whom?'

'MacCullum. On your mother's instructions.'

'He must have keys.'

'He gave them to your mother.' Sophie was leafing through the handwritten inventories. 'D'you have any idea what may be in the storage areas, in terms of valuable items?'

'She never told me. Even her jewellery's vanished.'

'Then, d'you mind me asking, why she was so firm about no one having access to the rooms? What's so significant about these problematic areas? What's hidden there?'

'It's to do with my father. The single overriding reason must be that the cellars house his biomedical research material into the supernatural. Archives. Specimens. He gathered biological samples and medical data. Much of it morbid. Most of it unfit for tender eyes. Mother was privy to it, though to what extent, I don't know. She was secretive, more often than not unreasonable. Who knows?'

'She'd taken leave of her senses, Hal.'

'I know. I don't expect you to understand, but I feel, well, responsible for her pain. It's inside me. I have to put her first.'

'No you don't. Put yourself first. Get her out of your system. Get on with your own life.'

'Which is what I was doing until Afghanistan. I wasn't here to care for her, was I? That's why we got in Teresa and Francesca. No one could've foreseen they'd get so close to her and vice versa and then steal her soul. You believe in the malignity of souls?'

She shrugged. 'Souls? I'm sceptical. Like you, I try to keep an open mind. I've got enough problems of my own. I'm not sure what the soul is. Does anyone? Let the soul look after itself. That's what ninety-nine per cent of the population does. Did you ever hear someone say: "I'm worried about my soul"? People say the soul is precious. The truth is, they don't give a shit about it. My so-called soul's been to hell and back.' She paused. 'Look at me. Closely.'

She edged near to him.

'What do you see?'

'You're beautiful.'

'You can see I'm not. Tell me the truth. I want to hear you say it.'

'You're beautiful.'

She toyed with the stem of her wine glass. The red varnish on her long fingernails sparkled. She gazed at the wine in the glass, then at Hal. They held each other's gaze. Her green eyes were tender. Hal knew she was beautiful.

'What if,' she said at last. 'What if I was to say I want you?'

43

'What do you think?' She stretched for her wine glass on the table and knocked it over.

He reached for the glass. He kept his focus on his grip, his handhold steady, staring at his hands before he moved them. He was watching for any involuntary twitch.

'It's all over me.'

'I'll get some salt and water.'

'I shouldn't wear white silk.'

'I'm glad you do.'

'You like white?'

'Particularly silk.'

'Me too.'

'More wine?'

'Just a little.'

He refilled her glass.

Suddenly her body shook. She burst into tears, covered her eyes with her hands and sobbed.

He moved his chair beside her and gently stroked her back, then held her close.

'Don't cry. It's okay. You're my friend.' She pressed

her face against his chest. 'Do you want to tell me what the matter is?'

'I've told you,' she said softly. 'I want you.'

'You want me?'

'You heard.'

'Yes. I heard. You know I have a girlfriend.'

'Yes. It doesn't stop me wanting you.'

'She's about to come up here for Christmas.'

'I know. Married, isn't she?'

'She is.'

'Do you love her?'

'Yes.'

'But?' she said.

'No buts about it.'

'Except you made love to those two.'

'They made love to me.'

'Takes two,' she said. 'In your case, if my arithmetic's right, three.'

'Is that a criticism?'

'No,' she said. 'It's an observation. You either love Sumiko or you don't.'

'I love her.'

'You don't sound convinced.'

'It isn't easy.'

'That's what all men say.'

'Let's change the subject.'

'Suppose she doesn't get here?'

'She will. Do you want to join us?'

'No, thanks. I'll be with Minti and Schadzi.'

'Then why don't the three of you come here for Christmas dinner?'

'It'd be too painful.'

'It needn't be. I'll make sure it isn't. I'd like you to join us. Why don't you?'

Tears formed in her eyes.

'What's the matter? Please tell me, Sophie. How can I help you?'

She pushed the chair back from the table and looked into his eyes. 'Look at me. Tell me what you see.'

'A beautiful woman who's very sympathetic. Someone I trust.'

The candle was burning low.

Maybe it was the candlelight that induced the adrenalin rush. Or even fear. *The gambler's excitement. Or the mountaineer's ... climbing some Alpine rock face without a safety harness. Or knowing that he did want her but making love to her would change their growing friendship.*

'Don't be frightened of me,' she said.

'Why should I be?'

'Because I frighten myself.'

'Why?'

'Okay. Look. I'm touched, more than that, I'm *moved* that you can't tell.'

'Can't tell what?'

'What I have to do every morning, every night. That

I have to ask myself: "Sophie, are you a man? Or are you a woman? Or are you both? Or are you neither?" You can be grateful at least you don't have to suffer that. What questions could be more cruel? To survive what Fate's handed me you need a calm and supportive world wrapped around you. Ask me.'

'Ask you what?'

'Ask me who I am.'

'Who are you, Sophie?'

'Pretend you're a police officer. Ask me who I am.'

'What do you want me say?'

'Try "May I see your driving licence?"'

'May I see your driving licence?'

'"Madam."'

'Madam.'

'"Please."'

'Please.'

She took her driving licence from her handbag.

He read:

1. CHAPE

2. PHILIP JASON GOLDEN

There was a small mugshot of Philip Jason Golden Chape in a shirt and tie. He was gazing straight into the camera lens.

'Why were you named Philip Jason Golden?'

'My mother was from Corfu. That's where I was born. My father was a travel agent with Thomas Cook. Mummy

named me after the Duke of Edinburgh and Jason
Golden after the Golden Fleece. Now you know what
I am, I want to know what *you* think. Because I
want you.'

44

The sheets were warm and clammy with their sweat.

Her long fair hair awry and propped up on the pillows, a blanket around her shoulders, she kissed his neck and ran her fingers through his hair. 'Tell me more about the work your father did.'

He told her about his clandestine exploration of the workshop of the spirit, the secret sanctum. She listened to him without comment or interruption. And once he'd finished for some time they remained silent.

Finally she said: 'Do you honestly believe your mother's still alive?'

'Both Yes and No. It's that I can't believe she's dead.'

'I'm sorry to speak ill of the dead,' she said gently. 'The truth is, as I understand what you're saying, that your father and mother had dead hearts. They put you through a lot of pain. And believe me, I know about pain. Just as people can be good-hearted so they can be evil-hearted. Just as the heart can nurture the finest feelings so it can harbour the worst and wreak havoc. Let's prove it. Visit the remains of your father's sanctum. Take a look at the *verboten* areas.'

'Later?'

'Later.' She drew aside the blanket. 'Scratch my back.'

He ran his fingernails across her shoulder blades.

'Lower. Lower. Here. Hold me. Inside. There. Don't stop.'

Flat on my stomach, mindful of the venomous snake, I look for a battery and a wire and the best place to break the circuit to the detonators. I can withdraw the detonators, unravel the wires, and disable the electronics. But cutting into the hardened foam will cause dangerous vibration.

   And for the third time you rose from the dead
   Ascended into heaven
   And sitteth on the right hand of the Father
   Whence he cometh –

45

'The séance,' she was saying. 'You want to join in?'

'Why not? We've got an hour to have a look around before they start summoning up the dead. Can't say I'm looking forward to it.'

He cursed. 'I have to get that Velamorphine from the Range Rover.'

'Then go and get it,' she told him. 'Don't look so scared. I won't vanish. Get dressed. Look at you! You're a wraith. You should put some weight on. But stay as sweet as you are.'

'No one's ever said that to me before.'

'It's true.'

'And you ... who taught you to be so gentle with your fingers?'

46

As a kind of bait, so that nothing would get in the way of Teresa or Francesca retrieving the NulFail, he had deliberately left the Range Rover unlocked. He had of course already told Teresa where his Velamorphine was.

Sure enough, Francesca had taken the NulFail, leaving his Velamorphine on the back seat. If and when WPC MacQuillan and her friends searched The Towers they'd find the illicit drug in the nurses' possession: a nugget of criminal intelligence that might prove handy down the line.

He opened up the garage storage unit, found a variety of metalwork tools and took two flat pieces of steel to raise the tumbler locks' five pins to breaking point. Most likely MacCullum would have used the most readily available five-pin cylinder locks. So he also selected an old-fashioned tension wrench to rotate the cylinders and release the locks.

On his way back to the kitchen to store his Velamorphine in the refrigerator he took the precaution of collecting the shotgun from the Gun Room. This, at any rate, had been his intention when he unlocked the gun cabinet.

The ancient pistols and rifles were there: the family relics from the Second Anglo-Boer War, the German Mauser automatic pistol, the Lee-Metford, and the two Lee-Enfield rifles. But not, definitely not, the Holland & Holland Badminton double-barrelled shotgun.

Teresa must have taken a leaf from his own book and removed the weapon to use it as evidence against him. Why remove it – why not simply leave the bloody thing there anyway? He doubted that either she or Francesca would know one end of the shotgun from the other. Then again, they might. Whichever way you looked at it, the shotgun's disappearance was disturbing. He couldn't imagine what complexion the rebarbative WPC MacQuillan would put on it.

Passing the Library, he heard the introductory chimes of BBC TV's *News at Ten*. A headline had reduced Teresa and Francesca to hysterical laughter. '*Heaviest snow in living memory . . .*'

The clangs of the BBC time merged with the chiming of the Winterhalder & Hofmeier UhrenFabrik clock: I – II – III – IV – V – VI – VII – VIII – IX – X

– the X's echo hanging in the cold darkness like a witch's sneer.

47

An abandoned world presented itself beneath The Towers. It had existed only in his memory throughout his adult life as an uninhabited exotic territory, the subterranean extravagance of his Victorian forebears.

He'd forgotten when it was, during childhood, that he'd found Turkey on a map and parted these barred gates; then tiptoed down these same stone steps in sandalled feet to the Turkish baths.

His hands shook as he began to pick the lock MacCullum had installed and it required all his strength to open the rusted gates for Sophie to enter the cavern that housed the swimming pool.

To his relief, he found the underground electric light system was in working order, and it revealed the dereliction in a haze of green.

Layers of viscous silt covered the floors and above the empty pool were remnants of a trapeze and rings. They dangled from rusted poles of a scaffold like a hangman's noose.

At the far end of the pool he could see the remains

of the diving board: a brownish stump protruding like a rotted tusk.

He glanced up at the Moorish arches and the cast-iron columns that supported pointed windows and the cupola on a miniature version of the dome of St Paul's Cathedral.

'This is very sad,' he said.

Then, with a sigh, he wiped away crusted slime to reveal a riot of painted flowers. 'The tiling was beautiful. I remember finding these ... carnations and hyacinths, roses and tulips; and Chinese clouds – look ... still here. And – up there ... nothing there now – I think there was a gallery with lattice-work ... so contented guests could sip cold wine and watch the swimmers.'

He led Sophie into the ruined rooms of the Turkish baths.

'Originally two were hot rooms heated by steam coils; two cool, with small central fountains ...'

On into what had once been the two hot rooms, each measuring some fifteen feet square. Beneath an octagonal dome were the broken marble slabs on which guests had dozed either wrapped up in hot towels or naked.

'This is the tepidarium where they soaped themselves ... The cool room's over here ... Here's what was the plunge room. Here, the douche room with showers. I believe the taps were gold-plated ... This is where the coal-fire boilers were housed ... between the two hot rooms. Dampers or valves regulated the flow of the heated air and temperatures ...'

The cold air reeked of decay and sewage. Sophie winced and shifted her balance uneasily on the slippery floor. 'The mouldiness is noxious.'

'Not surprising. It's been neglected for years. You think it's in danger of collapse?'

'Hard to tell. Is that why it's been off-limits so long?'

'The reason's bizarre. Two Turkish brothers who'd worked in hammams or baths in Istanbul were found dead in here. They'd been castrated. The murder was never solved. They were buried in the Moster Lees churchyard. Thereafter the use of the baths was forbidden. So they can't have been used for long. No one could be bothered to keep things in good repair. See for yourself. This is how I first saw it. The surfaces of pool and baths cracked; even back then there were pools of watery green scum and burial mounds for termites, cockroaches, mice and rats. My mother hated the pool with a vengeance. She had an obsessive detestation of Turkey, Turks and Turkish baths.'

'And you?'

'Me? I have dreams of their restoration.'

He led her towards the door to the Stirling family Crypt and Chapel and could smell its decades-old human decay.

*

As he entered, he felt a chill presence by his side.

He heard himself reciting in his father's unmistakable voice, word perfect: *'Repeat after me ...'*

> *'The Chapel may be found described in architectural*
>   *guides.*
> *Tiling plays an important part in the decoration of the*
>   *nave.*
> *Painted by Mallord Stembridge and manufactured by*
>   *Mansfield L. Foulkes and Sons, the panels from left*
>   *to right depict –*
> *Abraham, Moses, Daniel and St John the Baptist –*
> *The Nativity; St Mary Magdalene;*
> *and in the final panel –*
> *St Peter ...'*

'It's my father's voice.'

Sophie took him in her arms. 'Stop torturing yourself.'
    And drudge of all my father's house am I –
    My bread is sorrow and my drink is tears ...
    'Are you sure you can continue, Hal?'

48

The cellars smelled of chloroform blended with disinfectant and, to Hal's surprise, it was dry.

Powerful fluorescent light illuminated cardboard and plastic boxes, their labels completed with a librarian's skill in his mother's handwriting. His father had found the perfect archivist in his prisoner and the curator and scholar's widow in Priscilla had kept the flame of death alight. He was amazed that their vile industry had been so prodigious.

Arranged in alphabetical order, the boxes were stacked on floor-to-ceiling PVC shelving. The racks were firmly bolted to the walls so the boxes slid in and out with ease. The polished wooden and glass-fronted cabinets contained the biological specimens, manuscripts and correspondence, the latter labelled MOST STRICTLY CONFIDENTIAL.

More transparent plastic boxes revealed dated fragments of human skeletons, mummified lumps and body parts; mostly male and female sexual organs in apothecary jars; fused and individual human bones; skin samples, bladders and molecular analyses of fungal microbiota from human skin and psoriatic lesions.

The alcoves were jammed with embalming and autopsy slabs: cold chambers: emulsification and freeze-drying equipment. His mother had written a bold notice above one such alcove: WARNING | CPU: CORPSE PRESERVATION UNIT | −10°C (14°F) | −50°C (−58°F)

'Look at it,' said Sophie. 'Dear God – what the hell was going on in here?'

He'd seen it before:

SKOPTSY [скопцы]

Christian sect. Imperial Russia. *See*: Ritual Castration; REMOVAL OF MALE PENIS, TESTICLES AND SCROTA. Preservation of same. REMOVAL OF WOMEN'S BREASTS; *see also*: Grass, K. K. *Die geheime heilige Schrift der Skopzen*. Leipzig, 1904; *Die russischen Sekten Leipzig*, 1907.

– *Et cetera*

Sophie held out a wad of faded postcards, stamped and postmarked WORCESTER MASS.

Hal chose one at random and read aloud:

Dear Professor Stirling,

You again ask me to describe my castration by our beloved S—. I've told you, Stirling-san, this was many years after the castration of Ishida.

I cannot recall the actual moment S— cut IT

off or what she did with IT. If IT still exists I do not think whatever authority may possess IT will part with IT.

Do you really want IT? Why should they give IT to you? Cannot you establish sexual telepathic contact with S— and me through some other tangible medium?

Do NOT, Sir, beg me to keep on and on retelling the story. I've told you again and again that S— performed a ritual of great elaboration in ecstasy.

She drenched her white silken kimono in jasmine oil. As if it were yesterday I can smell it here and now. She mixed my blood with oil and drank it.

She demanded IT raise itself to resemble the Indian cobra head, the *Naja Naja*, and injected me with priafil inducing a priapismic condition in a narcotic opiate state.

She squatted on me and pleasured herself dementedly. Upon climax she used a sashimi knife to sever my genitalia.

What more can you possibly want to know from me?

I send you greetings from Worcester.

Sincerely yours,

Miss Yoshida.

Each postcard showed the identical view of a sprawling mansion, its architecture resembling The Towers: THE HOSPITAL FOR THE INSANE, WORCESTER, MASS. USA.

'What could he have wanted with another penis ... What do you think?'

Hal never heard her complete the question.

The acrid fumes overcame him and Miss Yoshida's postcards from the lunatic asylum in Massachusetts fluttered to the floor.

49

'*Hal* . . . can you hear me – *HAL*?'

Sharp lights pricked his eyes. His head had fallen forward and he saw the blur of Sophie's face upside down.

'Sit still,' she said. 'Breathe in. For God's sake, c'mon, *breathe* . . . slowly . . . deeply.'

She was seated on a stack of archival boxes. Soaked in sweat, he lay sprawled across her lap, his right arm dangling to where the postcards had fallen across the floor.

'We have to go,' she whimpered. 'I can't take it.'

The malodorous mixture of putrefaction, chloroform and disinfectant fumes made him wheeze: old man's gurgles, *click-clack*, sounded in his throat. His clothes had twisted around his torso; they constrained and trapped him like a straitjacket. His skin and genitals itched; his fingers had turned a purplish red. He whispered hoarsely to himself: '*Calm down.*'

He fought to control the twitching in his fingers and heard his mother pleading:

'Won't someone help me? I'm dying. Does no one understand? We are one in flesh and blood, my son ... My beloved son in whom I am well pleased ...'

Another voice called out: 'Is anybody there?' He heard his voice begging: 'Father, are you here?'

'It's me ... Sophie—'

She struggled to help him to his feet saying: 'I heard a woman's voice. A minute ago. Someone else here. Now. Over there, in the shadow, look.'

'I can't see.'

'There.' Her voice had risen.

'Where – what's she saying?'

'She's asking for you by name.'

'Where?'

Sophie was gripped by foreboding. 'I can't see ... the face ... it's hidden, she's hidden behind a veil ... Oh my God ...'

She drew her arms tight around her body.

'What's she saying?'

She clutched her throat and shuddered. 'Can't you hear? Listen – "I'm – Sada Abe."'

'I can't see her.'

'She's gone. There's nothing there. She's gone.'

Hal was breathing with great difficulty. 'You saw her?'

'You don't believe me?'

'Of course I believe you. Only I didn't see her.'

'You heard her?'

'No, I didn't.'

'She was in here. Standing there. In front of that alcove. Her withered paw on the rail of that autopsy slab. And so help me God – in the shadow – there was another figure – close behind her.'

He lowered his feet slowly to the floor and stood unsteadily, peering into the alcove.

'There was a pair of them,' she said quietly. 'Who are they?'

'I'll tell you once we're outside.'

He kicked aside the postcards and they hurried back the way they'd come, their shoes clattering across the tiled floor.

In the anteroom he gave her a garbled version of Sada Abe's murderous history.

50

Hal glanced at his wristwatch. 'There's five minutes until they start the séance.'

'Another time, Hal.'

'It's a chance to show them their telepathy is bullshit.'

'I can think of better things to do.'

'I'm curious.'

'You may be,' she said. 'Not sure I am. First light – and I'm off to the world of sanity and the living.'

The blizzard was battering The Towers.

'I don't want to disappoint you,' he said, 'but listen to the wind. You aren't going anywhere in that.'

'I'll get MacCullum to drive me to Carlisle.'

'In this snow?'

She shrugged. 'Maybe Teresa and Francesca can control the blizzard.'

'Those witches can control sod-all,' he said.

'Not me,' she said. 'Not those things in there, what-ever they may be. You mustn't let them get to you any more, Hal.'

'They already have. It's like some bloody awful tune you can't stop hearing in your head. The more my reasoning mind tells me Mother's not here, the more she occupies my brain.'

'Then don't let her torture you.'

'I can't help it. Like I said, Sophie, I'm drawn to look at her. To see her, touch her.'

'You musn't. We're talking dead, Hal. Departed souls, whatever. The incorporeal. No substance. No form. Intangible. Get it? They consist of *nothing*. *Nada*. You're seeing thin air. That's what all of us vanish into in the end.'

'They live here.'

'Hal – they do *not* live here. They're dead.'

'You saw them.'

'I honestly don't know what I saw in there. I don't – I don't know . . . I was just seeing things.'

'Too right,' he said. '*Real* things.'

'Unreal things, Hal.'

'If you say so,' he said. 'Let's not argue.'

On edge, gripped by unconscious indecision, they were hanging back from climbing the stairs to join the séance.

The German clock began to sound **XI**. The beating and booming of the wind against the windows drowned out the final chime as a beam of light flashed through the Great Hall.

They turned sharply and Sophie walked very fast to the nearest window. 'MacCullum,' she said, peering after the car's rear lights.

'Are you sure it's him?'

'I'm not sure of anything. Could've been Warren.'

'More likely MacCullum,' he said. 'What's he want now?'

'Perhaps I imagined it.'

51

The séance took place in the candlelit room that had been Priscilla's bedroom. The dim light was diffused by Satya Nag incense smoke floating to the ceiling.

'This Holy Sanctum,' Teresa said reverentially, 'where Priscilla passed over is now the place for us to contact Her. Contact must be the only thought we have tonight. Please speak now if any of you have *Contrary Purpose*. In that event, our circle's psychic energy will be too feeble and atunement impossible.' Hal, Sophie and Francesca were seated close together at the round table. Their faces were ghostly masks. None declared *Contrary Purpose*.

Hal averted his gaze from whatever of his mother's possessions remained there under the dust sheets and was grateful that the powerful incense obliterated any trace of her familiar lavender-scented talc that might have lingered.

Teresa drew layers of diaphanous white silks around her, adjusted her veil, and raised the amethyst and tiger's eye around her neck, kissing it as if it were a holy relic.

Candlelight sparkled on the scarlet varnish of her fingernails. 'Are we of single mind?' she asked. Without waiting for a reply, she said: 'Please, together say: "*I am.*"'

There was a low harmonious chorus: '*I am – I am – I am.*'

'*I am, we are,*' said Teresa. 'We will observe the silence and touch each other. Place your hands upon the unsullied cloth of virgin white. Touch. Hold hands. Let us pray. We put aside all thoughts of self, our fears, our problems, our thoughts of what has happened to us today, all thoughts of what we have seen or imagined or suspected from our minds.'

Sophie cleared her throat.

'We invoke love,' continued Teresa, 'so that we will share our innermost feelings for each other.'

Hal felt the suggestive pressure of Francesca's fingers.

'The doctrine of Our Circle shows us the nature and right use of those means which we have instituted to remit our sins, give us grace, infuse into and increase in us the virtues of Faith, Hope and Charity and the Life Herebefore.'

Francesca edged closer to him and sighed.

'We are joined together,' said Teresa, 'in a united bond of psychic energy, in our personal spaces, in the true circumference of each, and in the love and remembrance of Priscilla. The Living here tonight cry to the Living Dead for vengeance against those who do not freely give of their flesh in love and because their iniquity is so great and so manifest that it inspires the Spirits to punish them with the Severest Chastisement.

Let us watch the white light of the Seven Candles, as we ask for the presence of the pure light of Angels, our Guides, and our Gods. Focus upon the Seven Flames. Feel only the Sacred Energy of the candles' light as we seek the Divinity of Patience. Now please keep Sacred Silence. Flesh in Flesh. Silence Sacred.'

The storm beating The Towers seemed to Hal to be holding him in its possession.

Sophie squeezed his fingers. She too must have been alerted to the eerie reverberations from the Bell Tower causing dull, irregular shudders within the structure supporting the floor of Priscilla's bedroom.

He imagined that the bell was slowly swinging and booming in protest against the storm's assault. The vibrations seemed to emanate from the impact of some distant hammer blows within The Towers, low bass steel-on-steel accompaniment to the storm: rising, falling, rising once again as the storm charged at the walls like waves crashing on a beach.

During the briefest of silent intervals he heard faint rustlings, creaks of wood on wood, the smooth sounds of the seven sputtering candles.

How the danger sinks and swells, of the bells of the bells, bells, bells, bells, bells . . .

*

He stole a glance at Sophie, searching for some sign of equilibrium.

Her fair hair was shining in the candlelight, her full lips were moist, her eyelashes cast long shadows on her cheeks, her green eyes glinted, her white silk dress shimmered.

Sumiko – Sophie – Sumiko – Sophie.

Hands had surely begun to toll the bell.

. . . by the sinking or the swelling in the anger of the bells . . .

The rhythm beat in his eardrums and his head was spinning. The bell summoning him.

52

Hal and Sophie shifted tentatively on the upright chairs to make themselves more comfortable. Francesca, her thigh pressed against Hal's, did likewise.

Teresa sat very still; her eyes closed allowing the incorporeal voices of The Towers to possess the sickly bedroom of the living dead, inviting phantoms to find refuge with her and escape the vagaries and dangers of the natural world.

To Hal it seemed an eternity during which he fought to control his confusion, fear and anger. The bell beat on in his head. Inexplicably, the room filled with lingering insubstantial white shadows.

What new orgiastic depravity fuelled by Velamorphine and NulFail was forming behind these telepathic masks? Now so demure, her body pressed close to his, would Francesca with downcast eyes, her parted lips alive with spittle, begin some new seduction?

Where was the shotgun? Had MacCullum or even Warren been here to steal it?

Who or what were those deformed and loathsome succubae feeding on the detritus of the dead in the cellars, and why?

Had his mother and Saba Abe liaised to issue some perverse Declaration of Inhuman Rights and instituted a new regime, a Second Front of horror? No memory of the future offered itself to guide him.

When was Sumiko arriving? Would she get here through the blizzards to cleanse the evil from this crumbling mausoleum of resurrection? Would it now collapse, destroy itself and take the living with it into eternity?

Locked into the psychic life force connecting her to the world beyond: its past, its present and its future, Teresa Vale chanted: 'The *nearcoming* of Priscilla heralds Patience. It is but a little while that She will come and that She shall come to us in Her Fullness. Be patient, therefore, my Sisters Sophie and Francesca and my Brother Hal unto Her coming. Be also patient, for the Coming of Priscilla draweth nigh. Her redemptive spirit draws near us in neither suffering nor affliction. Her peace is as a river. Her words, the music of the flowing stream. And when at last She is come to honour us with Her Divine Presence I will pose questions for Her Answering made crystalline by the Psychic Life Force through me, possessed by Her Divinity and She will answer simply: "*Yes*" or "*No*".'

Francesca's fingers clutching his were moist: Sophie's dry and warm.

'We will say together the Most Sacred and Supreme

Invocation. Say after me: "Our beloved Priscilla ... We bring ourselves ... as gifts from this life into the Abyss of Death ... Commune now with your intimate loves, Priscilla ... and move among us ..."'

Hal saw spittle dribbling from Francesca's lips and then Teresa slowly slumped forwards, her face pressed flat against the white tablecloth.

'She is here,' she whispered. 'Keep silence so She may speak.' She began to talk incomprehensibly as though a claw had clamped itself across her mouth.

Sophie tightened her grip on Hal's fingers.

Teresa said: 'Can you hear me, Loved One?'

'*Yes.*'

'Are you in The Towers?'

'*No.*'

'In the storm?'

'*Yes.*'

'Hal is here with us.'

'*Yes.*'

'Hal in whom you are much pleased?'

'*Yes.*'

'May we talk of conception?'

'*Yes.*'

'Conception occurred after twenty-four hours of ovulation?'

'*Yes.*'

'Francesca is with child?'

'*Yes.*'

'Do you know who the father is?'

'*Yes.*'

'Is Hal the father?'

'*Yes.*'

Hal stared at Francesca. She gently removed her hand from his and drew her shawl over her inclined head so it formed a veil.

Simultaneously, Teresa raised a photograph to the light of the candles. Francesca bore an uncanny resemblance to the image of the veiled Virgin.

'Is this the image of Francesca with child?'

'*Yes.*'

Hal held Sophie's hand so tightly he could feel the bones of her broad fingers. Though the diagnosis of Francesca's state might be ludicrous, it was still distressing. Sophie looked startled and Teresa went on babbling.

Hal tried to speak. The words wouldn't come. He felt Francesca edging her legs close to his and her arm slide around his waist, a gesture of possession that brought a gloating tone to Teresa's voice.

His father's rocking chair had started moving.

Was the old boy about to have his say too? He was a man for plain speaking, *pace* the teachings of prophet, magician, poet and sexual adventurer Maynard Arcus, there was nothing amorphous about his father's views. There was always the touch of cruel truth in his sour candour.

The howling of the Jack Russell outside the bedroom connected his anxiety to the supernatural signals of distress emitted by the storm. Demons were gathering in the ether. The unexpected was to be expected. Nothing was impossible. As for Teresa, the sound of the puppy's pain acted as a balm.

She was asking questions in a tone of self-pitying frankness: 'Is it right that we are alone here this Christmastime?'

'Yes.'

'Is it wrong,' Teresa complained, 'that Mrs Sumiko Wright join us here?'

'Yes.'

The *Yes* became an echoing *Yessss* – and Hal felt it trigger the vibrations of his mobile phone in his jacket pocket.

He got up abruptly from the table, knocking his chair over backwards as he went, staggering from his mother's bedroom, fishing out his phone. Sophie looked at him and he saw an awful sympathy in her eyes. It was as if she feared for his sanity and recognized he was falling into an infernal trap he'd set himself.

53

Harsh and discordant sounds filled the Great Hall where the demented Jack Russell pup, terrified and panic-stricken by the screaming of the wind, careered across the floor. The lead from its collar whipped about like an IED's wire.

Maddened, the turning animal crashed into furniture: howling at the headlights of a car beaming through a window. Its drivelling mouth stretched open as though terrified by the sound of soot falling in a chimney breast.

Hal's mobile vibrated.

Above the deathly image of Planet Earth, he read the omen – BLOCKED – and tapped the screen – ANSWER.

EIGHT

Sunk in the caverns of insanity and pain
You howling creatures lie;
Sans sense to smile again,
Condemned to Satan's prey.
Confined by our unfeeling eyes,
Embodiment of British hell;
Shackled, maimed, in rusted ties,
You wait for God Almighty's summoning bell.

CLAUDIA HAYWORTH

54

Across the United Kingdom the temperatures had plunged to below minus 15°C. The ferocity of the weather showed no sign of abating. Snow blanketed the airports, roads and railways. Powerful north-easterly winds and blizzards added to the nation's misery and frustration.

Motorists fought against freezing snow and the majority of motorways and roads in Cumbria were impassable.

Sumiko was inclined to doubt the wisdom of her plan to join Hal at The Towers for Christmas.

It was Yukio and the promise of her new puppy that persuaded her to close up her house in Ashwell and pack her bags into her VW to embark on the perilous journey north. Lines from her adored Sawako Kyushi Jones exercised her mind:

> *About suffering they were always wrong*
> *The Old Masters: how little they*
> *understood*
> *of the falling sky.*

En route, she tried without success to let Hal know of her arrival. She never consciously intended it to be a surprise. In truth she was initially the surprised party.

She was considerably disquieted to find The Towers in total darkness and that no one was answering the bell.

On the verge of driving back to the welcome lights of the Moster Inn, she called Hal's mobile and finally succeeded in getting through to him as the séance was drawing to its close.

Elated, he ran down the stairs and heaved open the massive door.

There she stood smiling, with Yukio asleep in her arms.

'Captain Stirling-san,' she said. '*Santakukoru*.'

55

Sophie was torn between the choice of interrupting the séance and following Hal out of the bedroom, or staying until the bitter end; she shook off Francesca's attempt to hold her hand and remained seated at the table to hear the last of Teresa's questions and Priscilla's answers.

'She's a married woman?' Teresa asked in an accusatory tone.

'*Yes.*'

Now Teresa was COUNSEL FOR THE PROSECUTION: 'Married to Dr Wright of Cambridge University?'

'*Yes.*'

Now THE ABBESS: 'Does Dr Wright know of his wife's adultery?'

'*No.*'

Now CHILD WELFARE OFFICER: 'Dr and Mrs Wright have a young daughter?'

'*Yes.*'

ST MARK AND/OR JESUS CONFRONTED WITH THE INSANE: ('*What is your name?*' '*My name is legion, for there are many of us …*') 'Her name is Yukio?'

'Yes.'

BETHLEHEM INNKEEPER: 'Is there room in our hearts for Mrs Wright and Yukio to join us at The Towers?'

'No.'

THE VOICE OF MORMON WARNING: 'Is it dangerous for her so to do?'

'Yes.'

QUIDNUNC: 'Must I warn your son?'

'Yes.'

Teresa lowered her voice. 'The signal grows weaker. Priscilla is wearied.' She cleared her throat. 'Thank you, Priscilla. Thank you.' There was a long pause after which, seemingly much strengthened by Priscilla's revelations, she said: 'May we give thanks in silence. *Amen.*'

Sophie burst out: 'You're playing with fire.'

'Quiet,' Teresa said.

'You disgust me,' Sophie yelled.

'*How dare you—*'

Sophie got to her feet, leaned towards the candles and blew them out.

All three women held their breath.

'Sophie,' Teresa said with the nursing sister's practised steel of tenderness. 'You will be taken hence in Time's Fullness to the room in which you were last confined and from there to a place of execution where you will be hanged by the neck until you are dead and thereafter your body buried within the precincts of The Tower and may the Spirits have mercy upon your soul.'

Sophie stayed silent.

Francesca began to chant: '*Halfman. Halfwoman. DIE.*'

She was still chanting when Sophie left the room and closed the door behind her without a word.

56

He led the way through the Great Hall and upstairs to the rooms in the Victoria Tower, turning on the lights, smiling, speaking softly.

'Nothing's changed,' Sumiko said.

'Except it's colder.'

They could hear a clock striking and the sound of voices.

'Who else is here?' Sumiko asked.

'The nurses. They have rooms on the floor below. And there's a woman from the family solicitors, Sophie. She's stranded by the snow. You did well to get here.'

'In Japan I had Michelin X-Ice tyres.'

'You can recommend them to Sophie.'

'Is she your friend – this Sophie?'

'She's a great help to me. I want the two of you to be friends.'

Making the sleeping Yukio comfortable in her bed, Sumiko said: 'She's going to be wild with excitement when she sees the dog. Where did you find him?'

'In Carlisle. I got him from friends of Sophie's. His name was Bertrand. Now it's Arotiki.'

'Where's he now?'

'If he knows what's good for him he'll be in the kitchen.' His thoughts switched to the séance. *'Is it wrong, that Mrs Sumiko Wright join us here?' 'Yes.'*

Sumiko stood by the windows' parted shutters. *Two girls in silk kimonos, both beautiful, one a gazelle ...* 'The snow – it's stopping. Look, it's beautiful. A white Christmas.'

The wind had lessened and the light from the window shone against the wall of twinkling whiteness.

'Can I bring you a hot drink?' he asked. 'Or something stronger?'

'No thanks.' She kissed his cheek. 'I'm very happy ... where's your room?'

'Just through there.'

'I'm exhausted.'

'Do you want to go straight to sleep?'

'Do you mind?'

'No.'

They kissed.

'You're so sweet,' she said.

'Sleep well. Happy to be here?'

'Very.'

57

He found Sophie in her room in the dim glow of the single bedside light.

She was sitting cross-legged on the bed, her knees pulled up, wearing a white silk nightdress. The paleness of her skin, her glistening fair hair and the light reflected on the crumpled silk of the nightdress seemed to enclose her in an ethereal translucence. The only incongruity was the scarlet of her varnished fingernails. Her eyes were clouded with the defeat of a refugee.

'What's happened?' he asked.

'I don't want to talk about it.'

'Is it Sumiko?'

'I don't mind what she thinks.'

'I do.'

'You're not going to believe this. Those witches solemnly sentenced me to death.'

'They what?'

'Sentenced me to death by hanging. The sick daughter took leave of her senses. She started braying – *Die. Die*.'

'Ignore them.'

'I wish I could.'

'They're not serious.'

'I'd have said the same before that séance. I'm afraid that's exactly what they are. Venomous. Sick and dangerous. Hal, I can't stay here tonight.'

'You want me to take you home?'

'In this snow?'

'I can handle it.'

'I don't think so.'

'Then I'll stay with you in here.'

'With Sumiko across the landing – isn't that a bit cruel?'

'She'll understand.'

'I wouldn't.'

'I can explain things to her.'

'Explain about us?'

'Yes.'

'Talk to her in the morning if you must. Or don't talk to her about us at all. Don't you worry about me. Just another of my secrets. I won't say anything.' She turned her head aside. Tears rolled down her cheeks.

He took her in his arms. She kept on crying, her body trembling. She clung to him and he kissed her.

'I'll take you to Minti and Schadzi's.'

'You have to stay here with your Sumiko. And there's her little girl to think about.' She shivered. Then pulled the sheets and blankets across her. 'Why don't you fetch that gun?'

'Because it's gone.'

'It's what?'

'Someone's taken it.'

'Who?'

'Fuck knows.'

'Those two?'

'Maybe.'

'For God's sake. You must call the police.'

'Think so? They'll never get through the snow. Anyway, I've no proof they took it.'

Eyes wide, she sat immobile, frozen like a forest creature. 'I'm scared, Hal.'

'I know.'

'I'm frightened of what I can't see. Frightened of what's going to happen to us ... Can't we go downstairs, make some coffee?'

'No. We should stay here. Near Sumiko and Yukio. We don't want to risk encountering the others.'

She looked defeated. 'Don't leave me, Hal.'

'I'll stay with you.'

'Sure they won't come in here?'

He shivered. 'I'm not sure of anything.'

'Anyway, there's two of us. The bed's warm. Lock the door.'

'It hasn't got a lock.'

His fingertips felt gently round every one of those IEDs in Helmand, cautiously, tenderly. Her waist. Her curves.

Her erection. Her hips. Across the mounds. Into the shadows of valleys he couldn't see.

Maybe it's the risk involved ... Something induces the rush of adrenalin – I'm an addict. I'm addicted to fear. Maybe that's my good luck.

Two and a half hours later there was a beating on the door.

58

She didn't stir in his arms when he turned his head to check the time. The clock on his bedside table said **03.25**.

Neither did she wake when he left the bed and opened the door to find Sumiko in her pyjamas staring at him wide-eyed with fear.

'I've been looking for you. I don't like that noise,' she said.

'Don't worry. It's only the wind.'

She shivered. '*That* noise,' she said. 'Listen—'

'What is it?'

Yukio moaned: 'Mummy? I'm frightened.'

'Come here.'

Yukio ran to her mother's open arms. 'It's horrible.'

'It's nothing to be frightened of,' Hal said.

'*Listen*. The tolling bell.'

'It's stopped.'

'Was I dreaming?' Sumiko said.

'Perhaps. You two stay put,' he said. 'Try and sleep.'

'I'll stay with Yukio,' she said.

'I'll see you in the morning.' He stroked her forehead. 'Sweet dreams.'

'You too,' said Sumiko.

He watched her close the door.

He couldn't sleep.

The Great Bell was tolling; irregularly reverberating:
rocking slowly; the steel clapper swinging against the
rim.

Tuneless persistent thudding: muffled summons to
the unfaithful: mocking the early hours of Christmas
Eve: enticing him to discover what preternatural imbal-
ance in the mechanism had occurred.

59

Shortly after four in the morning he went to his own room, dressed hurriedly in cold-weather clothes, took a torch and picklock with him and headed for the stairs down to the Great Hall.

From there it only was a short walk through the cold dark passages to the northern entrance of the Bell Tower.

The doors stood part open. Beside them was a painted notice, red on white:

Danger. Unsafe Structure. Do Not Pass This Point.

The tower was constructed in brickwork, cast iron and limestone cladding. Its foundations were sunk to a considerable depth. Narrow flights of stairs spiralled to the top.

Cold mist exaggerated the otherworldliness of the strange sound from the rim of the bell high above him.

He tilted his head back and peered into the motionless veils of whitish gloom, watching the beam of his torch swallowed by the murk. He heard a distant thump overhead; the faintest rattle, perhaps a chain; a slight and distressing almost human screeching, and began to climb the spiral staircase.

A voice above him chanted: 'And behold, and, lo, in the midst of the throne and of the four beasts, and in the midst of the elders, stood a Lamb as it had been butchered in the shed, having seven horns and seven eyes, which are the seven Spirits of God sent forth into all the earth.'

His gloved hand felt wet against the iced surface of the curving mahogany handrail.

Round-and-round. Twisting. Rotating. Step-after-step, up-and-up, one-after-another. The onset of dizziness forced him to lose his balance.

'And I saw when the Lamb opened one of the seals, and I heard, as it were the noise of thunder, one of the four beasts saying: *Come and see.*'

He gripped the handrail fiercely.

His father was singing:

And when ye come, and all the flow'rs are dying
If I am dead, as dead I well may be

in time to the sound of his shoes on the stone steps:

– gedung . . . gedung . . . gedung.

His fingertips tingled.

Ye'll come and find the place where I am lying
And kneel and say an 'Ave' there for me.

Thin layers of ice fractured and splintered beneath his feet.

His breathing grew laboured, his mind closer to panic. He was drawn to peer over the banisters into the abyss hidden beneath the layer of mist.

He felt a ringing sensation in his ears; he was losing his sense of balance, the control of his equilibrium. His head was dizzy: The Towers' walls were spinning anti-clockwise.

He sat down heavily on a stair and gasped for breath.

He had no idea how long he'd been climbing the spiral staircase: he could only guess that by now he must have completed three-quarters of the climb.

Bent low, steadying himself against the handrails, he climbed on slowly.

– *gedung . . . gedung*

Narrow vertical windows let in a bluish light from the snowbound landscape. The faint light blended with the brightness of the torchlight as he reached the top of the spiral staircase.

There, above him, surrounded by a network of warped timber planks that had once been repairmen's scaffolding, hung the bell, glistening and squat. Its clapper, pendulous and weighty.

The clapper seemed to have been wrapped in cloth sheets for preservation. It bulged and he saw what his mind told him to believe: hanging branches. Only they were metal and rusted. The branches became tangled wires. The branches were twisted remnants of an old TV aerial.

He refused to believe the repugnant disfigurement staring him in the face. His eyes contracted involuntarily; the crushing pain squeezed out tears. His blood heaved up from inside his chest and heart and he felt a tightness in his arteries.

He was staring into dead and bulging eyes with broken blood vessels. Into ears filled with blood.

Not for a single moment can you afford to think of the victim as a person.

Tears and rage can't be allowed to get the better of you. If the terrible wounds scare you then fear will gnaw your heart. If it gets to your heart and head you will weep in the watch hours of the night and see visions.

He was *looking – not seeing*: he was *looking* at a corpse.

It had been trussed in industrial tape, electric cable wires; then wrapped in cotton shrouds. One leg was taped to the body. Yet another, like an insect's, hung loose. The monstrous thing was held in place by the lengths of TV aerial poles, the rods serving as splints. It was tied to the clapper dangling from the bell: hanging directly above the drop to the floor below shrouded in those veils of mist.

Inch by inch, he clambered up the creaking scaffold, testing the doubtful strength of each precarious bending plank, adjusting his balance, praying the whole structure wouldn't suddenly collapse and send him hurtling to the floor far below.

Settling his torch on a ledge, he reached out to touch the shrouded brownish bundle.

A single length of rope was tied beneath its scrawny neck. But the face was out of his immediate vision; he tried to turn it towards him, very gently swivelling the thing around. It clanked the bell's rim and produced a deathly *ding-dong-clang*.

He couldn't see the face. Or maybe his conscious mind was jamming his signals of recognition.

His fingers reached out to touch the waxy translucence of the facial skin: he looked into a sunken eye. The cornea was milky white, like cloudy marble; only slivers of its eyeball were visible, as if it had rolled up backwards inside the head.

The lopsided mouth hung open, fixed in a silent scream; its scabrous lips parched, small brownish pointed teeth protruding like a rat's, the grotesque bloodied opening emanating bacterial and faecal odours.

Beginning to loosen the clumsy knots, prising them apart with the picklock, he realized the corpse was giving off slight warmth. Death could have occurred only a few hours before.

Rigor mortis, the stiffening of the body muscles, begins between two and four hours after death. The corpse's neck and jaw were already rigid. After some eight to twelve hours the whole process of rigor mortis would be complete. Complete *rigor* then starts to disappear between eighteen to thirty-six hours later. After forty-eight to sixty hours it's gone. Back to normal dead.

He slid his hands beneath the legs; without rigor, they were warm. Death must have taken place less than three hours before: at about the time, say, he and Sophie began to make love.

He succeeded in heaving the corpse near enough to the edge of the scaffold, allowing him to rest it on a timber platform projecting into the darkness and to continue cutting and jerking aside the industrial tape.

Gradually, he settled its weight on the platform and drew it free from its constraints; tearing the shrouds as he jerked the lengths of tape away.

As he did so, the clapper swung away from him, creaking for a second as it swung; then hammered the bell to produce a boom. The report caused the scaffold to shudder and vibrate and go on vibrating.

He hung on for dear life: one arm straining over a wooden rail; his other around the dead bundle which swung and tilted away from him like some elongated ghoul in a daemonic dance of death.

The clanging faded and he prepared for the descent. His mind was seized, not by the proximity of the hideous load he was raising, trying to balance its weight across his shoulders – No. The bundle was light enough, its spine arched.

No. It wasn't the strain this fireman's lift imposed: it was its smell.

You can't *imagine* the smell of the freshly dead. You never forget it. People don't tell you how your loved ones smell in death. You smell it; or you don't. It's the smell of terror, *sheer* terror, virginal, unadulterated terror.

Up to this very moment, in the early hours of Christmas Eve, up the Bell Tower, his brain and all his senses had in part refused to tell him what he was seeing and smelling. No. No. I am in the wrong place. The barrier of fear bore a notice:

BLOCKED

His neck stiffened violently. Something was stabbing his olfactory nerves.

His sense of smell said:

ANSWER

What am I smelling?

LAVENDER

The swaddling clothes around the corpse smelled of lavender.

At the end of the dangling arm a sharp object was stabbing the side of his ribcage.

A platinum and diamond cocktail watch with blue steel hands.

He lowered himself, sat for a moment on a stair, and shone the torch at the tiny wrist.

His mother's ruby and fourteen-diamond cluster ring made by Cartier.

The gemstone: a 3.96-carat maroon-red Burmese star ruby.

He heard moans and realized they were his own—

'Is anybody there? Is anybody there? Your mother is the dog.'

Step after step

down

and

down

probing the darkness with the tips of his cold-

weather boots

brick sediment and rat shit

The combination of probing, edging downwards, telling himself to keep control of himself, the cold, iced slime, the extreme nervous tension: all of it made him retch.

He looked at his hands and saw them shaking with distressing violence. *I can't bloody keep them still.*

Then he dropped the torch.

And heard it roll down the stairs.

There was a second's silence before it struck the floor below and a fierce light blinded him.

The doors to the Bell Tower must have been opened, sucking in the cutting wind.

Still his heart lurched and pounded in his ribcage to the beat of his descending steps – *gedung-gedung-gedung.*

His forehead seemed to swell, the veins tightening unendurably; and he felt again that vertiginous dizziness and the sudden impulse to lash out with his fists; but the strength in his arms and hands was exhausted.

His thoughts in turmoil, he couldn't understand what was happening to him.

The darkness concealed shadowy figures watching him.

He fell to his knees like a prizefighter in the ring unable to withstand further punishment and felt himself losing consciousness.

He sensed spectral faces looking down at him. Powerful hands seized his wrists.

Firm hands lifted the weight from his shoulders without tenderness.

The needle found the *vastus lateralis* muscle on the outer edge of his thigh between the knee and hip bone.

As the chaos and the panic lessened somewhat I turned my mind to the collection of forensic evidence from the bloodstained clothing, the collection of body parts and smashed equipment to establish the trail of evidence leading to the hated bomb-makers, the shit-faced owners of the workshops and the evil little explosives smugglers.

The hand gripped him round the neck, the bone of the forearm tightening against his larynx.

'There-there,' the voice said softly. 'Didn't hurt, did it?'

62

The nurse said:

'Demons and souls in fire in clouds of smoke. Like they'd been struck by a bomb in the desert. Crying out in pain. Like animals. Dead dogs and cats.

'So Mother had me cradle and cuddle Priscilla in her lap. Like she was Jesus. And she says there needs to be another death, another hanging from the bell. The Bell Tower being a place of execution.

'It's prophesied.

'It's Holy Writ.

'There'll be a sacrifice to rid the demons here.'

The clock by his bedside said **09.00**. Twenty minutes after sunrise.

He awoke painfully aware of nagging anxiety. The comfort of the bed was skin deep, its protective warmth inadequate.

The walls of the room seemed to have tilted. In the mirror the landscape was reflected like a mirage. Long blue shadows fell across the snowy moorland hollows and rises of the snowdrifts.

The wind sent powdered snow streaming from the small summits, sucking them from the shadows for darker shadows to swallow. Garish, like an illustration from a winter package holiday brochure, the sunrise had been tarted up with Pentel colours, smeared with lavender and rouged; the snow land as barren as the Helmand landscape, the frozen heather harbouring creatures unseen.

His eyes cleared and he saw Sumiko smile.

'How are you feeling?'

The events of a few hours before began to unfurl in his mind. 'What did they do with my mother?'

'Sorry?'

'My *mother* – where is she?'

'It was Akitoki. He'd gone completely mad.'

'Where's the body?'

'How would I know?'

'Haven't they told you what happened?'

'Yes, of course. They found you in the Bell Tower. You could have died. Why did you go there?'

'Why I went there doesn't matter. I found my mother's body – they murdered her.'

'You're imagining things. Please. They found you. You, no one else. No one else was there.'

'Who found me – was it Francesca?'

'Francesca and Sister Teresa along with a man from the village, MacCullum.'

'MacCullum, what's MacCullum doing here?'

'They needed to take you to hospital. You're not well, Hal. MacCullum's the only person who could get out here through the snow to ferry you to the hospital in Carlisle. Then Sister Vale decided it would better you stay here. With me.'

He pushed aside the bedclothes and sat awkwardly on the edge of the bed. 'MacCullum too, eh? Those bastards killed my mother.'

'Hal. Calm down. You're hallucinating. You haven't been taking your medication.'

'Where's Sophie?'

'Downstairs. There's a meeting in an hour.'

'What meeting?'

'With your solicitor and some other people. Thank God you didn't injure yourself. They thought—'

She stopped abruptly, caught her breath, thinking better of what she was about to say.

'They thought – thought what?'

'You'd tried to commit suicide.'

'Oh, for Christ's sake.'

'I don't want to believe you tried to kill yourself.'

'What the hell are they talking about? They're trying to scare you.'

'They don't have to try.'

'I'm getting rid of them.'

'And go back to Headley Court?'

'Headley Court's one thing. They are another. As soon as I can fix it they're out of here.'

'There's the meeting. They need you there.'

'You've spoken to Sophie?'

'We introduced ourselves. You're right; she's a good person. Very fond of you.'

'She told you about what happened in the Bell Tower?'

'In a manner of speaking.'

'Listen, Sumiko, you must believe me.' He fought back tears. 'They must have kept my mother here . . . a living skeleton . . . a demented, pitiful soul.'

She put her arms round him. 'You're exhausted, Hal.' She kissed his cheek. 'You're going to be okay. I promise.'

He stared at her in silence.

'Now,' she said, 'if you do what I tell you, there are lots of things we have to talk about. And—'

'And what?'

'I have a special Christmas present for you.'

'Tell me.'

'Tomorrow. Christmas Day.'

'I'll do what you tell me, Sumiko. Leave the practicalities to me. Only, I won't go on about it now – but did Sophie tell you *everything* that happened in the night?'

'Why should she?'

'She must know the truth.'

'If she does, she feels no need to tell me about it.'

'Please go and fetch her.'

'Now?'

'Please fetch Sophie. Tell her I insist she see me. It's urgent.' He got up unsteadily. 'Don't say anything about what I've told you . . . about my mother.'

'Be careful, Hal. They gave you a very powerful sedative.'

'Don't worry. I'm becoming immune to powerful bloody sedatives. What I'm not immune to is my own people destroying themselves. Fetch Sophie. And hurry.'

64

'I was there at the crematorium,' Sophie said. 'I was there when we scattered her ashes in the Moster Lees churchyard over your father's grave. The Vicar was there. Ryker and Betsy MacCullum. Warren. Teresa, Francesca, the Schmidt-Kingsleys. Dr Mackle and his wife along with WPC MacQuillan.'

'We saw her in the cellars, Sophie.'

'We saw a spirit. A body-out-of-body.'

'There's no such thing. Listen to me – in the early hours of this morning I carried the dog's corpse down the spiral staircase of the Bell Tower. It was wearing my mother's jewellery.'

'There were no witnesses, Hal.'

'Other than the nurses and, I daresay, MacCullum too. So what was the needle Francesca stuck in me?'

'She was trying to relieve your panic.'

'If you have all the bloody answers, you tell me. Where's my mother's body?'

'I've told you. She was cremated. Fact.'

'And common sense says she wasn't in the coffin.'

'Then who was – one of MacCullum's dead pigs? I'm

telling you ... her ashes were scattered in the churchyard.'

'Who handled the formalities?'

'If you really want to know, I did. I had all the necessary personal details.'

'Like what?'

'National Insurance number, NHS number et cetera. Dr Mackle as GP knew about it. We had the Will. MacCullum made the funeral arrangements. We registered the death. A post-mortem wasn't required. We got the green form. Permission for the body to be cremated. She was receiving her state pension so we had to submit the BD8 form for social security purposes. And we dealt with the bank and insurance broker. That's about the sum of it. It was left to Teresa to inform you as and when she felt appropriate. And, Hal, it was expected.'

His mind was fogged. 'Unexpected.'

'What's been *unexpected*?'

'The missing jewellery. It's on her corpse.'

'Did you see her?'

'Yes. And I heard my father.'

'If you say so, Hal.'

'How do you explain the jewellery?'

'You tell me.'

'What else is missing?'

'Apart from the jewellery, according to the inventories, true enough, quite a few other things are missing.'

Actually, a couple of eighteenth-century ormolu-mounted bow models of tawny owls. A pair, same period, of Meissen white porcelain herons for the Japanese Palace. A seventeenth-century fragment of a William and Mary Mortlake tapestry. A possible Van Dyck of Samson and Delilah. An 1890 Tiffany silver, copper and niello loving cup. More besides . . .'

'Worth what in total?'

'Hard to say. In all, give or take half a million. The problem is that your mother gave a lot of stuff to charities. UNICEF. Oxfam. Ahmadiyya Muslim Jamaat International. Spiritual centres in India, mainly to a Mr Mouthful—' She read out loud from her notebook. 'Mr Bochasanwasi Shri Akshar Purushottam Swaminarayan Sanstha when he's at home in Ahmedabad or Amdavad, Gujarat. Though mostly her dealings were with a man from a North London Gujarati travel agency.'

'How do you know?'

'Teresa told me. To be fair, she tried to stop your mother parting with even more valuable items. Apparently Priscilla would hear nothing of it and started sending very sizeable sums of cash through the regular post.'

'Why haven't you mentioned this before?'

'I didn't want to hurt you. Anyhow, I needed to double-check before this meeting.'

'Who'll be there?'

'Warren and a man called Stefan Nielsen. An auctioneer.'

'Well, well. Whose idea is this?'

'Warren's. He thinks Nielsen will have some helpful advice to offer.'

'Good,' said Hal. 'Because I've more or less made a decision to loosen the bonds.'

'You what?'

'You mean *how* – by selling up.'

'What – leave?'

He shrugged.

'You're going to auction it off?' She searched his face for some further clue to his confused thinking. Finding none, she asked: 'When did you decide?'

'I don't know. It must have been at the back of my mind for months, years even.'

'There has to be a reason to have tipped you over the edge.'

'Perhaps there is. Perhaps there isn't. Perhaps at last I know I want to leave. Sir Glendower built this. Other Stirlings kept it going. Still more Stirlings achieved various degrees of insanity here. I will be the one to say enough's enough. If he's any use, the man Nielsen can be the one to say going-going-gone.'

'And then what? What will you do with the rest of your life?'

'*Begin* it, Sophie, *begin* it.'

– and deny the solemn promise I made you, Mother, that I

would live here throughout my lifetime. And he heard the voice saying: ' ... *the person or persons responsible for The Towers' sale will become insane, be struck down, committed to eternal damnation and hell-fire.*'

Sophie continued: 'I've asked Schadzi and Minti to bring working clothes and help me continue the work of listing things. I don't think you should suffer any more visits to the cellars. I went down there again early this morning.'

'Did you see those—?'

'No,' she interrupted, 'I didn't.' She took a folder from her briefcase. 'Have a look at these ... notes for books your father planned to write. Sorry about the smell – chloroform, death, and God knows what else ...'

Hal glanced at the papers:

EMBALMING PRACTICES IN 19TH & 20TH C. ENGLAND.
Perfection of long-term structural preservation of organs and tissues to ensure minimal shrinkage or distortion.

· THE HAUNTING OF THE TOWERS

'The epigraph's from Jung,' she said. '*Knowing your own darkness is the best method for dealing with the darknesses of other people.*'

He sifted through piles of illustrations of vampire bats.

'Even the pipistrelles have left the Bell Tower.'

There was a self-portrait made from dead spiders,

clearly the work of a madman; the account of a visit to an inmate of Broadmoor lunatic asylum; a man confined for life for eating his wife. A monochrome watercolour of his mother made with his father's own blood and semen. Anatomical drawings his father had made of his own penis, both erect and flaccid. Each signed *Stirling*.

'It's repulsive.'

'I wonder . . .' said Sophie. 'Spectres, evidence of obsession – madness surround the deranged man's death – I wonder . . . whether he might literally have scared himself to death?'

Like father like son, thought Hal.

'The nurses told me how worried they are about you.'

'They can worry about sod-all and those damned séances.'

'And I can walk out any time I like. You can't. Because, if what you say is true about your mother, you have to tell the police. You're caught between a rock and a hard place. If the police begin a murder investigation, who the hell is going to buy this pile? No one. Not in a month of Sundays. And its reputation as an asylum for the living dead is grisly. No one in his right mind will buy it. And anyone in his wrong mind won't have the money. To coin a phrase – you're buggered.'

'What would you do?'

'Me? Do what you're doing already. Get your strength back. Enjoy being with Sumiko who, by the way, is as intelligent as she's beautiful – and obviously adores you.'

'And you?'

'We'll see.'

'Is that all you have to say?'

'No. As a matter of fact it isn't. The rest can wait. Meanwhile get a grip on The Towers. Get it sorted, Hal. That's what I'm here to help you with. To finish the job.'

'What do we do with Teresa and Francesca?'

'What do *you* do? Do you by any chance keep a written record of what they do – what goes on?'

'No.'

'Then make one. Write down in detail what happened last night. To be frank, if you don't mind me saying so, I think there's only one chance in a hundred that your version of events is true. But write it down.'

'I leave the writing to you.'

'As you wish. Remember – I've made an enemy of them. So have you. The enemy of my enemy is my friend. To the rest of the world they're sweetness and light. When it comes to us, they're the enemy. Quite how dangerous they are remains to be seen.'

65

There remained his long-term plans, however sketchy, for Sumiko to live at The Towers with him; a happy fantasy, perhaps still realizable, from which he derived considerable strength.

He reflected that the rest of the world would dismiss the record of the night's events as the raving of a madman.

At its worst, Teresa and Francesca had, in so many words, increased the pressure on him at the point where his sensibilities were most vulnerable. They were conducting a vicious form of aversion therapy, anti-counselling. His mother's spirit, some *dead* not *living* ghost, was fired up to torture him to death. If she failed to possess him in this world she was making sure she would in the next.

Like long-term patients in the bin, the others seemed to be enjoying troubled peace of mind; each in their own way trapped by the joyous threat of the Cumbrian Christmas Day tomorrow.

Midnight mass at the church in Moster Lees.

Presents round the tree in the morning.

Traditional Cumbrian Christmas Lunch. (Inmates Menu: Thornby Moor Blue Whinnow Cheese. Cumbrian Christmas Vegetable Broth. Cumbrian Turkey with trimmings piled high. Cumbrian Christmas Gin-soaked Damson Pudding.)

The Queen's Christmas TV message, not that Cumbria would get a mention.

Wintry sun filtered through the windows of The Towers, bringing temporary relief from the horrors cowering unseen within its depths.

He had no abhorrence of danger, only in its absolute effect – in terror. He told himself not to let tears and rage get the better of him. If the phantoms terrified him, these viruses of the supernatural, then fear would gnaw at his heart. As he put it: 'If it gets to your heart and head you will weep in the watch hours of the night and see visions.'

Certainly, in choosing a Christmas present for Sophie, a prize item from the first-floor gallery, he discovered a fleeting sense of pleasure.

He knew she would love the delicacy and innocence of the small early-twentieth-century signed print of a young girl by Kate Lilley as much as he did. No. 1 from an edition of four.

No. 2 he set aside for Sumiko.

No. 3 for Yukio.

No. 4 he kept for himself.

66

He took an instant dislike to the auctioneer, Nielsen. Ruddy, pot-bellied and bespectacled, Nielsen sported an unsubtle pepper-and-salt toupée. To quit his smoking habit he had a dummy cigarette nipped between his thumb and forefinger, the little finger of his right hand extended in the air as if he were holding a precious teacup.

They were seated in a semi-circle facing the Library's fireplace. Warren and Sophie occupied what Nielsen enthusiastically described as 'a very desirable nine-teenth-century antique oak-framed French settee' to one side. Hal sat opposite, next to Nielsen on 'an early nine-teenth-century Biedermeier burr walnut settee. Rather plush.'

Teresa was at a sideboard with a thermos flask of coffee, cream and hot milk; taking an age to pour the coffee, fiddling with a nest of mahogany coffee tables, stringing out her service to overhear as much as possible of the discussion.

Nielsen was keen to hear out Warren's 'update of the situation'. The latter outlined the 'new tasks' faced by

Sophie. He spoke warmly of Minti and Schadzi. At Sophie's request they'd be joining The Towers' staff as 'supernumeraries in the near future'.

Hal noticed Nielsen stretching his jaw and tightening the greasy knot of his dark- and light-green and white diagonally striped Old Shirburnian tie.

Warren was saying: 'We're not here, Hal, to try and persuade you to change your mind about The Towers' future; rather, we thought we'd put down a few strategic markers. Yes? Hence Stefan's visit.'

'Captain Stirling,' said Nielsen. 'It's a privilege to be here to give you the benefit of my advice. I gather *entre nous* that sale isn't actually an option you'd welcome?'

'I'm open to any ideas to save The Towers.'

'Oh, absolutely. *Ab-sol-ewt-lair*. One always goes the extra mile to meet the major clients' objective.'

'Give us your considered view of the present country house market for the next twelve months,' Warren said.

'Between ourselves,' said Nielsen, 'the mega end will continue to be in short supply. Talking The Towers is talking *crème de la crème*. Top-end *par excellence*. Think Russians. Pop stars. Chinese. The *yuan*'s twenty-two to the UK pound. Our Shanghai branch can't get its hands on UK domestic properties fast enough. We're taking a go-get entrepreneurial approach to delivering value—'

Hal cut in: 'Are you perhaps suggesting a silent auction?'

'I'd need notice of that question. But it has appeal. Absolutely.'

'At what price?'

'Good day, fair wind. Could be looking at between fifty and a hundred.'

'Fifty and a hundred what?'

'Million pounds.'

Cloud cuckoo figure.

'A little more than one thought,' said Warren.

'Maybe more,' said Nielsen. 'I'm giving you the no-strings ballpark figure.'

Hal could see Teresa's reflection in the fireplace. She was standing motionless, silhouetted against the window, holding up the coffee thermos.

'It only needs two major players to increase the bidding,' continued Nielsen. 'We're talking History. Look about. Family pedigree. Parkland. Farmland. Fine art and furniture. Books and manuscripts. Japanese art, Chinese art. Clocks. Collectables. Silver, rugs and carpets, garden statuary and architectural items. The whole shebang. Week-long sale. *Country Life*, quality press and TV coverage.'

Cloud cuckoo.

'What makes you so confident?' said Hal.

'Gut feeling. Think spring. Not winter. The Towers – cleaned, painted, fixed, clutter removed. Bluebells, daffodils and apple blossom have greater pulling power than pretty Japanese ladies playing in the snow.'

'What do you think, Hal?' Warren asked.

'I like the optimism.'

'I remember old Beaumont,' said Nielsen, grinning with regret. 'The Memory Man. Beaumont used to say he'd come back to haunt The Towers here. Right here. You don't want ghosts scaring off the bidders. Keep an eye out for Beaumont. The People's Republic of China believes in ghosts. That's official. One point three billion Chinese. A ghost for every Chink. Imagine. List as long as a Chinese menu.'

Hal looked at his watch deliberately and Nielsen seemed to read the gesture. 'Confucius he say: "Respect ghosts and gods, but keep away from them." Wise, very wise. No fools the Chinks—'

Hal interrupted: 'What's your commission?'

'Seven and a half per cent of the purchase price. Plus expenses. Plus jolly old VAT. Cheap at the price. Though we're always open to negotiation.'

'So am I,' said Hal.

Nielsen got to his feet. 'Absolutely. Anything I can do to help, call me. Twenty-four-seven.' He stooped forward with the solemnity of the courtier to shake Hal by the hand. 'Selling one's home is finally a personal matter. Especially property like this. With its million living memories, private and personal, like most things in life that matter to a gentleman.'

His handshake was limp, his palm cold and moist, and Hal was reminded of something the pharmacist had said about things that matter to a gentleman.

'The happy ghosts of Christmas past,' Nielsen added, sucking on his bogus cigarette. 'The Ghosts of Christmas Past. Robert Louis Stevenson, isn't it, Captain?'

'Dickens,' Hal muttered. '*A Christmas Carol.*'

'I'll show you to the door, Stefan,' Warren offered.

'Allow me,' said Teresa.

Nielsen gave her a knowing smile. 'Sister Vale, one of life's little treasures. Where would we be without Teresa?'

She held out an ashtray for him to dispose of his dummy cigarette but Nielsen palmed it into his jacket pocket. 'Dear Sister Vale, you should know by now it's everlasting. Like love.' He carefully adjusted his nautical Breton cap to avoid skewing the set of his toupée. 'Happy Christmas one and all,' he added with the auctioneer's impatience to get on with the sale of another lot.

By giving his vast and cuckoo-land estimation of The Tower's worth, Nielsen had shot himself in the foot. His firm, a provincial outfit, had few if any of the resources required to handle what might or might not be a major auction.

Hal was about to take the line that it would be

more sensible to consult a major London firm instead, when screams rising in the Great Hall brought about a further complication.

'It's the little girl,' said Sophie.

NINE

Truly the universe is full of ghosts, not sheeted church-yard spectres, but the inextinguishable elements of individual life, which having once been, can never die, though they blend and change, and change again for ever.

H. RIDER HAGGARD
King Solomon's Mines

67

Francesca was at the entrance ushering in Mrs Warren and the Choir of Lakeland Angels in full voice:

> *Once in royal David's city,*
> *Stood a lowly cattle shed . . .*
> *Where a mother laid her Baby,*
> *In a manger for His bed—*

accompanied by Yukio's screams—

The sight of Yukio, hysterical in her mother's embrace, confronted Hal in the Great Hall. Sumiko was weeping.

> *Mary was that mother mild . . .*

The comfort of the hot bath couldn't stop Yukio shivering. In clouds of steam, the cowering child was inconsolable.

Sumiko was scarcely in control of herself. 'We went to play hide-and-seek. Yukio went off first. I counted to fifty and went to look for her. I picked up a trail in the snow and followed the footprints. Then Yukio called out to me, said she could hear voices.'

'Where?'

'She was outside the stables.'

'What voices?'

'The voices were from behind the stable door. Yukio tried to open it and couldn't. I was about twenty yards away when the door opened. This bloodied hand hurled a mangled lump out – aimed directly at Yukio's head.'

Sumiko lifted her out of the bath and began to dry her.

'I'm cold. I'm *cold*.'

'You'll be warm in a minute. Do you want to go back in the water?'

'Yes, Mummy. Can you hot it up for me?'

'What was it – lump, what mangled lump?'

'The headless dog. Whoever was in the stables threw it in Yukio's face.'

There was a knock at the door.

'Hello? It's me.' It was Teresa. 'May I come in?'

'Wait a moment,' Hal said. 'You've no idea who did it?'

Sumiko shook her head.

Hal opened the bathroom door and barred Teresa's entry.

Sumiko and Yukio were looking at her with fear and loathing.

'I'll wash the child's clothes,' Teresa said.

'You won't touch them,' Sumiko shouted.

*

Hal closed the door and leaned against it.

'Who did it, Teresa?'

'Your father's Japanese lover.'

'Bullshit.'

'Face the truth.'

'Stop this. There's no such person.'

'Don't you shout at me. Fetch the child's clothes. I'll burn them.'

'You'll do no such thing.'

'Mam?' Francesca was calling from below. 'Will I fetch the mince pies?'

'Hand them round,' Teresa called back. 'One each, mind.'

'What are you doing, Mam?'

'Never you mind. Down in a minute.' Teresa turned to stare at Hal. 'It's not safe for them here. Tell them to go away. To leave. Now.' She tugged at his sleeve. 'Come away. Before anything worse happens.'

Hal tried to grab her wrist. Teresa turned suddenly and almost overbalanced. They faced each other in silence broken only by Yukio's sobs from behind the bathroom door.

'Who killed it, Teresa?'

'Killed what?' she said hotly.

He clenched his fist. 'The puppy – the puppy's blood was all over Yukio. Her own dog's blood.'

'What dog?'

'Now look – I am asking you straight. Who killed the puppy, Teresa?'

She clutched her arms round her as if she'd suddenly felt a chill draft. 'You did.' She lowered her head with a look of pity. 'You're behaving like a dead person, Hal. I wish I could communicate with you. Your mind – it's *DEAD*. You're going to be all right. Together, you and me – we'll make everything all right, won't we?'

Hal followed her along the landing.

She walked with her shoulders back, straightening the hem of her tight black skirt.

'You come to me,' she whispered. 'You need me.' Suddenly she stopped in the shadow, her face very close to his. Her lips were parted. She raised her hand to his mouth, caressed his lips with her fingers and looked closely into his eyes. 'You want me, Hal. It's natural. You want me, don't you? You must come to Mummy. Teresa won't tell a soul.' She was growing breathless. 'Just you and me. You dream of me, don't you? You're guilty for me, aren't you? We have our secrets, don't we? You can have me, baby.'

'You don't know what you're saying, Teresa. Who killed the dog?'

'You need your Teresa. I love it when you ask for me.'

'I'm asking you for nothing.'

'You are. You're asking for me.' She turned and caught sight of herself in a wall mirror. 'You're asking "Is anybody there?" And I am. You don't know it ... you want me. I know. Because, see, I want you. Look at me.'

He looked at her dark reflection.

The unexpected.

The succubus to convert the shame of infidelity into pleasure and allow him finally to abandon himself to shamelessness?

'Teresa, I'm warning you – I want you and Francesca out of here.'

'Why?'

'The dog. The drugs. The gun's been stolen. You're in every kind of trouble.'

'We're all of us in trouble here,' she said to her reflection. 'That's why you must ask your friend to leave and take the suffering child with her. Now. Right away.'

'There's no question of that,' he said firmly. But firm though he may have sounded, he was frightened. 'They stay, Teresa.'

'Why?'

'Because I say so.'

'You want to drive them mad? As for me and Francesca. *Leave*? Oh no, dearie, I don't think so. We aren't going anywhere. If *you* want to leave, then go on, please yourself. Like you did with my daughter. Don't think actions don't have consequences. And I'm the one intended for you. You're my lover. My spirit and my body. Our heated streams have flowed into each other. I have swallowed your seed. Your juice. Your blood. I am your shrine.'

'What the hell are you saying?' There was helplessness in his voice.

'*Saying?* Do you want me to sit down with that Sophie – and tell her? And give your Japanese the full story? And Francesca. Don't think Francesca spared me any details. You enjoyed yourself inside of her. She didn't take precautions, did she? Because you told her – "*I love you, Francesca.*" I heard you begging her.' Her lips quivered. 'I was in bed with you myself. You were inside me too. We pleasured you inside of us.'

'What are you trying to prove?'

'*Prove?* I don't need to prove a thing.' She stepped up close to him. 'You killed that dog.' Her breath was hot and moist, her fury rising. 'You slept with my daughter,' she shouted. 'I've photos of you two naked. And you having her like she was a dog in heat. And you took me from the rear like I was a dog.'

Her shout brought Sumiko from the bathroom at the moment Teresa struck him across the face.

He grabbed her wrist; he wrestled with her briefly and she retaliated by kicking wildly at his legs so he was forced to step back, his elbows and back thumping against the mirror hanging from the wall.

The mirror didn't fall at once. It tilted, juddered, the heavy frame's wire snapped, then the whole thing toppled face down to the landing floor, the glass shattering in a burst of jangling splinters.

The report of the mirror's exploding glass petrified Yukio and she began to whimper.

A moaning sound came from Teresa's closed mouth. Her dark eyes stared at Sumiko with hatred. Sumiko didn't flinch.

Teresa was glaring at Hal. 'I will never leave you,' she said.

'Get away from me,' he shouted.

'Never,' Teresa shouted in return. 'I am Sada Abe.'

He saw Sumiko's eyes focus fiercely on Teresa's. Her small hands trembled and rose up to the sides of her head like a bird's beating wings, palms pressed against her ears.

Yukio clambered out of her bath. Dripping bathwater, she stumbled across the slippery floor into her mother's protective arms, her eyes gazing fearfully at Teresa whose full dark hair framed her face and accentuated her glistening eyes.

Teresa's mouth was stretched into the smile of a well-satisfied lunatic.

She stooped to retrieve a shard of the mirror's glass. She fixed the terrified Yukio with her eyes. 'Child, you are like the puppy,' she said conversationally, 'you are cursed to die in your mother's blood.'

She began to walk away and just before she reached the top of the stairs she let the shard of glass drop to the floor and began to grind it into dust beneath her shoe. 'To avert seven years of blood and death,' she announced, 'we should grind the broken mirror's glass

to dust and bury it in the cemetery. Now it's too late
– too late.'

At the top of the stairs she reached out a hand to
steady herself against the handrail with a gesture of
proprietorship and raised her right hand, the thumb
beneath her middle finger, the Sign of The Hornéd
Satan, God of the Witch.

Then she gripped her nose, the thumb and forefinger
grinding into its bridge until blood began to flow,
streaming from her nose and eyes, her face contorted,
twisted horizontally; her skin stretched, pitted and
convoluted like a lizard's.

Sumiko pulled Yukio back inside the bathroom,
slammed the door and locked it.

Blood streaming down her face, Teresa smiled: 'My very
blood is shed for you, Hal. We are of the same blood
and spirit.' She began to chant some half-remembered
song. '"Tonight you're mine, completely." As I am your
body and soul, I am the keeper of your future.'

*The damaged body can offer a clue to the performance and
construction of a bomb. So I have to look at it up close.*

'Give me your love. My body will be waiting in white
silk. Caverns measureless to man. Come inside . . . come
inside me. I am Your Coming.'

– *I stare into dead and bulging eyes with broken blood vessels.*

– *Into torn ears filled with blood. Multiple twisted fractures.*
Fragmented splintered bones.

– *Not for a single moment can you afford to think of the victim as a person.*

– *Not for a single moment can you afford to think of the person as a victim.*

Her eyes exerted a terrible hypnotism.

– *I am going to her . . .*

To his horror, Hal heard a voice saying: 'Wait . . . I'm coming to you.'

'I always knew you would,' Teresa told him sweetly. 'You and me together, Hal. Only we can remember the future. Tonight I will be yours. I will be waiting as I've waited a thousand years for you.'

68

Sumiko packed her bags in silence and Hal loaded them into her VW along with Yukio.

Then he led the way in the Range Rover to Moster Lees where Sumiko had agreed to take a room at the Moster Inn.

Smitty greeted Hal with patronizing flummery. '*Is there room at the Inn?* This isn't Bethlehem.' He lowered the reception desk flap and settled a grimy ledger on it. 'Bear with me. What have we here now? Every room vacant, every one a winner. You, Sir, can take the pick of the very best. How many will there be staying with us?'

'Two. One adult, one child. If you could arrange a room for the two of them to share.'

'Glendower Suite's vacant. En suite shower. Wall bracket TV.'

But when Sumiko and Yukio appeared in the entrance hall, Smitty's lizard eyes blinked. He untangled the gold chain dangling from his neck and adjusted his glasses on his nose. 'You'll have to forgive me, Captain. I'm looking at next year's ledger. My mistake. Cock-up. Sincere apologies. *N-C-D. No-Can-Do*.'

'Not a single room?'

'Chock-a-bloody-block.'

'Does anyone else nearby have rooms?'

'You could try the Vicar. He's got a spare room or two. Mind – what with Midnight Mass and tomorrow's services . . .' He drew his hand across his throat as if it were a blade. 'He's up to here with Christmas—'

'Can we telephone him?'

'My pleasure.'

Smitty wiped his fingers on his handkerchief and tapped in the number. 'Hi-yer. *How are yew*? I've got Captain Stirling here. Yes. *The* Captain Stirling. Have you a spare room for tonight? Oh, good. Good. Hang on a sec while I hand him over . . .'

Hal took the phone. 'Hal Stirling. Can you help two of my guests with a room tonight?'

'Of course I can,' the Vicar said. 'Bring them round.'

'All done then?' said Smitty. He beamed at Yukio. 'You'll be happy with the Vicar. He's very good with kiddies. This old house gets noisy after Midnight Mass. That's when the big drinkers get in pole position for the off. Must be much the same in the Army, Sir.'

'I daresay.'

Smitty coughed into his hand. He'd sensed that Hal knew perfectly well the Moster Inn wasn't expecting a single guest. Examining his phlegm, he leaned close to Hal's face: 'If I could have a quiet word?'

'I'll join you outside,' Hal told Sumiko.

'No offence, Sir,' Smitty spluttered. 'The wife lost her grandfather in 1945 at Hellfire Pass. The Japs cut off his ears and fed 'em to the other POWs. No way are we having yellow bastards under our roof. I'm a Kipling Man. White Man's Burden. Nothing personal, mind. This being Christmas. Good Will To All Men with some exceptions, matey. Any road, I don't hold with Christianity. I'm what they call a humanist. There's not much in the Bible about Japs.'

Hal felt his hands forming fists. *'Was ist mit Deutschen?'* ('What about Germans?')

The hooded eyes flickered. *'Verpisst euch – raus hier!'* ('Get the fuck out of here!')

69

The Vicar said Sumiko could have the run of his kitchen, 'for what it's worth, which isn't much. I'm afraid I'm vegetarian. I do have a spot of fish. Coley. The Japanese like coley, don't you?' He didn't wait for an answer. 'Please, can I talk to Captain Stirling a moment . . . in private . . . would you mind?'

Sumiko left them alone in the kitchen.

'How much do I owe you for the room?' Hal asked.

'Just give me a cheque made out to the Cathedral Church of the Resurrection in Lahore. Some other time. I'll send it on.' The Vicar closed the kitchen door and leaned against it. 'I was going to phone you anyway.' He frowned. 'It's just that we won't be having your reading at Midnight Mass. The service is far too long as it is.'

'Is that the real reason?'

'Well, not exactly. Only that one or two of the locals think it would be inappropriate. I mean, do attend. Don't get me wrong. Bring your lady friend and the little girl too, though I fancy it'll be a bit past her bedtime.'

'What are you telling me?'

'There are rumours going the rounds.'

'About what?'

'About you.'

'Me?'

'About you and Francesca Vale.'

'What rumours?'

'What you'd expect when a man and a woman are involved. Need I explain?'

'We're both adult.'

'I know. But there's an understanding among the clergy that there's an inviolable confidence between the individual priest and the parishioner.'

'The penitent?'

'The penitent. Though you haven't asked me for God's forgiveness.'

'Try me. I might. You're talking to someone who's a signatory to the Official Secrets Act.'

'What do you know of Sister Teresa's parentage?'

'Nothing.'

'Is that true?'

'Yes.'

'I don't know whether this is ultimately a matter of regret or not. But I regret that what I have to tell you isn't going to make your life any easier.' He spoke as if to the ceiling.

'Tell me and we'll see.'

The Vicar folded his hands together. 'I'm told your father was a secretive man,' he said.

'In professional matters,' Hal said. 'Yes. He was.'

'And, it also seems, in more personal matters.'

'What do you mean, *more personal matters*?'

'It's about Sister Vale.'

'What about her?'

'I found myself in the unfortunate position,' the Vicar said, 'of being asked to help establish Teresa's parentage. What d'you know of it?'

'I've told you already. Means nothing to me.'

'What I must tell you is about to change that.'

'It isn't any of my business.'

'I'm afraid it is. It seems to me, now's as good a time as any to let you know the truth of things.' He began to finger the crucifix dangling from his neck. His eyes look frightened. 'You and Teresa are your father's offspring.'

Hal clutched his throat.

'I don't want to upset you,' the Vicar said. 'I'm afraid it's true. Your father paid regular sums of money by way of what you could call child maintenance. In that respect he was an honourable man.'

'How d'you know this?'

'My predecessor told me. He saw the legal agreements, the relevant bank statements, details of credit transfers and so on.'

'How did he get hold of them?'

'He didn't get *hold* of them. He only *saw* them. His brother was branch manager of your family's bank in

Carlisle. There was a problem with the Inland Revenue. Documents required witnessing. My predecessor obliged. He also, by the way, baptized Teresa and her daughter. Both of them confided in him. Your father likewise, though perhaps that wasn't entirely in character.'

Hal closed his eyes. 'I'd like a glass of water.'

The Vicar filled a tumbler from the cold tap and handed it to him. 'Your father also formed a relationship with Teresa who in turn gave birth to Francesca. The outcome of your father's philandering. Francesca's your half-niece. Perhaps – who knows? – this explains a little of The Towers' evil.'

'What else do I need to know?'

'That Francesca wants to have a child with you. She and her mother want The Towers.'

'They'll to have to wait till hell freezes.'

'That's not what they believe. I'm afraid you'll find the villagers are on their side. The Moster Lees community is close-knit. So close you can't even see the stitching. More or less all the villagers seem to be hapless victims of The Towers. More practically, given the estate owns their houses, as tenants they're in thrall to its contagion. They hint at secrets of violence, incest, abuse, torture, murder even.'

'They discuss all this with you?'

'Of course.'

'Do you believe them?'

'I don't know what I believe.'

'You're the Man of God. You either believe or you bloody don't.'

'That's a matter between the Almighty and me. Sometimes it seems the cauldron of The Towers is their sole demented topic of conversation. The gossips huddle together in different covens. Teresa, Francesca and MacCullum are one such. I'd say, as a more or less neutral observer, whose business is pastoral care, Teresa and Francesca have formed an unhealthy attachment to MacCullum.'

'To little Ryker?'

'I wouldn't underestimate him, Captain Stirling. Ryker MacCullum's possessed of the charm that accompanies low cunning. The born undertaker who relishes dealing with people at their most vulnerable. The natural chancer. Oh, I know he's *Good Old Ryker*. Everyone's friend, to be pitied for his drunken wife. He casts a spell. He's also a creature who spends solitary hours prowling around in the wasteland of the disused mines, obsessively haranguing witless Carlisle crematorium assistants or any demolition man or passing soldier from Catterick about his repressed passion for military weapons, arms and explosives.'

'He hasn't harangued me.'

'He wouldn't, would he?'

'Why not?'

'Because he loathes you.'

'What makes you think that?'

'Betsy told me,' the Vicar said wearily. 'She takes comfort in hatred.'

'She a penitent too?'

'Simply addicted to mendacious gossip. Like the majority of the sullen people in these sad parts, smouldering with quiet hatred for the Stirlings. They blame their misery, their perceived enslavement to the landed gentry on the Stirlings, and everything The Towers represents. Nothing changes. Perhaps it's a class thing. As Smitty says: *Neid frisst nichts als seine eigene Herz.* Envy eats nothing but its own heart. It's been the same for generations.'

'I find it very sad.'

'So do I,' the Vicar said with a sigh. 'When I see The Towers from a distance, even on a clear and sunny day, I think it symbolizes a certain sadness, a kind of pain. It's like one of those cathedrals in north Germany. A vast structure filled with piety and fine intentions, a house of God that's seen too much evil and has been quite unable to cope with it. When one sees your family home in the rain it seems to weep. It reminds me of my visits to the dying. You'd be astonished how often they say: "I wish this would end. Can't we get it over with?" You see, there are more people than you'd ever imagine who don't want to go on living. The instinct for death is innate. More so than life. That's something Our Lord teaches us. The Towers exemplifies death and the living dead. You should know that too. More often than not, death shows us the friendly face. As Mark Twain tells us: "All say, How hard it is that we have to die – a strange complaint to come from the mouths of people who have had to live—"'

A gentle knocking at the door interrupted the drift of his Christmas homily.

70

It was Sumiko. The Vicar greeted Sumiko's return as a sign that he'd heard Duty call. 'I'd be more than happy if the three of you stay tonight. I won't be back until the early hours. Midnight Mass and all that. And I have to put in my traditional appearance at the pub. Anyhow, make yourself at home.'

'What about joining us tomorrow at The Towers for Christmas lunch?' suggested Hal.

'I already have an invitation from Dr Mackle and his wife. Thanks all the same.' He gave Hal a troubled look. 'I wouldn't go back to The Towers tonight.'

'I have to be there. Throughout its history it's never, even for a minute, been uninhabited.'

'Will you mind staying up there alone?'

'No,' Hal lied. 'I won't. After all, it's home, and there'll be the nurses for company—'

The Vicar shook his head. 'They're staying with the MacCullums.'

'They didn't tell me.'

'They didn't? If I were you I wouldn't sleep at The Towers alone.'

'We'll be all right here,' Sumiko said. 'Yukio will be happier here.'

'Then I'll leave you two to make your own arrangements,' the Vicar said, stuffing papers into his briefcase. His face was grey with tiredness, his smile kindly, but Hal could read the fear in the weary eyes: fear; as well as a kind of relief. The Man of God had unburdened himself, and had passed the pain like a relay runner handing over the baton to the next person who had no other choice but to run with it.

71

'Serve immediately,' was Sumiko's kitchen catchphrase. She was the kind of woman who thought good food conquered the cruelty of Fate.

All the better when it was her lover's favourite food, cooked according to her equations and consumed without delay.

She'd brought the ingredients in an icebox labelled: HAL'S FAVOURITE MISO SOUP; HAL'S FAVOURITE PAN-FRIED TUNA STEAKS; HAL'S FAVOURITE SAKE.

They dined by candlelight at the scrubbed pine table in the centre of the austere kitchen.

There was no mention of Sophie.

Afterwards, Hal gave Sumiko the print by Kate Lilley and she obviously adored it.

'And now for your present,' Sumiko announced demurely. 'Guess what I have for you?'

'Show me.'

'You're looking at it.'

'Well – where is it?'

'Christmas quiz first. Questions. Who wrote: "I ache

to see you. Your lips upturned. Your long eyelashes. To find the air filled with your lingering scent. To brush away the hair from your eyes."'

'I think we know.'

'Who wrote: the poem 'Funeral Blues'?'

'Auden.'

'Who knew he was alive when he heard a voice telling him: "Captain Hal Stirling . . . 101 Engineer Regiment, Explosive Ordnance Disposal. Counter-IED Task Force"?'

'You're looking at him.'

'Who told who: "We are each other"?'

'I told you.'

'And – final question. Who's expecting our child?'

For the first time in months, his world turned the right way up.

He held her close. 'That's wonderful,' he said. 'Wonderful.'

Understandably in the circumstances, Yukio had pleaded with Sumiko to leave The Towers. But Sumiko wasn't prepared to risk the snow and icy roads.

Upset by Yukio's request and mindful of Hal's state of mind, Sumiko was fraught with indecision and fearful of what else The Towers might hold in store.

Hal suggested an alternative; that she go to Carlisle straight away and take a room at the Holiday Inn. In other words, sit things out at arm's length. But Christmas Eve was no-room-at-the-stable time. Hal was still trying to offer her reassurance when he saw the kitchen curtains move.

Though he *knew* the face of the person peering in he didn't *recognize* it. Instantaneously they locked eyes.

The mask froze him. It blinked in recognition. Man or woman? It was impossible to tell.

He could *hear its silence*: the *silent voice* muttering threats: the tones distorted as if a door entryphone was amplifying the announcement of arrival, speaking his name. *It was seeking to gain entry.*

As in a nightmare, the disconnected narrative shifted abruptly without logic; he felt Sumiko's warmth beside him, sensed the aura of her perfume.

'What do you want?' he asked.

The living death mask was pursuing Sumiko, hell-bent on seizing her.

Snowflakes floated towards him like spikes on the wind. Through the shifting barrier of whiteness the one certain form was the mask's phantasmagorical mouth fixed in a joyless smile.

He felt compelled to stare it in the face. Eyeball to eyeball. A pair of prizefighters engaged in a prebout staredown of intimidation. The mask generated the electricity of fear, challenging him. *I am waiting for you.*

The voice warned: *'Don't Touch'* – and he asked: *'Why Not?'*

As the mask closed its lips, he felt a wave of freezing air literally slap his face, its effect identical to cold spray from a canister: clamping an anaesthetizing mask across his mouth.

He swept aside the curtains, knocking a rank of Christmas cards to the floor.

'What are you doing?' Sumiko said quietly.

He opened the window and stared wordlessly into the driven snow. The light from the room illuminated veils of silken white.

The mask had gone.

Sumiko reached past him to close the window. 'We'll catch our death of cold.'

Death of cold was waiting there outside.

'Did you feel the wind?' he whispered.

She looked at him in puzzlement. 'The window's closed.'

'It opened.'

'No, it didn't, Hal. You were gazing at the snow.'

'Yes. Perhaps that's what I was doing.'

'You're deathly white.'

'Didn't you see it outside?'

'See what?'

'You felt that sudden blast – that wind?'

She stooped to help him gather up the fallen cards and together they aligned them in ranks.

The largest was a singing Christmas card. Hal set it back in place and it began to threaten him: '*Brightly shone the moon that night, Though the frost was cruel . . .*'

'It was only the wind,' she said with a smile.

*

'You want to go back there?' she said.

'I'm worried what else might happen if I don't.'

'I know. Well, Yukio and I will be fine here. I don't mind if you go.'

'You don't object to me leaving you two on your own?'

She smiled. 'You should mind about leaving Sophie on her own. You'd better go and see she's okay.'

'Only if you don't mind.'

She didn't and said she wanted him to do what instinct dictated. She recalled the Japanese proverb: '"*One kind word can warm three winter months.*" And,' she added, 'Yukio still has to get used to seeing you in my bed.'

He told her he'd bring Christmas lunch provisions to the vicarage early in the morning. She said she was sure she could persuade Yukio they stay on, at least until Boxing Day.

They mulled over plans

– to ask Sophie and her two friends to assume the role of caretakers at The Towers until things returned to an even keel.

– to offer a good sum to Teresa and Francesca to move out with immediate effect. If needs be he'd pay for them to stay at a Carlisle hotel until they found alternative lodgings.

'Soon enough,' he said, 'I'll have to go back to Headley Court.'

'You can stay with me,' she said. 'Let me look after you. You have to relieve yourself of the burdens of The Towers and—'

'And what?'

'– familiarize yourself with impending fatherhood . . .'

Mobile phone signals permitting, they agreed to call each other at midnight.

The Range Rover's warmth intensified the aroma of her perfume. Overjoyed by her announcement, the elation induced new confidence and resolution.

The headlights' beams dipped and dived across the wilderness of snow, the drifts rising and tumbling like cascading Arctic waves.

The vertiginous facades of The Towers held no fear for him.

No light shone from the ranks of windows.

He didn't give the statue of Sir Glendower in the portico a second glance. Sir Glendower was no longer murmuring encouragement: '*Capax Infiniti – Capable of the Infinite*.' If the patriarch was pondering the isolation, he wasn't spoiling Christmas by sharing any of his thoughts with his only surviving heir.

It was time to bathe The Towers in light.

His hands were warm and the entrance door swung open so easily it might have been an omen.

Click-and-click-and-click. He ran the palm of his hand down the light switches in the hallway.

He walked back and forth across the flagstone floor turning on yet more lights. In the long passages leading to the Victoria Tower he repeated the procedure, ignoring the eerie sound of his shoes clacking on the stone floors; sometimes muffled when he crossed the threadbare floor rugs.

As he passed the vast wooden staircase rising to the gallery on the floor above, the familiar scent of damp soot greeted him as a friend. Lights went on here too, sparkling across the largest window of the ground floor. If his mother was chattering, he didn't hear her. There was no remembrance of things future. *'We Stirlings have lived here perfectly happily for a hundred and fifty years. And, as long as there is a Stirling, we will continue to do so until hell freezes. Capax Infiniti.'*

The ceilings filled with kindly light. Lights went on in the Stone Drawing Room. They illuminated the doubtful works by Rubens, Van Dyck and Claude Lorrain.

On they went in the nineteenth-century Baccarat six-arm Napoleon III crystal chandeliers.

The nineteenth-century Italian gilt metal chandelier hung with crystal drapes and drops came on in the Gothic Library, its reflected lights sparkling in the glass of the bookcase fronts.

Lights shone across the Billiard Salon and the Music Room where the 'Elgar Piano', rotted like a broken coffin, stood against the curtained double doors.

The lights of Christmas forced the devils of ill fortune to seek refuge in the luminous ether pervading space to infinity.

The demons had quit the haunted stage of the expanse of unsullied snow across the lawns.

Tiny sparks of Christmas lights in Moster Lees, in the hamlets further afield in Stonsey, in Gretan and Warely had exorcised them.

Silent night, holy night
Son of God, love's pure light
Radiant beams from Thy holy face
With the dawn of redeeming grace ...

Between The Towers and the world beyond the wall of darkness parted.

76

22.00

2 hours till the Birth of Jesus to the Virgin Mary:
fulfilment of Messianic prophecy.

2 hours till Sumiko and I
wish each other Happy Christmas.

TEN

As fear rises to an extreme pitch, the dreadful scream of terror is heard. Great beads of sweat stand on the skin.

CHARLES DARWIN
The Expression of Emotions in Man and Animals

77

The lights flickered. Filaments became dull red. Then faded. Off, then on. Wary of an imminent power cut he found a torch.

In the silence of the kitchen he prepared a box of Christmas foodstuffs to take to the vicarage in the morning.

He wanted music to break the silence. So BBC Radio 3 echoed through The Towers.

So far as he could tell nothing in his room had been disturbed.

The room that had temporarily been Sumiko's was much as she'd left it. Some of Yukio's bloodstained winter clothing lay in the broken wicker laundry basket.

Sophie's bedroom was empty. Pillows and sheets lay neatly folded on the bed.

Surprised and hurt that she'd abandoned him without so much as a by-your-leave, he went in search of Teresa and Francesca.

He made a brief and unrewarding inspection of their rooms.

Except for a residue of the stale aroma of scented candles there was no sign of them either. Likewise, no explanation for their departure.

He looked into the bedroom that had been his mother's. No change there.

To begin with he felt no unease about being alone in The Towers.

Where was Sophie?

78

Outside his mother's bedroom, shortly after he began to search for Sophie, a pair of long-bodied white-and-fawn odd-eye rats startled him.

With pink left eyes and black right eyes, about ten inches long, the rats leapt away from him, skittering for cover in a brownish linen dust sheet hanging from the frame of the mirror Teresa had smashed.

He grabbed a corner of the dust sheet and shook it, intending to stamp on the vermin when they hit the floor. Too quick for him, the rats pelted across the landing to the sanctuary of the shadows.

Had it not been for the rats he might never have made the discovery that drew the future closer.

He'd caused the frame to slip its moorings. It fell to the floor, taking the dust sheet with it, exposing the rims of a false door.

The door opened without difficulty to reveal a second. The door of a combination safe.

Like the first, he'd never seen the door before. Here

was another of The Towers' secrets he wasn't going to leave undisturbed.

Was this the reason Teresa had attempted to create such a repulsive diversion – to prevent him from seeing that the wall safe held dirty secrets?

Manufactured by Ludovici of Milan, the safe was steel-plated with welded seams. Only once before, in training, had he disabled a similar repository for weapons, bombs and high-explosives.

He took a long look-see.

The Ludovici's doors were of solid steel plate. No tell-tale wires. The safe had a pair of locking bolts on its front rim fastened into a drill-resistant frame. The doors were suspended on hidden pivots. He reckoned he was facing locks with four or five levers; maybe, for good measure, an additional and alternative locking system comprising a two-wheel combination lock: the model of Italian deviousness.

Ludovici here I come.

He turned the dial three times right, then rested it at the first number. To the left. Gently through the second number. Stopped. Back to turning it left, through the second combination number, just the once. The second time around he stopped the turning.

The likelihood of guessing the right release numbers was non-existent. You're talking millions of combinations. You can't press your ear against the lock, fiddle and listen for telltale clicks like some safebreaker in the movies. But, by stroking at the skin of the locks, teasing out the nerve of least resistance, exciting the thing's glands, you can squeeze in.

With heavy-duty bolt-cutters from the garage, he could cause enough damage to persuade the Ludovici to surrender to his advances. It takes a knack for seduction. Such knacks were part of the professional armoury of his vocation. Anything that's been put together can be taken apart.

He hurried to the garage and returned with bolt-cutters.

Within ten seconds the Ludovici gave up its last attempts at resistance and revealed secrets that froze his bones.

ELEVEN

Here, and here only, the traces of the past
lay deep – too deep to be effaced.

WILKIE COLLINS
The Woman in White

79

Three hundred miles south.

The sign at the gates of Headley Court said: COUNTER-TERRORISM RESPONSE LEVEL: HEIGHTENED.

To his embarrassment, the counsellor's mobile started ringing during the Headley Court Christmas Eve Mass.

He left the service to take the call.

'Fear not,' said he, for mighty dread
Had seized their troubled mind,
'Glad tidings of great joy I bring
To you and all mankind.'

'Where are you, Hal?'

'The Towers.'

'You all right?'

'Yes and no. Listen, write this down.'

'Write what down?'

'No questions. Move it. Write it down. A list of materiel I've found. If anything untoward happens to me you're to pass the list to the police.'

'What's happening, Hal?'

'Listen to me. Write this down. *Do it.*'

'I'm listening.'

80

FIGURES:

ONE. Mobile phone with charger.

TWO. Cache of photographs of Sumiko wrapped in pages from the *Cumberland News*.

THREE. Jewellery.

FOUR. Photographs of Sada Abe.

FIVE. Xerox inventory listing major works of art, furniture and rare valuables plus sale estimates.

SIX. Photographs of Sister Teresa Vale with St John Warren *in flagrante delicto*.

SEVEN. Copy. Mother's Last Will and Testament.

EIGHT. Sister Vale's digital camera containing images of self and Francesca Vale.

NINE. Xerox plans Family Chapel and Crypt.

TEN. Xerox copies *Counter IED Task Force Manual*. With reference to specifications for use of ammonium nitrate, graphite blades and incendiary chemicals comprising non-military and military components, platter charges, two to six kilos plus same-weight plastic explosive.

ELEVEN. Victim-operated improvised explosive device/ booby traps incorporating pressure pads, tripwire, release spring-loaded, push, pull or tilt.

TWELVE. Xerox copies. *U.S. Special Forces. TM 31-210 Improvised Munitions Handbook.*

THIRTEEN. Photographs of pigs gnawing at what resemble human remains.

'Got all that?'

'Yes. Want me to read it over?'

'There's no time. Also, note in your own words, I'm looking at two small steel cylinders packed with high-explosives. Others have been prepared and removed.'

'What is all this?'

'Evidence of intention to blow this place to hell.'

'Have you called the police?'

'It's too late.'

'You can't handle it alone. Get out of there and *now*.'

'That's what I'm going to do.'

'I'll call the police.'

'Too late. Do what I say. It's an order.'

The line went dead.

The counsellor read the list. Either: *one* – his patient was imagining things and had altogether lost his mind. Or, if not: *two* – his patient was about to lose his life.

00.00
Time to wish Sumiko Happy Christmas.

She wasn't answering.

His call was diverted and he left a message.

'You'll be asleep safe and sound. I wish you and Yukio and the one-to-be A Very Happy Christmas. If anything happens to me tonight please call the one-to-be Sumiko. *Watashi wa anata o aishite imasu.* I love you. I always have. Always will.'

No more calls.

He turned off his mobile. *Home and Not at Home.*

00.05
In the garage, he assembled a make-do kit of emergency basic IED disposal equipment. He looked at his hands. Strangely, they were steady.

Antichrist. False Keeper of The Towers' Satanic Grail. Show me your eyes that you be tormented with fire and brimstone in the presence of the holy angels—

Crouched in subterranean silence, the Crypt was waiting for him. Piles of haemorrhaged waste and faeces
carpeted its cavernous bowels.

Peering into the gloom, he walked slowly, yard by
yard, through vaulted passages. Watery slime ran down
his face.

A rotted catafalque rose to face him, its skeletal frame
erect in mute protest. Locked gates of wrought iron
barred his entry to the vaults, final home to the eldritch
remains of subhumanity.

At one curve of the main passage a narrow stairway
could be seen. Moistened brickwork blocked the
slanting ceiling exit to the Chapel overhead.

Still narrower passages led to more vaults lined with
stone shelves. Occasionally he glimpsed geometrical
shapes of open coffins lined with lead. The coffin lids
lay discarded beside them. Above them iron wall-ladders
rose to the ceilings.

It seemed to him an age had passed within the deathly
interconnected chambers when he finally paused to
assess the progress of his reconnaissance.

Water pattered near the entrance to a tunnel a few metres distant. The passage to it reached out before him, lit by electric light fittings from the postwar years.

The light bulbs offered up a clue; namely, that they'd been fitted and connected to the mains electricity supply in recent times to cast dim light. Satan's handiwork.

Then he saw it . . .

83

In the guttering.

Satan's handiwork wove its sinister route along the corridor.

The fine red line wriggling a few metres ahead, circling the staircase elevation at the point you reached the exterior wall where the indentation suggested a doorway leading to steps: steps out-and-up-and-away to the central courtyard adjacent to what had once been a coal store. The way in and the way out. The discreet and discrete entry to the resting place of Stirling dead.

The wire made no immediate sense. It had a redundant look about it.

He tested it with his tick-tracer; it didn't light. No current flowed through it. Not, then, a command wire linked to hidden IEDs.

Walking steadily, glancing over his shoulder, he heard the whirring.

nnng-whhhhrrrrrr-whhhrrrrrrrnnnnng

Animal, human or mechanical?

It warned him. He was not alone.

*

At the end of the passage the *nnng-whhhhrrrrrr-whhhrrrrrrrnnnnng* grew louder.

He paused and glanced at his watch.

01.18 was blurred.

As it flicked to **01.19** he looked down and saw it . . .

. . . the telltale wire . . . *if it is a wire. Might be a come-on. Might be another one buried in the shit connected to yet another. Wire might have degraded in the filth making the bomb unstable. Moving in the lightest air current the wire might produce an electrical short and trigger an explosion.*

nnng-whhhhrrrrrr-whhhrrrrrrrnnnnngwhrrrr

He began to visualize the IED even before he reached the point where it ended abruptly outside a heavy door.

The wire had been set deep in the wall patchily covered with rough plaster. A few feet to his right he saw the flight of stone steps leading upwards to the courtyard exit.

He heard the rumbling of a generator. Powering what?

nnng-whhhhrrrrrr-whhhrrrrrrrnnnnngwhrrrr

The surface of the bottom steps gave the clue.

There were muddled patterns outside the door where the slime had been disturbed. The footprints were fresh.

Crawling on hands and knees, he examined the footprints further up the staircase.

Unknown Person &/or Persons had come down the steps, then left the same way.

Person &/or Persons had dragged a wire: the wire that, looking down, he saw running all the way to the door and then beneath it.

The steel padlock was reinforced with a Vaselined steel chain.

He crouched before the door and stared at the wire.

It goes beneath the door to left.

And

– to the right it comes out again

– goes into the brickwork, up a bit, and

– eye-level:

– six inches from my face: the IED, attached to a fine trip-wire among a patch of shit and slime.

– no tripwire. A singleton.

– original: organic local Cumbrian produce, no sell-by date, shelf life zilch. Civil warfare at your fingertips: one false touch and it's

N

One cut. You're paraplegic.

Three cuts with bolt-cutters.

– **1** high-strength low-alloy steel padlock and **1** chain hit the floor and the door opened

nnng

– and a howl of panic.

84

The wild disturbance racked his peripheral vision. Eyes were staring at him. Voices rose in chorus above the *nnng-whhhhrrrrrr-whhhrrrrrrrnnnnngwhrrrrnnng* – '*Spiritus Aeternitas et Dominus*. I believe in the Life Beyond, Almighty Creator of Heaven and Earth.'

He saw his mother walking towards him, arms outstretched, singing in lubricious tones: 'The Eternal Spirit of Our Mansion. The Only Begotten Son, My Son.'

Naked, her marbled lips recited:

'*Two Souls in One One in Two.*'

He inhaled droplets of rotted lavender, maternal physical odours that appalled him, stupefied by the imminence of inescapable incestuous union.

'*Two in One in Spirit and in Flesh.*'

The neurotransmitters in his brain signalled an unholy crescendo of static.

Ferocious sounds of exploding head syndrome: *nnng-whhhhrrrrrr-whhhrrrrrrrnnnnngwhrrrrnnng*, the physical and mental trauma mismatch between visual and tactile signals.

It was as if he were *outside* himself, positioned in two entirely distinct places simultaneously.

Adrenalin filled his bloodstream, causing his skin to emit a froth of sweat heavy with the stench of rotted flesh.

He felt a sleep jerk, a hypnagogic jerk between his legs and the wires across his thighs squirmed like silken vipers squeezing his genitalia. He saw rank upon rank of IEDs, actually grinning tombstones in a war cemetery, and they sang out with the sad fervour of a Remembrance Day congregation: '*Captain Hal Stirling. Come to Mummy, Hal.*'

> '*Long years ago, as earth lay dark and still,*
> *Rose a loud cry upon a lonely hill,*
> *While in the frailty of our human clay ...*
> *Here lies the man who calls himself the bomb disposal*
> *expert.*'

Conceived, Born, Suffered, was Crucified, Dead, and Buried:

He descended into Hell.

And very slowly the two strange women finished their disrobing. The moaning voice was his: synchronized with exactitude: '*Is anybody there?*' It went on and on whimpering. He heard moans and realized they were his own – '*Is anybody there?*'

A woman's face materialized through veils of blood

and a line of verse looped in his head: *Two girls in silk kimonos, both beautiful, one a gazelle* – eyes fixed, struck dumb.

Cowering on the cell floor, wrists tied with industrial tape to a whirring butcher's heavy-duty slicer.

nnng-whhhhrrrrrr-whhhrrrrrrrnnnnngwhrrrrnnng

She looked at him in stupefaction like a madwoman.

Please: Don't Die.

85

03.01

Out of the Crypt and into the light.

He carried her through the passages across his shoulders, her weight evenly distributed.

The lights flickered.

On and off. On again . . .

He set her on the floor . . .

. . . the lights went out.

He groped around the walls for a half-remembered switch.

It clicked.

No light.

The electricity supply must have been cut off at the mains.

Through a veil of tiny stars pricking at his eyeballs he saw a shape glide across the Great Hall in the thin light from the snow outside. Its feet seemed to rise, two, perhaps even six inches from the floor.

The figure of a woman faced him. There was the faintest gleam of a hypodermic's plastic; its needle threatening.

Her sunken eyes mesmerized him; her wide mouth opened, either with a smile or an agonized grimace, he couldn't tell.

There was the sickly scent of jasmine oil and lilies in a funeral parlour ... and she drew a wristband of white silk thread towards his eyes so he was forced to look at the glow of the diamond ornament dangling from it.

He was looking at the image of an Indian cobra's head, a *Naja Naja*'s severed head.

Kill. Kill it.

'Who are you?' he pleaded.

There was no reply.

He stood rigid in the darkness. *It's so dark. I can't have seen this spectre.*

It dawned on him that all the while his torch had been on the darkness swallowed its light.

Something fell.

Earth hard as iron?

Water like a stone?

'Who are you?'

Frosty wind made moan.

'Is anybody there – won't someone help me?'

86

Carrying the heavy-duty bolt-cutters in one hand, in the other his torch, he headed slowly through the darkness of the Great Hall approaching the kitchen, alert to the slightest sound.

He stood outside the kitchen door without touching it: listening for any movement from inside: searching the surrounds; feeling the rims and handle for the signs of the booby trap.

He tucked the bolt-cutters into his belt beneath his jacket and slowly squatted on his haunches; then flattened himself on the floor, peering through the minute crack afforded by the entry–exit hole a rodent had clawed. His fingertips touched cold plastic.

Suddenly, he heard he generator rumble into action and the world exploded with savage light.

He raised his hands to shield his eyes.

A blur, the hooded figure's face was masked: the deathly mask he'd seen in the driving snow outside the vicarage window. Gloved hands held a shotgun aimed steadily at his chest. Others seized the bolt-cutters and they dropped to the stone floor.

'Who are you?'

No reply.

'What d'you want?'

The silent figure drew closer.

He could smell the acrid breath. It gestured at him with the gun's snout to place his hands on his head.

The shotgun lowered, level with his groin. The figure turned slowly and sideways to steady the weapon, managing to keep it aimed at its target.

He tensed his arms and elbows, clenched his fingers together on his head allowing the gloved hand to explore the inside of his thighs.

As it transferred exploratory fingers to his right thigh, he twisted violently, bringing down his fists like hammerheads, the full force of the blow striking the carotid artery.

The shotgun hit the stone floor, its impact triggering the firing mechanism: the report of both barrels shattered the silence.

87

The shadow twisted noiselessly like the Levantine viper.

'*Where's the bomb?*' He edged towards the unloaded shotgun and lifted it from the floor. '*Where is it?*' He looked at the kitchen door. 'The door? In the bloody kitchen? A timer? There'll be a fucking heap of body bits and no one will know what's-me-what's-you. What's wrong with you, fuckface – w*here is it?*'

Silence.

Only the beating of his heart.

'You scared of dying – ?'

An arm clamped around his throat. The gloved hand smothered his mouth.

needle

stabbing in the thigh

squirting venom into his bloodstream.

The death mask –

booby trap linked to more up the riverbed flowing into the kitchen.

He reached out to steady himself

touched luminous ether with his fingertips

*

Remembering the future. He thought:
Sophie's crawling towards the kitchen and oblivion –
and felt no pain.

TWELVE

In the bleak midwinter
Frosty wind made moan,
Earth stood hard as iron,
Water like a stone;
Snow had fallen, snow on snow,
Snow on snow,
In the bleak midwinter
Long ago.

Angels and archangels
May have gathered there,
Cherubim and seraphim
Thronged the air,
But only His mother
In her maiden bliss,
Worshipped the Beloved
With a kiss.

CHRISTINA ROSSETTI

88

Sunlight.

Shimmering whiteness on the frosted window panes.

Here I am.

A wood fire burning in the grate. The smell of burning pine.

Here I am in my bed.

With a splitting head. Drenched in cold sweat.

In my room, my room. Once my nursery:

– with its Japanese six-panel folding screen, the early nineteenth-century *byobu* of the Edo period with its delicate black-and-white images of figures dancing on a golden floor holding fans. Here are the African hides, Indian rugs, lace curtains, the crochet blankets.

For a hundred years or more this is how the Stirlings have liked their bedrooms.

Now with Sophie.

– sitting on his bed looking at him with a worried smile.

'Happy Christmas,' she said.

'Happy Christmas,' he croaked. 'Are we – okay?'

'We're alive.'

'What happened?'

'The good news is they've gone.'

'Teresa and Francesca?'

'Left at dawn.'

'Don't . . .' he said. His eyes closed. 'Don't go near the kitchen.'

'I already have. Made breakfast. Porridge and cream. Bacon and eggs.' (He remembered Teresa's breakfast menu. Or had it been Francesca's?) 'Toast, marmalade and a glass of freshly squeezed juice. Coffee and hot milk.'

'*In the kitchen?*'

'Where else?'

'There's a whole lot of explosives down there.'

'They didn't go off, did they?'

'There are wires. Tubes. Canisters.'

'The bad news is there's a bloody awful mess. Some-one . . . they shit themselves.'

'Did you speak to anyone?'

'There's no one here,' she said. 'Just us.'

'No one?'

'All gone.'

'Hold my hand,' he said. 'Are you okay?'

'Bruised and shaken.'

The night was coming back – 'I thought they'd killed you.'

'I guess that's what they intended. And you too.'

'I think you'll find it was their last throw.'

'Who knows?' she said. 'Thank God you found me.'

'What time was it, where was I?'

'Dawn. You were in the hall.' She cradled him in her arms. 'Can you face breakfast?'

'I'll try.' He dragged himself from the bed. 'We'd better check on Sumiko. Are you up to Christmas lunch with the pair of them?'

'You decide.'

'No, you.'

'Let's do it,' she said.

'I stink of the crypt.'

'So do I.'

'You want to bath with me before breakfast?'

'If there's hot water.'

Shrouded in steam, she said: 'You know what my Christmas present is to you?'

'Don't make me guess.'

'A room with a double bed tonight. The Hallmark in Carlisle.'

'Not here?'

'No, Hal. Not here.'

'I'm thinking of Sumiko.'

'So am I. It may be for the best you don't tell her.'

'And best I call the police – except, no mobile.'

'Mine's down.'

'We'll call from the village and wish Moster Lees a Happy Christmas.'

89

The Towers stood alone eyeing their departure with a kind of triumphant indifference.

For the first time in centuries it looked serene, very still: as frozen as the enormous icicles in its windows – bars of an asylum – the whole resembling a prehistoric corpse frozen for eternity in some cavernous mortuary's refrigerator.

He drove the Range Rover carefully down the icy roads.

'I know when I'm beaten,' he said. 'It was always going to beat me in the end.'

'That's not true.'

'It is. I won't return.'

'In the New Year perhaps?'

'Next year? No.'

'Sometime?'

'Never.'

'Perhaps you'd have been better off without it in the first place.'

'You're asking my opinion?'

'It seems so.'

'You give evil hearts and hands too much credit.'

'Think so?'

'That's how you've been seeing things.'

'Like what things?'

He thought of the nurses, of MacCullum and the rest rejoicing in their Christmas victory. 'You know what I'm talking about.'

She seemed to read his thoughts. 'The possessed – Teresa and Francesca – God knows who else, they haven't won either.'

'Think not?'

'They haven't gained possession of The Towers, have they?'

'No one has, Sophie. No one's got The Towers. No one's got anything.'

'Matter of fact,' she said, 'we've still got each other.'

The sun shone across the moorland bathing Christmas morning in pale pink, blue and pink.

He couldn't resist one final glance at the old enemy. It returned his glance like an incarcerated high-risk lunatic, its face literally vacant and without regret. If it saw what he saw, it wasn't saying.

Sophie looked back too. She was peering through the rear window in a crouch when she suddenly straightened up.

'Someone's following us.'

'Who?'

'Don't know.'

He gradually decelerated. 'When you put that box of food in the boot did you notice anything?'

'Like what?'

'A box, say – anything you didn't put there yourself?'

Even 1lb of high-explosive would blow the Range Rover to kingdom come. Say, even an old-fashioned mix of nitrobenzene and sodium chlorate. But nitrobenzene has a very powerful, unmistakable odour. Unlikely, but it could have been packed in an airtight container to disguise the telltale smell. The bomber couldn't have forced a way into the Range Rover. But MacCullum could've. He had keys.

'Did you check inside the food boxes?' he said.

'Check – what?'

'Did you notice anything?'

'No.'

'When you got into the car – notice anything then?'

'Like *what*?'

'Handmarks in the frost. *Think*, Sophie. Footprints in the snow?'

'Don't think so,' she said, once more peering through the rear window. 'It's there. The hearse.'

Hal pulled up sharply. 'Jesus Christ ...'

He looked back.

In the distance – at the top of the hill, the hearse was drawing to a halt.

Making to turn off the engine, he thought better of it. 'Sophie. Do exactly as I say. Move slowly – very slowly. No hurry. Watch your step on the ice. I want you to get out ... carefully – so as not to rock the suspension, okay? Now open the door – carefully.'

'What is it?'

'Just do it, Sophie.'

She did as he told her.

'Cross the road. Take it easy. Into the field. Stay calm. Keep listening to me.'

She stepped over the frozen ditch, up into the field and blundered through the snow.

'Stop there,' he shouted. 'Lie down — *flat*, flat in the snow. Go on. *Flat*. Don't move again until I tell you. Cover your head with your arms. Right down. *Further*. Good. *Don't raise your head.*'

In slow-motion he got out of the Range Rover, walked to the back of it and looked inside.

He saw a low pile of greasy blankets. Protruding from them was the edge of an unfamiliar blue rug neither he nor his mother had ever possessed. Unfamiliar, yet familiar. The bright blue of a Carlisle United Football Club rug with the club motto *Be Just and Fear Not*.

With slow deliberation and the lightest touch he slowly raised the rug.

90

The open cardboard package lay beneath it

– laced with detonating cord, Cordtex, its penta-erythritol tetranitrate explosive core coated in plastic: gelignite, commercially produced Frangex. Used in quarries—

He found a terminal: an Eveready Energizer PP9 battery, and a Casio alarm clock.

The clock was timed to fire the bomb in six minutes. 6 minutes = a very short time.

He looked closely at the circuitry. Traced its path. The tiniest inadvertent movement would close the contacts = N.

He took a step back. From the corner of his eye he saw a movement.

Sophie was peering at him

'Get the fuck down,' he shouted. 'Lie flat.'

'What's happening?' she said.

'Get down. Don't move.'

His fingers were steady. The adrenalin rush caused his eyes to widen, his pupils to dilate.

He watched for any involuntary twitch. No nerve signalled fear. He visualized how he'd take the bomb apart, what needed touching, where to move things, how to finish: the disconnection.

He slowly removed the battery from the clock, then the Cordtex from the charge.

Matched by the brightness of the snow, the minutest rainbows dancing on the frost, the rush of pleasure was luminous.

Euphoria = Big E

The hearse had disappeared.

He walked slowly across the road and stepped across the ditch. Following her tracks, he waded through the powdery snow and crouched down beside her.

'The hearse's gone?' Sophie said.

'Don't count your eggs. My guess is there's another bomb. Means he may have tried to trigger the first bugger by remote control, failed and fucked off out.'

'How do you know?'

'I can read bastards' minds.'

'How?'

'Because it's my business. That's what I do. It's the only thing I know about, see? That and disabling bloody bombs like that fucker. I guess there's more of the same – enough stuff inside it to blow the Range Rover to what Paddy calls *smidirín*, a.k.a. holy shite.'

91

'We just wait?'

'For as long as it takes.'

Nothing moved.

'We go on waiting?' she said.

'Other man's move.'

'Where is he?'

'Waiting up there, that's what *I'd* be doing. Shielded by the hill, that's where *I'd* be waiting.'

'You think he's alone?'

'Doubt it. I'd have taken precautions. I'd have witnesses to it.'

'Witnesses to what?'

'The fact we blew ourselves up.'

'Sorry?'

'That's what he wanted.'

'*We* blew *ourselves* up?'

'You and me. He wanted *me* to do it – while the balance of my mind was disturbed. He's thinking Coroner. Self-satisfied old fart, always *satisfied*. Ever heard of a Coroner who isn't fucking satisfied? *Satisfied* that the deceased was "capable of forming the intention to take his own life. Oh yes, by the way, neither drugs, alcohol nor psychiatric illness played a part." But I didn't. I didn't blow myself up. I didn't blow you up. I didn't even blow up my mother's fucking Range Rover. And you tell me – is the balance of my mind disturbed?'

'The forensics will tell another story.'

'That's not what I said.'

'Forensics will show who planted it.'

'Exactly. That's why he's waiting. The shit is waiting to finish the job. Waiting. When it goes up he'll come down here and make very sure the evidence is obliterated. Witnesses will help him complete the job. Believe me, he'll have Francesca and Teresa with him. That's what nurses do best.'

'Do what?'

'Clean up. After the living and the dead. Clean up Unholy Shite. That's what one of them told me. She said: "That's what we do twenty-four-seven, we handle hurt." Could've said shite. "Not like the people who've died hereabouts. MacCullum says this place has a history of distress and hurt and misery and madness and demons. They've brought pain here each time there's been building works, even minor repairs to old pipes and electric wiring. You tell me why the workmen don't want to come up here. This place scares grown men shitless. They hate coming here. Too many people have died here . . .." That's more or less what she said.'

'Teresa or Francesca?'

'I don't remember.'

Still they waited.

'You know what – I mean about who said what about hurt and misery and madness and demons?'

'What?' she said.

'I no longer give a fuck.'

'How much longer, Hal?'

'I've told you. As long as it takes. It's a game of cat and—'

'mouse' he was saying when the second bomb exploded.

92

Snow, steam, grit, metal parts, fragments of fabric and tyres blasted out a mass of spurting flames and burning smoke. Blew the Range Rover to *smidirín* . . .

Covered in snow, they waded through the field to the ditch.

Except for the billowing cloud of black-and-bluish smoke and spouting flames, nothing moved.

When they heard the gun's report from the car up the hill, they shuddered.

She grabbed his hand.

He barely flinched. There wasn't a flicker of anxiety in his face. He had the air of the man on guard. Well used to clearing up other people's shite. The quiet pleasure of the explorer, well used to No Man's Land, frustration and disappointment, who's finally arrived. The solitary hunter home from the hill. His hill. His home. Back in charge. In charge of himself absorbed in the game he knew best.

'Let's take a look-see,' he said. 'You prepared to look?

She grimaced. 'Yes and No.'

'It won't be a pretty sight.'

93

Blood drenched the warm interior of the hearse. The stench of burning flesh filled the air.

The shotgun lay near MacCullum's head. Rather it lay where his head had been connected to his body a few minutes before. Actually the jellied blob was scarcely recognizable as a head.

Blood had soaked into MacCullum's Christmas Day suit, his Sunday best.

He wore a tie, still neatly tied beneath the chin. You could see the crest of the Cumbria coat of arms on it. The Parnassus flowers on the green border representing Cumberland interspersed with white roses of Yorkshire superimposed with the red roses of Lancashire.

To the left, the bright red bull with nasty-looking horns. To the right, the bright red dragon with a pointed tail. The dragon was sticking out its tongue at the head of a ram. Beneath the coat of arms was the motto: *Ad Montes Oculos Levavi*. 'I shall lift up mine eyes unto the hills.'

Not any more you won't.

Francesca's eyes must have filled with terror at

MacCullum before he killed her. There weren't any eyes left, just scarlet and purple and black bloodied craters filled with ooze. You couldn't say they were staring death in the face because there were no faces left.

The turmoil of the spilled blood and flesh made it impossible to tell immediately who'd killed whom and in what order.

Hal wiped blood from his hands.

Neither of them noticed the bright red nurse's cardigan. It lay in the snow next to the waist belt with its nickel-plated clasp.

Hand in hand, they walked slowly back down the hill.

She said: 'I hate to think . . .'

'Of what?'

'Of all that might have happened.'

'I hate to think of all that did.'

'Is that what you say to people whose lives you've saved?'

'The dead? Let's not talk about them now. I tell the living I'm an ordinary person doing an ordinary job.'

'That's not entirely true.'

'Isn't it? They listen but they don't hear, Sophie. The dead – they can't listen but they hear.'

'How about you?'

'It's quiet now,' he said.

'What can you hear?'

'Silence.'

Broken by the crescendo of a searing cry.

The wail was terrible. He'd heard such screams more times than he cared to remember.

He began to run –
following –

– the trail of dark red smears in the snow.

The cry reached up through the still of the day to the sky.

The questions that would remain unanswered were three-fold:

How had she got there unnoticed?

How had she stumbled unseen from the bloodied hearse to the Range Rover's smoking wreck?

Why?

The answer to the last question could be found in what she was clutching in her hands.

Hal saw:

The original Second World War Japanese naval dagger and

scabbard in mint condition.

The blade, razor sharp.

He saw her standing there: eyes wide as if now at one with Priscilla and Sada Abe.

His strange memory of the future came back a final time.

'Teresa,' he said gently. He knew full well what she was about to do. 'Teresa – *DON'T*.'

The gentle wind gusted snowflakes across her haunted face.

She must have heard Hal's plea. But she didn't heed it.

Falling to her knees, she toppled slowly forwards. Her body accepting the blade through her white silk dress, drawing it into her, right up to the hilt, puncturing veins, arteries, lungs and heart.

THIRTEEN

– I faced what I had to face.

HENRY JAMES
The Turn of the Screw

96

Few tears were shed at the funerals, presided over by
the Vicar who'd taken his sermon's text from Isaiah:

'The wolf also shall dwell with the lamb, and the
leopard shall lie down with the kid; and the calf and
the young lion and the fatling together; and a little
child shall lead them.'

Outside the crematorium, a sober Betsy MacCullum
showed Hal a bitter face.

'You've won,' she said.

'There are no winners,' he told her.

'Only losers,' she said. 'You've got what you always
wanted. Nothing changes in these parts.'

'I wish it had turned out differently.'

'And what do you think I wish?' she said.

Before he could answer she turned her back on him,
adding as an afterthought:

'It's not over yet.'

For the time being, along with Sophie, Minti and
Schadzi, Polish 'Concierge Officers' from Secure Property
Services of Carlisle (SPSC) were taking care of The Towers.

Like its past, its future was uncertain. Following 'the emergency incident', the police reminded Hal it was his responsibility to ensure the property was secure. They offered to assist SPSC 'with measures to prevent vandalism and theft', and fire service officers said they would advise 'on protection against further weather damage'.

He had grown accustomed to fear and as the days grew longer and the evenings lighter, so the intensity of the horror on the hillside faded. He felt perhaps it was terror, the gnawing anticipation of horror, that The Towers embodied. The terror it generated was indeterminate but not, he felt, essentially negative. He had a vague recollection that he'd reached that conclusion many years before. To his surprise he remembered it was none other than Ann Radcliffe who'd given him the insight. For the first time since childhood he turned again to her essay *On the Supernatural in Poetry*. 'Terror,' she explains, 'expands the soul and awakens the faculties to a high degree of life . . .' whereas horror 'freezes and nearly annihilates them'.

What of fear?

The truth was that it excited him.

Where now could he find it?

FOURTEEN

It's spring fever. That is what the name of it is. And when you've got it, you want – oh, you don't quite know what it is you do want, but it just fairly makes your heart ache, you want it so!

MARK TWAIN

No reason was given to him by the Army for the order to be on parade at Headley Court on the sixth of January. Coincidentally it was Epiphany, the twelfth day of Christmas. Perhaps this was the military's little joke that his future would be revealed on the same day Christians celebrate the Adoration of the Magi, their recognition that the Incarnation of the Christ child really is the Son of God.

Was this the day they'd chosen to tell him his bomb disposal expertise was no more required?

Or were the powers that be in the Ministry of Defence about to offer him a numinous experience, to reveal a *mysterium tremendum*, invoking fear along with *mysterium fascinans* to draw him back within the fold?

Sophie drove him to Leeds Bradford airport for the southbound flight.

She kissed him three times and explained it would be bad luck to see him enter the terminal building. 'Don't look back,' she said.

It seemed to be an omen.

'*Ladies and Gentleman. May we have your special attention for the following safety instructions.*'

Given a fair wind the flight time from Leeds Bradford airport to Gatwick above the spine of England is about fifty-seven minutes.

It's a distance of about three hundred and eighteen kilometres or one hundred and ninety-eight miles. From Gatwick it's a short taxi ride to Headley Court.

'*Please make sure that your hand luggage is securely stowed under the seat in front of you or in the overhead locker . . .*

'*Emergency lights on the floor show you the way to the emergency exits. Fasten your seatbelt whenever the FASTEN SEAT-BELT sign is on. The belt can be opened easily whenever necessary.*'

He looked down to the landscape and saw flood waters covering long stretches of the countryside.

WAKEFIELD
the eastern ridges of the Pennines
SHEFFIELD
built on seven hills

'*For safety reasons we advise you to keep your seatbelt fastened while seated.*

'*In case of loss of cabin pressure, oxygen masks will be automatically released above your seats. Pull down the nearest mask, place it over mouth and nose and secure it with the elastic band. Your life vest is located under your seat. In the event of a water landing, place the life vest over your head, fasten the straps at the front of the vest and pull them tight. Do not inflate the vest inside the aircraft.*'

His mind was far away.

HELMAND
Islamic Republic of Afghanistan
Latitude: 32.07 Longitude: 64.8
23,000 square miles of it
say, about half the size of England, roughly
NOTTINGHAM & SHERWOOD FOREST
once home to Robin Hood
LEICESTER
motto *Semper Eadem*, Always The Same
MILTON KEYNES

City of Seven Choirs

LUTON

once home to Taimour Abdulwahab al-Abdaly

(2010 Stockholm suicide bomber)

99

Shortly after sunrise, Ops Room receives a tasking message. My No. 2 tells me what I've already guessed. It's an IED shout. The sixth in five days on the trot.

I've slept fully dressed.

I grab my kit and join the others at the team vehicles. The rest are donning Kevlar helmets and combat body armour; activating radios, making ready electronic counter-measures gear and loading weapons.

The '10-liner' that's alerted us to the incident gives the details of the IED and a brief assessment of what may be additional threats. The route is planned.

Accompanied by an infantry escort, we head out from the base into the low morning mist.

I'm on the road, back in business in clouds of dust, bound for the wastelands and the bomb in a riverbed.

The sun dazzles me. The roaring engines taunt me. Every shape I see harbours danger. The rim of the seat-belt is another slithering viper; a streak of dried chewing gum, a scorp, then turns into a wire; a wire connected to another IED.

When I see the lizard on the patch of desert shale pretending to be dead, I blink.

The lizard flinches.

'Ladies and gentlemen, we have started our descent to London Gatwick. In preparation for landing please make sure your seat backs and tray tables are in their full upright position.'

'As you leave the aircraft, pull down the red tabs to inflate the vest. If necessary the life vest can be inflated by blowing through these tubes.'

'Bear with me a moment ...'

The flight attendant is reading from the wrong hymn sheet.

The lizard springs into a tangle of bamboo roots narrowly avoiding the dusty package.

Wise move, *trapelus agilis.*

'Sorry about that, Ladies and Gentlemen. Make sure your seat-belt is securely fastened and all carry-on luggage is stowed underneath the seat in front of you or in the overhead lockers.'

Maybe it's fear that induces the adrenalin rush. I crave fear like the gambler; or the mountaineer climbing some Alpine rock face without a safety harness.

*

He unfastens his seatbelt.

The flight attendant sashays along the aisle and doesn't notice.

'Please turn off all electronic devices until we are safely parked at the gate.'

'It's not over yet.'

'The flight attendants will shortly pass through the cabin to pick up any remaining cups and glasses.'

100

Defence Medical Rehabilitation Centre
Headley Court
Counter-Terrorism Response Level: Low.

POST TRAUMATIC STRESS DISORDER
NAME: Captain Hal Stirling

WRITE YES. NO. DON'T KNOW.

1. Have you suffered trauma?
    Yes
2. Did you witness death or serious or minor
    injury?
    Yes
3. Did you face death or major injury?
    Yes
4. Did you experience fear, terror, horror or
    paralysis?
    Yes and No
5. Have you regularly experienced fear,
    helplessness or horror since trauma?

Yes and No

6. Do you have troubling thoughts about the event?

    Yes and No

7. Did you witness violent death or fatal injury or the threat of same?

    Yes

8. Do you regularly experience unease, panic, fear or terror or horror?

    Yes

9. Do you have nightmares about all/any of the above or have disabling thoughts of same?

    No

10. Did you actually witness death or serious threat of death?

    Yes

11. Do you feel helpless/powerless/relive the trauma?

    Yes and No

12. Can you remember the traumatic event/s in detail?

    Yes and No

13. Do they constantly appear in your head?

    Yes and No

14. Are your sleep and rest patterns normal?

    Yes and No

15. Is your diet normal?
    Yes

16. Are your bowel movements normal?
    Yes

17. Has sexual activity been reduced or
    impaired?
    No

18. Has it increased?
    Yes

19. Do you have an alcohol problem?
    No

20. Do you have a drug problem?
    No

21. Do you have a satisfactory
    domestic/emotional partnership?
    Yes

22. Do you consider yourself completely fit
    mentally and physically to return to unit?
    Yes

'I can think of no better news than your return to Afghanistan,' the counsellor said. 'Can you?'

'Not immediately.'

The counsellor smiled. 'One turns off the computer in the head. Mother Nature turns it on again. Shutting the brain down is Mother Nature's cure. Most minds restart just fine if turned off properly. One heals oneself.'

They shook hands.

'Safe journey, Hal,' the counsellor said. 'Good luck. Mind how you go. Any other problems?'

'None that I know of.'

Closing the file on his desk, the counsellor said: 'One never knows what goes on in a brave man's head.'